The Lost Coin
by Samuel Hayes Sherwood

© Copyright 2015 Samuel Hayes Sherwood

ISBN   978-1-63393-140-4

This is a work of fiction. The characters are both actual and fictitious. With the exception of verified historical events and persons, all incidents, descriptions, dialogue and opinions expressed are the products of the author's imagination and are not to be construed as real.

Published by

SHERWOOD
PRESS

yetnotibutchrist.com

THE
LOST
COIN

Samuel Hayes Sherwood

SHERWOOD
PRESS

1

THE OLD MAN AND THE COIN

SAM LAY IN A quagmire of mangled and confused dreams, twisting, turning, futilely fighting back as evil phantoms swirled around him, jabbing at his consciousness with flaming swords of accusation. He was no stranger to these importunate psychopathic minions. These faceless cowards always took flight in the drunken half-light of morning when their victims were most vulnerable, obfuscating good and evil without compunction, set into motion by the Accuser of the Brethren.

Sam moaned. "No!" he yelled, yet no sound came out of his mouth. "Not true! Leave me alone!"

They paid no heed to his pleas, but shoved the hot swords deeper into his soul. He tried to fend off their allegations, to deny and stop their threatened disclosures. But he had no defense. They mercilessly sifted him like wheat. The more he denied and resisted, the louder their accusations became. The noise became unbearable. He covered his ears; he couldn't breathe; he was going under.

As he grasped for consciousness to break the spell, a still, small voice said, "Agree with your adversary quickly in the way."

"What?" he cried.

"Agree with your adversary quickly in the way," it repeated, "lest he deliver you to the judge and the judge cast you into prison. You won't come out then until you have paid the last farthing."

It was his grandfather's voice.

Okay, he conceded silently, *you've got me. I'm guilty.*

Their power neutralized, the phantoms vaporized into the morning light. His clenched muscles exhaled all their built-up tension. Sleep started to drift back over his eyes, but it was short-lived.

The peace was shattered by an excruciating crescendo. Sam's eyes opened in a tiny slit, enough to see the black box on the night table. He started to reach for the snooze button but his hands were bound in a self-made cocoon of sheets raveled around him. He finally wrangled one arm out of his straight jacket and pounded the black plastic box into silence.

"What the hell?" he cursed. "Damn!" His still-inebriated brain struggled to guess the day. It was Sunday. "What an idiot," he muttered.

He lay there staring at the ceiling, exhausted, slowly getting his eyes used to the dim light. At least the phantoms were gone. *Cowards,* he thought. *Can't stand the light of day.* How he wished for more rest, but his pounding head disallowed that.

He ripped off the sheet. His body was wet with sweat. He realized he was naked.

What's this? he thought. *Too drunk to put on PJ's?*

He got up and headed to the kitchen. His foot knocked over an empty beer can. He shook his head as it kept rolling with a tinny rumble until a chair leg stopped it. John's door was halfway open. He was still passed out. *Wonderful,* Sam thought, *to be able to sleep through that alarm.* His girlfriend lay next to him. Half of her naked derrière and one long leg hung limply down the side of the bed. He reached in and closed the door for her modesty and his. He was pleased to find two Advil in the kitchen cabinet. He popped them in his mouth and chased them down with a handful of water. He walked quietly back to his room and splayed himself back on the bed to wait for some relief.

After the throbbing started to recede, he moved on to the next priority—coffee. *Yes, need some coffee.* He pulled on his jeans and grabbed a shirt off the floor and walked back to the kitchen.

He fumbled through the cabinets for the coffee. *Where did John put it this time?* he wondered. His anger started to kindle. He was afraid to open any cabinets that John had been in for fear of what might fall out. "What the hell," he said. *Gotta do what I gotta do. If it wakes you up, it's your own fault, buddy.* Luckily, he found the foil bag on the first try. No avalanche.

Sam crashed into the old overstuffed chair and let it percolate. Hope revived as the aroma filled the room. Finally, it stopped percolating. He ventured into another cabinet for a cup. This time one stray cup fell out and bounced off the wooden floor with a thump. *At least it didn't break,* he thought. *Thank God for wooden floors.*

Sam sunk into the well-worn chair and slowly sipped the strong coffee—no such thing as too strong. It washed the latent taste of scotch from his tongue.

The morning light revealed the wreckage from the previous night. The reminder of a bad idea lay before him on the coffee table. A "dead soldier," as his mother called it, lay on the coffee table beside a cadre of empty beer cans.

"Something has to give." He sighed. "This ritual is killing me." He stared at the empty Cutty Sark bottle, hoping it wasn't he alone that polished it off. Joe was there last night. No one loved free booze like he.

There was a time Sam hated the taste of scotch. Now his newly acquired taste drew near each night like a siren, beckoning, seducing, and eventually breaking his resistance.

He shook off what he couldn't remember. Other aromas attracted his attention to John's ashtray. It was never full, never emptied. The butts just fell to the floor. The aroma cocktail of spent tobacco, whiskey, and beer fueled his hangover.

John's yard-sale ashtray was a sore spot between the roommates—a huge ceramic, blue maple leaf about the size of a basketball cradled in a brass-metal stand. The tips of the maple leaf were like the fingers of a hand reaching out to hold butts.

To escape the depressing sights, smells, and lost memories, Sam stepped out on the veranda to finish his coffee. It was a rickety wooden structure overhanging an alley between two apartment buildings. The cool fall air slapped him in the face. It felt good. He was finally feeling alive. Sam relaxed into his favorite plastic chair to enjoy the view: the backside of his equally classy neighbor's apartments towering high above an alley lined with trashcans and dumpsters. The nascent sun was peeking over the roofline. He could feel the warmth on his face.

The coffee helped, but it was no cure for the Sunday blues or the hangover. The loneliness of Sunday always triggered the same nagging questions. *What was wrong with him?* he kept wondering. Everyone else seemed fine with the status quo. His brother sure fit the mold, racing off after things the world envied. Sam wondered if they weren't more like a bunch of lemmings hurtling mindlessly over a cliff into the sea, robots programmed by some arbiter operating behind a curtain. What was it he didn't get?

Church wasn't an option. That path had dried up long ago. He just couldn't bring himself to sit through one more boring self-help sermon that didn't help. He wondered at all these faithful parishioners sitting there week after week with glazed looks on their faces. *Why did they go? What were they getting out of it other than an attendance award? Another group of lemmings?* He tried prayer. That didn't work either.

He had no answer. His grandfather was the only one who seemed to know. "The truth," he remembered him saying, "was hid in plain sight." That seemed to make sense but at the same time didn't. *This is goofy,* he thought. He let it go, releasing his mind to random thoughts. He had a plane reserved for the afternoon to practice maneuvers, so he focused on that.

†††

A movement across the alley caught his eye. A young lady was watching him from the apartment building on the other side two units down. She was bundled up, but he could see that she was very pretty. Steam from her coffee curled up around her face like a halo. She smiled at him, and he forced a smile and looked down. A look from a pretty girl for Sam was like a vampire being flashed by a cross. Suddenly self-conscious of his ragged appearance, he looked for a way to escape. He gulped down the last of the cold coffee. How he hated cold coffee, but it was the only way to save face. He stole one last glance at her before going inside. *She's still smiling, maybe laughing,* he thought.

Sam showered and stood in front of the mirror with his shave cream. Staring back at him was a red-eyed, puffy-faced young man who looked older than he should. Looking down at his belly, he pressed in on it with both hands. It returned to its original shape. Grimacing, he lathered his face.

The shower and clean clothes made him feel somewhat revived. His head was only slightly fuzzy now. John and Molly were still sleeping as he left. *Must be nice. Wish I could do that.* He navigated the three levels of narrow stairs of his walkup apartment and proceeded toward his favorite dive diner.

The sun was now bright in the east, prompting Sam to take a shortcut through an alley. Generally, the alley was to be avoided given the reputation of the neighborhood, particularly at night. Despite the bright sky overhead, he was surprised how dim it was between the narrow apartment buildings. He moved decisively, navigating through trashcans, old cars, and dumpsters.

As he was passing the second dumpster, he was startled when a hand reached out from behind and touched his jacket. Sam jumped back, not sure if he was facing a knife or some other malevolent intent. An old man stood there. His smile immediately disarmed Sam. There was something familiar about his blue eyes. The many lines in his face portrayed kindness. His hand was extended out to Sam.

Sam reached into his pocket and pulled out an empty lining. "Sorry, sir, no change," Sam said. "Wish I could help, but I can hardly help myself." He started to move on, but the man pulled gently on his arm as he tried to leave.

"Sam," he said. It wasn't a question.

Startled, Sam stopped and turned back around. "Do I know you?" he asked.

The old man's hand was still extended, but now he noticed it was not empty. It held a small round object. "This is for you, Sam," the old man said quietly, inserting it in Sam's jacket pocket.

Sam stared in bewilderment as the old man turned to walk away without saying another word. *What just happened?* Sam wondered. *How did he know my name?* He reached into his pocket to see what he placed there, but it was empty. *A trick?* He checked his wallet. It was still there. Sam looked back down the alley. The old man was gone. *How could he move so fast? Weird.*

Sam hurried to the end of the alley and into the light. Across from the outlet was an old church. The bells started to toll, and it smelled like someone frying chicken. *Really?* he thought. *Who actually fries chicken in the morning?* The tune of "Sunday Morning Coming Down" stuck in his head, along with a bad feeling.

He stopped and watched the faithful walking up the steps in their Sunday best. He felt so disconnected. There was a time he enjoyed the days in church with his mom and dad—a long time ago. He wasn't sure what happened. Shaking off the bad feelings, he marched onward to his cheap, greasy destination.

The name *La Grande Bouche* was the only thing French about the diner. The owner was an Italian from New York and the food he served was about basic American cuisine. The morning menu was simple—bacon, eggs, toast, sausage, no substitutions. No eggs benedict here. The only greeting offered here was a "Watta'l it be?" Which meant you had the choice of fried or scrambled, crispy bacon or not crispy. It also meant you better know what you wanted before he came to your table. Take it or leave it. Those of sensitive dispositions probably didn't frequent *La Grande Bouche*, but the New Yorkers around loved it.

Sam walked in and glanced around. The place only had a half dozen tables and a counter that would hold twelve. There was one cheap painting of the Eiffel Tower. The tables were filled with people looking about as ragged as he felt. No church people in here. No diamonds. No minks. *My kind of people,* he thought.

Sam took a stool at the counter.

"Watta'l it be?" the owner, Joe, asked, looking down at his pad.

"Two eggs over medium, medium bacon, and wheat toast," Sam said, hoping the meal would be the final cure for his hangover.

"Drink?"

"Coffee."

"Guido," Joe yelled, "cluck and grunt medium, wheat raft." Old Guido stood right behind Joe and nodded like he already heard the order. Guido's spatula pushed a healthy bead of grease toward the trap with one hand while the other masterfully cracked the eggs laying them sunny side up on the surface. The bacon sizzled as it hit the grill. Sam could have subsisted off just the aroma.

Guido stabbed the bacon off the grill and soaked up the excess grease by folding it between two paper towels. He did the same with the eggs and slid the plate in front of Sam.

"Anything else?" he asked. The New York tone was almost like a dare.

"No, thank you," Sam replied, sticking his fork into one of the eggs.

Things were looking up. The migraine started to subside as he dug into his delicious breakfast. He wondered why it tasted so good. *It has to be that grill.* The Lord knows how many years it had been seasoned by tons of bacon and sausage. It looked like it may have been the first one after the discovery of electricity. Maybe, he fantasized, it was converted from a coal stove into an electric grill and was a hundred years old. *Whatever,* he thought. *It's mighty good.*

Joe set the check in front of Sam: $7.39. He reached into his back pocket for his wallet. It was empty. Sam panicked. *Did that old man pick my pocket?* He was sure there were a couple twenties in it the last time he looked.

"Dammit!" he mumbled as he went through his other pockets. His hand hit an object in his jacket pocket. *What's this?* he asked himself, and then remembered the old man put something in there.

He pulled it out and examined it. It was an old, tarnished coin. By the look, feel, and weight, he thought it could be silver, but quickly dismissed that idea. *No one in his right mind hands out silver coins.* He thought about biting it like in the movies but he wasn't sure where it had been. The inscription grabbed his attention. One side of the coin had a figure of a human bust with a crown. He wondered, *Greek, Roman, or what?* The other side looked like sheaves of wheat. He didn't know much about coins, but somehow he was pretty certain he wouldn't find this in any coin book. He was also certain Joe wouldn't take it as legal tender.

Sam frantically fumbled through his other pockets as his anxiety increased because Joe didn't suffer bums, and he was sure that Guido wouldn't hire him to wash dishes. He shoved the coin back into his jacket pocket and felt some paper bills. Two twenties. His mind swirled with questions. *How did they get in that pocket? It was empty a few seconds ago, except for the coin? Am I still drunk?* Relieved, he thanked God and plunked a twenty on the counter in front of Joe who quickly snatched it up.

Sam picked up the ten and told Joe to keep the rest. Joe nodded. Then Sam jumped up and stepped outside into the cool air, trying to clear his head. The sun felt good on his face.

"What a weird morning," he said to himself. "I must be really losing it now."

Sam decided to take the long route back to the apartment and walk the rest of his haze off, and to avoid that alley. He checked his watch. He had a flying session scheduled at noon. He had just received his solo certificate and was nervously looking forward to taking the controls alone for the second time.

The traditional route took him down Church Street, which was lined with churches that were starting to come alive. Cars circled for parking places as people crisscrossed without looking or speaking. Each headed robotically for their particular worship site like schools of salmon programmed to swim up their separate home streams oblivious to any other fish or where they were going.

There were seven churches. *Unbelievable,* Sam thought, *all worshiping the same God but needing seven different houses of worship to make it happen. Explain that!*

The first was a Baptist church. They were already in the mode, sort of. He could hear "Just As I Am" faintly emanating from inside. *Could use a little more enthusiasm,* he thought. Sam had a soft spot for Baptists. Their hearts seemed to be in the right place, but it was just too hard to get to heaven. That wasn't for him. Anyway, he was sure alchies were not welcome.

The next was the Episcopal Church. He grew up in one of them. Most of these people showed up in minks and Cadillacs and those who didn't were not in any way shrinking from their superiority complex. No, he decided some time ago he was a misfit among them. Ragged jeans and unkempt appearance weren't greeted with much warmth.

Then there was the Catholic Church, one of Sam's favorites. He had to give them credit. For a church that was drowning in myriads of do's-and-don'ts, venal and mortal sins, they sure seemed to be much less burdened than the Baptists who, despite being saved by grace, carried tons of guilt around on their faces. For those Catholics who didn't get their sins absolved Saturday night, they had a second chance on Sunday.

Then there was Unitarian Universalist. No comment there. He passed the Methodist and the Lutheran churches and was coming up on the darkened doorways of the Seventh Day Adventists when his cell phone rang. Caller ID showed it was Steve, his brother.

"Damn," he muttered. "Guess I'll get a sermon with or without church." Sam's head started to hurt again. He wondered how his orthodox brother was able to tear himself away from his church duties to make a personal phone call. Then again, he was always able to make time to sermonize, chastise, criticize, or otherwise lecture him on his deviant lifestyle.

"Hey, Steve," he answered.

"You in church this morning?" Steve blurted, not wasting time on salutations.

"I'm fine, Steve. How are you?" he replied, ignoring his question.

"Don't be smart," Steve fired back. "How am I going to get through to you? You get wasted again last night?" Without giving an answer a chance, he fired at him some more. "You're headed for hell, buddy boy, if you don't get your act together."

Sam could see this picking up steam and going nowhere.

"What did you really call me for, Steve? I'm sure you're worried about my spiritual wellbeing, but I doubt that's why you stepped away from your solemn duties to call me on a Sunday morning."

"Go ahead, Sam," continued Steve. "Be a smartass. But you're right. I'm only calling for Pop. He's not doing all that well and, for whatever reason, he keeps asking about you. Says you haven't been to see him for quite a while. It beats me what he sees in you, considering how you wasted his money."

Steve's remarks hit home. Sam had neglected his grandfather. Pop was the only one who continued to believe in Sam, who had taken seven years to finally get an engineering degree. When he needed money, Pop was there; no questions asked. That was in contrast to his father who, though also generous, needed an executive summary, then the details, before handing out the bills. Sam was never turned down, but somehow he felt he earned every dollar his father provided. Now that he had graduated and found a real job and seemed to finally be on his way, he hadn't been around to show his gratitude; yet, he was very grateful to both of them.

"I don't know about how wasted his investment was, Steve," Sam fired back. "You've got some nerve, but you tell him I will see him this week. And you know what you can do with your little talk."

"You are right about one thing, there probably is no point in talking," Steve replied and then hung up.

Sam picked up the pace, fuming. His brother knew how to get under his skin. He was tired of righteous preaching from someone he didn't consider all that righteous. Steve was ten years Sam's senior, and it was clear as far back as he could remember that Steve wasn't the one that invited him into the world. He was perfectly content being an only child and garnering all the attention.

"You're a quitter, Sam. A quitter!" Steve reprimanded Sam the first time he left school.

Sam thought it was overrated whether it took him four years or seven to finish. And when he did, all that mattered was that he had a responsible job. His only penance was constantly having to hear Steve go on and on about how he had busted his ass in college and Sam was a ne'er-do-well slacker, never to amount to anything in this world.

††

When Sam returned to the apartment, John was lumbering around and looked like hell; his girlfriend didn't look much better. "My head feels like it's stuffed with cotton," John mumbled as he headed for the medicine cabinet.

"I'm with you, brother," retorted Sam. But he at least was starting to feel much better.

John was Sam's cellmate, as he called it, in college. Both had meandered their way through the university, meeting in Heat Transfer class. Their friendship took off and they started sharing living quarters and expenses. John was still looking for a full-time job. His anti-establishment hair and attitude didn't match up with employers' vision of an engineer. Nevertheless, John didn't seem concerned. He had always been the rebel, particularly with his father who was an Army officer. When straight-lace meets ambiguity, the result is always the same. John and his father basically had a stalemate, and that was where they left it.

"Hey, I've got a plane reserved this afternoon," Sam told John. "Want to go for a ride?" He laughed.

"I may still be drunk," John replied, "but not that drunk . . . By the way, I thought you had to be sober for twenty-four hours before flying?"

"Nahh, I think that's just for commercial pilots. It's less than .02 percent for private. I think I'm close to being legal." Sam laughed. "Anyway, I'm heading on over. I'll catch you this afternoon."

"Good luck. Don't crash it." John laughed.

"Funny." Sam headed to the street to his car.

Sam pulled into the private terminal and sauntered over to the office. It was a small regional airport that at least had a control tower. His instructor was not there, so Sam signed in and got the keys to the yellow Cessna 152 he had been training in.

He began to tense up. They could say it was like driving a car, but that was bull. There was nowhere to pull over in times of trouble. Fear was a good thing as long as it was mixed with the enjoyment of flying. He enjoyed the maneuvers, particularly the engine failure exercise where you simulated a loss of power and had to glide onto the runway. You had only one shot at it since theoretically the backup plan was to crash.

What a perfect day, he thought. The sun was shining. Visibility was great.

Sam slowly walked around the plane doing the preflight inspection. He checked everything: the pitot tube, the elevators, rudder, wheels, tires, and ailerons. Once satisfied, he hopped into the two-seater and put the key in the ignition.

"Clear," he yelled, popping open the window. He always felt a little foolish yelling into the wind since no one was within a hundred yards of the propeller. The little plane reverberated as it started and smoothed out as the engine revved.

He keyed the mike. "Ground control, this is seven-zero-four-hotel-tango, ready to taxi."

"Roger, seven-zero-four-hotel-tango, you are cleared to runway three-zero," came the crackling reply. It was difficult to hear over the engine noise. There were no other planes in sight.

Sam revved the engine and it started to pull out on the taxiway. The plane lurched like it was being pulled by a rubber band. He slowly taxied up to the runway and revved the engine again to check the carburetor heat. The engine quickly sputtered. Carburetor heat off. *Check*. He operated the rudder, elevators, and ailerons. *Check*. He ran the flaps wide open and back. *Check*. The trim was set for takeoff. He was ready to go.

Switching over to the tower frequency, he keyed the mike one more time. "Tower this is seven-zero-four-hotel-tango, ready for takeoff."

"Roger, seven-zero-four-hotel-tango, you are cleared for takeoff," came the same voice.

Sam squared the plane onto the runway and pushed the throttle all the way in. He used the rudder to compensate for a brisk wind from the left. The plane was quickly up to fifty-six knots as he began the roll, the wind shifting it to the right as he left the ground. Banking slightly to compensate, he climbed to four hundred feet at seventy knots and banked left, heading out over the hills. He climbed to three thousand feet and leveled off, resetting the trim and adjusting the throttle to regulate his speed. The houses were reduced to toy size while the roads snaked through bright fall colors. There was enough turbulence to bounce him around in the cockpit. He firmed up his grip on the stick.

Sam started out with some easy maneuvers, keeping his eye on the airport. He liked to leave mental breadcrumbs of landmarks to make it easier to navigate back. He practiced the usual maneuvers, banking to the right, banking to the left. This was very routine. After a while he was a little bored. *Need to spice this up,* he thought.

He decided to practice a power-takeoff stall. This was more interesting and required some real skill. One of the first things

Sam learned was that an aeronautical stall had nothing to do with stalling the engine. It was the minimum airspeed required to keep a plane aloft. Anything less, the plane falls. There is no gradual loss of lift. When a plane stalled, it fell from the sky like a rock.

He pulled the nose up, thrust the throttle all the way back in and reset the trim to takeoff position. He inched the nose up, slowly, watching the speed drop off and keeping his eye on the little white ball on the lower left-hand side of the dash. That indicated that enough right rudder was being employed to compensate for the torque of the engine and keep it level. As the plane speed slowed, more and more rudder was applied to keep the ball in the center. He waited apprehensively for the plane to stall, which would be a quick dip of the nose.

As he approached forty knots, he knew he was getting close to stall speed. The right rudder was pushed to the floorboard. And then the stall. The nose dropped. He pushed the stick forward and quickly recovered, level and flying straight. He was proud of himself. It was textbook.

Suddenly, without warning the plane dropped. It fell like a rock. No lift. The strings cut. No control. Straight down with full throttle. The plane went into an immediate counterclockwise spin. The earth rose up to meet him, a kaleidoscope of greens, oranges, and browns in a dizzying blur.

Sam immediately reacted. His instructor had shown him how to recover, but he had never done it himself. He struggled to remember.

The altimeter was spinning, only two thousand feet left to recover. *Full right rudder to stop the spin? . . . Yes . . . that's it.*

Sam pushed the right rudder to the floorboard. No effect. The plane continued to spin out of control, as the rotating earth loomed larger and larger. He pulled on the elevators as hard as he could. No effect. They would not budge. He turned the ailerons clockwise hard. The plane continued its downward spin. Sam was out of ideas—helpless.

Sam's life started passing before him. Even in his panic, he could hardly believe the old cliché, but it was true. He remembered his childhood, his acrimonious brother, and the loving eyes of his father, mother, and grandfather. He wished he could see them one more time to say . . . to say he was sorry for not living up to their ideals.

Something fell out of his pocket and hit the windshield. He wondered why it caught his attention above the roaring noise. *That crazy coin. What good is that?*

The plane seemed to spiral downward at supersonic speed. No time to pray. Sam resigned himself to his fate as he twisted and pulled on the controls.

2

God and Mammon

STEVE SEASON RAMMED THE phone in the cradle as he hung up on Sam. "That unappreciative little shit. Little leech," he mumbled as he walked into the bedroom. "I don't even know why anyone fools with him. He's drained Dad and Pop dry and has the nerve to talk back to me. I'm the only one who cares for them, cutting grass, fixing things around the house, getting them to appointments. He's nowhere around when you need him."

"Honey, did you say something?" asked Sue from the bathroom.

"No, just talking to Sam," Steve said, composing himself.

"Sam? How is he doing? We haven't seen him in a while."

"He's fine," he said as he put the final adjustments on his tie. He liked the way the red tie was set off against the dark-gray, three-piece, pinstriped suit. Pretty good taste, he thought. He turned sideways to admire the cut, smoothing his hair with his hand. He was a fine figure of a man—and he knew it. Six feet, one-eighty, jet-black hair. He was very proud of how well he had maintained his shape in his mid-thirties. And then he thought of his slovenly brother and wondered if he really was his brother.

"Honey, I'm taking off now," he said to Sue through the door. "Sorry to make you drive alone, but I have a Finance Committee meeting after church. Then I have to run to a meeting at the office. Then I have to go cut Pop's grass. Hopefully, with my superpowers, I can do all that and be at Mom's in time for Sunday dinner."

"Okay, sweetie," she replied. "I'll be right behind you."

Steve was drawn to Sue at first sight when he met her in church. Steve was attracted to her beauty; Sue was mostly attracted to Steve because of their like faith. They had been married five years and were now contemplating their first child. The prospect excited both of them—she more than he.

Steve got into his new 740i BMW, his present to himself for his recent promotion. He sat there for a moment soaking in its luxury. His hands reached down and stroked the black leather. Everything felt so different. He felt different. The smell. The ambiance. The success. Sue wondered how they were going to pay this along with their other debts, but Steve assured her a bright future was theirs for the taking. The new CFO of a prestigious accounting firm had to dress and live the part, he told her. The clothes, cars, and lifestyle made the man. Image was everything. You had to spend money to make money. This car was just a small investment with a huge payback, he had convinced her—and himself. And it said he had arrived, at only age thirty-five. He started the engine and listened to the muffled purr.

Steve looked to see who was watching as he slowly motored into the church parking lot. Sue was right behind him in her BMW X3. Greetings were accompanied with metallic smiles and robotic handshakes as they made their way to the choir room, where they donned their robes and waited for show time.

Finally they could hear the pipe organ's big voice start with "Holy Holy Holy." An opened door beckoned them to start the procession. A big cross led the way followed by swinging incense, the choir, and tailed by Father David. Each choir member genuflected to the eternal light as they turned to take their assigned seat in the loft above the pulpit. The choir led solemn songs. Rote prayers were read, alternating verses between the choir and the congregation, then silence ensued as Father David stepped up to take the pulpit.

Father David made an invocation and started his message. The theme was the dignity of man, showing respect, and not doing unto others what you would not want done unto yourself. A few recognized this as a remix of previous sermons. Some listened. Some didn't. Eyelids started to sag. When a barely audible snore started to become audible, a nervous wife elbowed her husband to attention. Many spent the time making mental checklists of plans for the afternoon as the sermon droned on. Steve thought about what to say during his Finance Committee meeting. Sue listened to Father David's every word.

Steve enjoyed the prestige of being the chairman of the Finance Committee of St. Paul's Episcopal Church of Murrysville. He controlled the purse, signing all the checks and handling all the financial affairs for the church and its school. He called a special meeting that Sunday right after the service to discuss the ever-widening gap in the church's expenditures versus revenues. He wasn't looking forward to that. The church was running in the red each week. Attendance had been steadily declining for the last five years.

After thirty long minutes, Father David finished his sermon and began preparation for the Holy Eucharist. The faithful were invited to the altar to kneel in groups.

After the last parishioner had partaken, Father David consumed the last of the transubstantiated wine. Final prayers were said, the candles extinguished, and the ceremonial procession began its reverse trek to the back of the sanctuary, mirroring their entrance. The choir trailed behind the cross-bearing layman while another swung the sweet-smelling incense in the faces of those lining the aisle. The glassy-eyed priest brought up the rear. Once the priest disappeared, the congregation started winding through the pews toward the exits, making banal small talk. Father David met them at the doorway and shook each person's hand. A smile would come across his alcohol-laced lips with each gratuitous review of his sermon.

The choir room picked up a head of noise as they disrobed. They were excited to get out and enjoy a beautiful fall day, with its peaking autumn colors.

Steve could see his committee members starting down the hall to the conference room. He nodded to Sue to say he would see her later in the afternoon. She acknowledged and walked out chatting with one of the ladies.

Four of the five members on the committee were long-time members of the church. One newly nominated member had recently moved into town from out of state. He was about Steve's age, had some business acumen, and tended to ask a lot of questions. Steve was used to presenting his recommendations and having them rubber-stamped, but this guy was a wild card which he took as a threat to his authority.

Father David would sometimes sit in on these meetings as an ad hoc member and was counted on as a favorable voice. But today was communion, and Steve knew that rendered the padre unavailable. Father David gladly performed his duties on communion days, but it always resulted in needing more of a nap than concern about worldly details.

Steve handed out the year-to-date profit and loss statement and gave a short PowerPoint showing declining cash flows and increasing expenses over the last several months. It was short on specifics as he felt there was no need to burden these lay people with the technical details of each line item. The shortfall, he pointed out, was about thirty thousand a month. They were drowning in red ink. Reserves were getting critically low.

"To sum it up," Steve said, "church attendance and membership continue to decline, but it is clear the remaining parishioners are not living up to the commitments they made at the beginning of the year when we put our budget together. The other main source of revenue, of course, is the elementary school, but it is barely breaking even. We need to come up with some strategies to balance the budget—soon. One thing for sure, it will take more than a cake sale."

Phil Martin, a charter member, spoke up. "Well, for one thing, those who committed their tithes to this church need to be talked to. The Bible is clear. If you make a vow, you better well keep it. That's the same as robbing God."

"True," said Mary Gilbert. "But I think it should be done privately to maintain their dignity. No need to embarrass them. We can talk to Father David. He can meet with them privately or subtly reprimand them in his sermons. Where is he this morning?"

"Other church business," Steve answered.

"Sermons on tithing give a short spike in giving," Phil said, "but it has proven not to be a long-term solution. It wears off quickly."

"Maybe so," said Gordon Blankenship, "but tithing needs to be taught. We should tithe because God commanded us to. I tithe because it's my obligation. 'Put me to the test, says God, and see if I will not open the windows of heaven' in Malachi. It's worked for me and it will work for them. There are consequences to our actions or inactions. 'For whatever one sows, that will he also reap' it says in Galatians."

"I disagree with sermons on tithing," piped up Mark Sutton, the resident scholar. "Tithing is not a New Testament mandate. That's old law stuff. The New Testament church isn't obligated to tithe and, in my opinion, it actually sets a limit on what people will give. If people give out of true love and a glad heart led by the Spirit, there is no limit to their giving. Ten percent just holds them back; puts a ceiling on it."

"That's very spiritual, Mark," Steve replied, hoping to avoid a full-blown theological debate, "and I totally agree. But I have been around numbers and these parishioners quite a while and, not to offend anyone, they are not close to the spiritual level required for them to open the windows of their hearts and pour out all their money spontaneously. They need a catalyst, a goad to prompt them. Let's just say Father David should address this from the pulpit. Agreed?"

Mark nodded his grimacing head in agreement.

Everyone nodded except Tim McCreary, the new member, who was still perusing the two sheets of paper Steve handed out, waiting for the theological discussions to finish.

"We definitely need to address the revenue side," Tim started. "I agree, but what about the expense side? That is just as important. To be honest, I can't really tell what is going on with these statements. I see a miscellaneous line item with a big number with no detail. Maybe a credit card account?" He looked over at Steve, pointing to the account.

"Yes," Steve said after looking. "That covers a lot of things. Gas, repairs, the communion wine, supplies . . . just a lot of various things."

"I see," said Tim. "I'm new here, so I apologize if don't know everything that is going on, but one thing I have heard from several is their giving is down because they don't know where the money is going. From some of these numbers, I have to say I can understand their concern."

"What is that supposed to mean?" Steve asked, glaring at Tim. "It's all transparent. Is someone accusing the staff of impropriety?"

"No, no," he replied. "I'm just saying, they don't think there is enough transparency, like these numbers that are presented. They don't have any detail. No one knows what it actually is being spent on. Any time there is a gap in information, human nature fills it, usually with misinformation. I've heard rumors, only rumors of course, of extravagant lunches, party expenses, personal expenses, payments to people for doing volunteer work. Stuff like that."

"All they have to do is ask," Steve replied. "Any uses of church funds are for church business and done appropriately. If some money is not used say . . . as efficiently as it should be in someone's opinion . . . we shouldn't be splitting hairs when you consider that none of us are paid for our services. Don't muzzle the ox is what scripture says. It sounds like a lot of pettiness based on rumor and innuendo."

"No one is accusing anyone, Steve," Tim said calmly. "Just for my edification, who has the credit cards? I understand just you and the pastor?"

"Yes," Steve replied, daring a follow up comment.

"I see," Tim said. "The other thing I can't figure out is the school costs. They seem awfully high given the number of students. The total salaries are extremely high. There isn't a breakdown, but I understand this little school has a superintendent and an assistant superintendent?"

"Well . . . yes," Steve answered, "but that operates more as a business. We don't typically tackle the operation of the school in this committee. I have reviewed all the numbers and the ratios are within norms for a school of this size. It might be a little beyond your scope."

"Maybe," Tim said not showing offense, "but I run my own business and this one seems to be top heavy, too much overhead.

I could be wrong. Anyway, can we get our hands on the actual budget detail? I might be able to help."

"I'm sure we can do that," Steve said, trying to control his frustration. "I'll see what we can do for next time."

"I'm not sure we accomplished much in this session," Steve said abruptly, quickly moving to adjourn. "I wanted to make everyone aware of the situation. Let's all pray about it and bring some more ideas to the next meeting. Thanks for coming." Steve's toothy smile masked his fury as he got up to leave.

"No closing prayer?" Mark asked.

Steve was half way out the door and didn't look back.

"Guess not."

Steve went straight to his car, passing a few others in the hall without speaking. He sat in it for a few moments to gain his composure. *Easy, Steve,* he coached himself. *Never let them see you sweat. Who is that wet-behind-the-ears SOB to come in here and start hacking away at our operations? Accusing me of how I handle the finances! Really! Challenging expenditures! One thing I know, worrying about nickels and dimes is not the answer. I've busted my ass for this church for years, even as an altar boy, and then this little pissant comes in worrying that someone might have gotten something they didn't deserve? Worrying about a tank of gas for church business. This car doesn't run on air.*

He started the car and slowly pulled out down the road toward the office, but his mind still raced. *And the accusation of nepotism. Tim knows my wife is the assistant superintendent. That was a smartass jag. She's only part time. Did he know that? She's more than qualified. Bachelor's in English and Master's in Reading. Who better to develop the curriculum?*

As he got closer to the office, he knew he had to shake off his emotions to set his mind on the next meeting, which was expected to be no more pleasant. As the CFO for MacNeil and MacNeil, an accounting firm, he planned on doing great things: reducing costs, improving productivity, and making a name for himself. This was only a stepping-stone.

After being in the job only two months, he decided to start by reengineering his entire department. That meant eliminating redundancy, the modern term for downsizing. In reality, it was a guise to justify ridding himself of non-team players. He had a meeting set up with Erik George, the director of HR, to go over the severance package for one senior accountant, Dick Masterson. Dick, a longtime employee, was passed over for the promotion and, in Steve's opinion, was disrupting his strategies and authority. He had to go.

Erik was already in his office going over a file. Erik suggested doing it on a Sunday afternoon to assure confidentiality.

"Afternoon, Erik," greeted Steve. "Ready to make short work of this?"

"Afternoon, Steve," returned Erik. "I don't know how short. I have some definite concerns about this termination."

"Such as?" asked Steve.

"Well, Dick Masterson is a longtime employee. He's been with this company since the old man started it thirty-five years ago. From all accounts he's been very effective, has had good reviews, and gets along well with others. True, he has exhibited an attitude at times, but I sure hope that is not the motivation here. That could backfire."

"Of course not, Erik," Steve lied. "He has been here a long time, long before me, and made positive contributions no doubt. But he hasn't kept up with the latest in accounting standards and methods. Jim is younger, but he has exceptional knowledge of the craft and new techniques. What he does will go straight to the bottom line as I explained to Mr. MacNeil. He also had concerns, but in the end, even he could see my logic. Dick is not the most qualified person to handle this job, and I don't need two people doing the same thing in two different ways. That makes his position no longer necessary. That is unfortunate, but we are in business to make money."

"I am not going to argue the technical aspects of the job or your organization, Steve," Erik said. "My part in this is the legal aspect—to protect the company and to protect Dick if appropriate. You know he is in a protected class. He's fifty-eight, which automatically puts him in a difficult position to obtain a similar job. We can say age discrimination is against the law, but it's alive and well with us in very subtle and covert ways. I can't worry about what discrimination he receives after he leaves here, but I have to be certain it is not an element of what we are about to do here today."

"I certainly agree," said Steve. "I can assure you that his age was not taken into consideration."

"Okay," Erik said. "I'll of course take your word for it. Now, I did hear from a couple persons, unsolicited by the way, that you might have made some age-related comments. Specifically calling him an "old fart" one time and a "dinosaur" another time in the hearing range of others."

"I don't recall ever making comments about his age publicly or privately," Steve said. "If they thought they heard something, it had to have been a joke taken out of context and before I became his boss. I would deny it."

Erik did the best he could to discourage him, but he could see that Steve was set on proceeding. The younger and elder MacNeils had signed off. It was a done deal.

"Okay," Erik acquiesced. "Don't take offense to my questions. They had to be asked."

"Understood," Steve said.

"Just be prepared," Erik continued. "This is a very fair severance package. Nevertheless, there is no sure thing he will accept it and sign a release. He does have a reputation of being hardheaded, and if he decides to lawyer-up, you will need to defend the decision. No offense, but you are new to management. Let's hope this isn't a mistake. If a court found in his favor for discrimination, it would hurt this company substantially."

"I'm sure," Steve said with some impatience. "I may be new but I know what I'm doing."

"Okay," Erik said. "When do you want to do it?"

"Let's get it over with," Steve said. "I'll grab him first thing in the morning."

"Good enough. Bring him right here. I'll have all the paperwork ready."

Steve got in his car and shook his head. *What a hellacious day,* he said to himself. Now one more task—cut Grandfather's grass.

Norman Season had a mild stroke a year earlier and needed help with the house chores. Steve to the rescue, again. *Where*

the hell is that worthless Sam—the favored one—when work is involved? "Damn him," he mumbled, "and the twelve acres waiting for him." But he lightened up when he considered its worth. Serious money was a good presumption. Steve had watched over the last few years as housing developments and strip malls had encroached closer to his grandfather's property. He knew developers had made lucrative offers, but he wasn't sure how much. He just knew Pop had declined to consider any of them. Steve planned on getting his just due for all he had done for his grandfather over the years. Sam should get his just due also—*Nothing!*

How Steve hated cutting grass, but today it would be good therapy.

Norman was not home. He was at Steve's parents for Sunday dinner. Steve brought some clothes to change in and mounted the tractor. *At least this will be the last mowing of the season . . . I'm glad he got a decent size tractor.*

Steve had a couple hours to let his mind float and forget the conflicts of the day, but there was no relief. *Why,* he wondered, *is he always the dutiful one with no help?* It never seemed to be appreciated. *Why is Sam the favorite? He was shiftless. He never did anything in school. At least I was the Eagle Scout.* Steve had carried the family's name to some glory in sports. He was salutatorian, the one Most Likely to Succeed. But the praise never seemed commensurate with the achievement. The "other one," on the other hand, didn't seem to mind getting all the handouts he could. He was in and out of college, a quitter. Wasting his father's money. Spending his time partying, drinking, and smoking. It disgusted Steve. *What a loser. Why do I have to compete with him?*

The two hours passed in an instant.

Steve carefully hung his suit on the rear passenger hook of his car and headed toward his parent's house for Sunday dinner. It was an open invitation every Sunday. Sam never seemed to be there, which didn't bother Steve.

Steve pulled into his father's gated community, which wound its way through a golf course. As soon as he passed the gate, the course sprinklers lit up and drenched his shiny black BMW with muddy re-circulated water. Anger shot through him like a bullet.

"Damn," he said, burning. How he wanted to go up to the pro-shop and light into them and stand over them while they re-waxed the car that he had labored over just the day before. How he would have made them get on their knees and wax it, square inch by square inch—if only he could.

The anger didn't have much time to subside before Steve was in the driveway. He got out and walked around his beautiful possession glaring at the muddy spots. The garage door was open, so he grabbed a rag, wet it, and started to wipe it down, cleaning it as best he could. Finally satisfied, he entered the house forcing a smile.

The smile quickly faded when he entered the kitchen. His mother was talking frantically on the phone. His father was sitting at the table, his head in his hands. Pop sat across from him silent, listening.

"What?" His mother was asking. "What?...When?...Where? ... How?"

"Hey," said Steve. "What? What's going on? Why the faces?"

"It's ... it's Sam ..." his father stammered.

"What's he done now?" Steve demanded. "Lord only knows what damn-fool predicament he got himself into this time."

His mother hung up the phone. "Sam ... " she said quietly, "he crashed that damn airplane ..."

Faces went white and lost all expression—except Steve's.

3

SEEING THE LIGHT

SAM WAS FISHING ALONG a lazy riverbank. He had no idea where he was or how he got there. A yellow sun blazed overhead while white cumulous clouds drifted across a deep-blue canvas. The azure river snaked through a mountain valley of forty shades of green. *This must be heaven,* he thought. Off in the distance downstream, a wriggling horny, green tail was propelling what appeared to be an alligator-like creature toward him at a slow but steady pace. When it was very close, the clouds suddenly turned dark and thundered. The water turned black as coal. The alligator, with eyes like burning red coals, stood on its hind feet in front of Sam. Sam threw his rod to the ground and turned quickly to run, but the river monster grabbed him and pulled him back. Sam bit the beast's arm. Unfazed, the monster wrapped both arms around Sam and started squeezing like a boa constrictor, tightening its death grip. Sam could not breathe. This must be hell he concluded as he passed out.

A dim light appeared in the distance. It kept growing brighter like it was approaching. *Was this the legendary light referred to by so many near deaths?* Sam wondered. It was always associated with heaven, but now Sam wasn't so sure. Maybe it was another deception like the river, a cruel trick. "Let's stop the games," he yelled to God. "Which is it? Heaven or hell? I know what I deserve. Let's just get it over." Sudden pain shot through every fiber of his body. His heart sunk with the final answer: *Hell!*

††

Sam's eyes popped open; a ceiling light shined in his face. It wasn't heaven and it wasn't hell. It was earth. He was in a hospital room with lines and tubes running every which way into his body and down his throat.

He tried to move but couldn't. Was he chained up? Was it another trick? He struggled to free himself, but only his left arm and leg seemed to obey. Then he could see the casts. He was bandaged up from head to toe. His right arm and leg were encased in plaster. He was mummified, but not dead.

Sam struggled to remember how he got there. Random images flashed in front of him. The pain became more and more real as the drugs wore off. It helped shed some of the fuzziness. It all started to come back. The plane, the nosedive, the spin, and how he was jerking and pulling at the controls. The whirling earth rushing at him with no chance for escape. Those last few seconds. The panic and then the peace. He made his peace with God in the last seconds. How did he escape?

Then he remembered the end. The spin started to unravel into a diving spiral as the redlined engine roared like a WWII dive-bomber. The nose began to respond and lift, finally leveling off just a few feet from impact. It was too late to climb. The woods were right there in front of him. No, they weren't woods. Just a thick row of trees planted as a windbreak between two fields. The last thing he remembered was rocketing through the tree limbs at what seemed like supersonic speed, ripping the wings off. It was as if the hand of God had grabbed that plane, swung it around like a father swings a child, and hurled it in the direction of those trees and that field.

He was alive! He couldn't believe it. What had he done to deserve this?

There were voices coming from the corner of the room. Figures started to hover around him. A tiny light flashed into one eye and then the other. His eyes recovered long enough to reveal a beautiful face smiling at him, and then he could feel a needle sink into his arm. That angelic face was the last thing he remembered.

Sam slept. Sleep without dreams. Everyone's prayer. No tormenting dreams this time. Just peaceful rest. The first time since he was a child.

When Sam awoke, he could see the same pretty face like time had not passed. So it wasn't a dream. She was adjusting some IV's. His eyes and mind were clearer. He tried to lift his head to speak, but the pain, the lovely evidence that he was still alive, brought it back to the pillow. She wasn't aware he was staring at what he thought was the most beautiful woman he had ever seen. Or had he seen her before? There was something familiar.

"Now I know I'm in heaven," he said, eking out muted words, "for mine eyes have seen an angel." Sam blushed through his bandages at his unusual boldness. *Was it the drugs?* he wondered.

She turned and giggled. He managed an awkward smile. It hurt.

"Ahhh," she teased, "the sandman liveth. You've been out for quite a while."

"Really . . . how long?" he asked.

"Four days," she replied. "You've had company the whole time. Your parents and grandfather just stepped out to get some lunch. I'll send them a message you're awake."

She stepped out and gave some directions to one of the orderlies.

She came back in and sat next to Sam. "How do you feel?" she asked.

"Pretty much how I look," he replied, surveying all the casts, bandages, and tubes with what little he could move his head. "Is it as bad as it looks?"

"I won't lie. It was serious. Touch and go for a while. You're very lucky. Someone was looking out for you. Someone not of this earth, I suspect. The doctor's been called and he will give you all the specifics, but it was one of those just save his life, stop the bleeding, and then worry about all the broken bones. You had broken ribs, internal hemorrhaging, concussion. They kept you in a coma to start the healing. But you're out of the woods now. You're going to need a lot of rest. You won't be going anywhere for a while. I've been praying for you every night."

Nice, but odd, Sam thought. Some stranger praying for him. Now he knew she was an angel.

"Thank you. How did they find me? The last thing I remember is crashing out in the country. I just remember some trees, closing my eyes, and praying."

"I can only tell you what your family told me. They are such nice people. Apparently you crashed into a farmer's field while he was planting winter wheat. If that farmer had not been out there when you crashed, they never would have gotten there in time. He said he was just driving his tractor on a beautiful Sunday afternoon when this bright-yellow rocket crashed through the trees out of nowhere right in front of him. It had no wings or landing gear and hit the freshly plowed field like a bobsled. He said you plowed a mighty nice furrow for a while until it flipped end for end with a few twists in the air and finally planted itself nose first in the ground. It sounded like you did a double gainer with a twist that would have made Greg Louganis jealous." She giggled again.

"You're funny," Sam said. "What's your name?"

"Mo."

"Mo? What is that short for?"

"It's not short for anything," she replied. "Just Mo. M-O."

Sam laughed, but the pain brought the seriousness back to his face.

"Uh . . . sorry," he said. "Just an unusual name. I like it though. There must be a story."

She giggled again. There was something about her laugh. He loved to hear it.

"Don't worry," she said. "Everybody asks. My dad came up with it. I'm named after a Chinese prostitute." She watched his face for a reaction.

"Interesting," Sam said. "I think there's more."

"There is. If you knew my fundamentalist father, you would never imagine this. He abhors any kind of sin or appearance of sin, but apparently there were at least two prostitutes he was willing to forgive: Rahab who assisted the Israelites in Jericho and Yu Mo, a Chinese prostitute who gave her life during a Japanese invasion to save the lives of young convent schoolgirls who would have been raped and killed. I'm kind of proud of it. Kind of proud of my dad."

"Well, I would be proud of it," Sam agreed. "You look familiar. I don't want to embarrass myself, but have I seen you before?"

"You probably should." She laughed. "It's possible I was one of the last persons you saw before you tried to kill yourself. Remember Sunday morning? Coffee? I was sitting on the veranda across the alley from your apartment. You looked at me and got up and left. Was it something I said?" She laughed again.

Sam turned a new shade of red. "Ohhh . . . Yeah. Sorry. Wasn't in too good a shape that morning."

"Kind of looked that way even from a distance," Mo concurred, smiling. "I'm not judging. Been there."

Sam's family filed into the room. "Sammy," his mother cried as she entered. How he hated her calling him Sammy, but somehow it didn't seem to matter now.

"I'll leave you in the good hands of these wonderful people. I'll be back with the doctor shortly," Mo said. She stood in the doorway for a minute to see Sam's family reunite.

His father and grandfather stood back smiling with simple relief. His mother rushed over with tears in her eyes. She bent over and kissed him softly on the cheek. She didn't know whether to touch him or not.

"Does it hurt? I thought I lost you," she cried. Then her face transformed into that old familiar motherly look. He knew he was about to get it.

"What in the world were you thinking," she started.

He winked at Mo. She muffled a laugh and disappeared.

Her lecture was short lived as she sat staring at her son thankful he was alive.

"Well, you'll have to tell us what happened," Sam's father said. "All we know is the ending, and thank God for that farmer."

His dad's recounting of the crash from the farmer wasn't as colorful as Mo's, but it was consistent. Sam did his best to explain what happened, but his father had no idea what he was talking about—stalls, spins, ailerons, elevators, and dive-bombers. His father was an accountant like Steve and as such knew about balance sheets—not aerodynamics.

"I guess the best way to sum it up, Dad, is I flew too close to the sun." Sam tried to laugh but it was too painful.

"I'll sum it up as a miracle," his father added. "Just a plain old-fashioned miracle."

"For sure," replied Sam.

"What's Steve got to say?" asked Sam. "I know he doesn't suffer fools, but thankfully God does."

"Oh, he didn't say much," his mother chimed in defensively. "He was here the first day with Father David. He didn't stay long. They prayed over you, talked to the doctor, and said he'd be back."

Sure, thought Sam.

Grandfather Season, always the quiet one, just sat and listened contentedly as everyone debated.

"Pop, I'm so sorry I haven't been over to see you. What do you think?" Sam asked. "A miracle?"

"Most assuredly so," Pop replied.

The doctor came in and waded through the family. He smiled at Sam. "Lucky man," he said.

"That's what I hear," Sam agreed.

The doctor checked all his vital signs. He was pleased with what he saw. He gave him a shot. "You're going to need a lot of rest," he said. "You are officially upgraded from critical to fair." He patted him gently on the shoulder and left.

When Sam awoke, the clock on the wall showed it was just after three in the morning. He looked over to see his grandfather still sitting in that little chair looking at him.

Norman was a quiet man, always staying in the background, unnoticed except by a few. But everyone knew he was the anchor holding the family together. His steady demeanor never failed despite the worst of situations, and he had had a few. This time was no different. When the news came with the possibility of the worst, he just prayed and thanked God, the God of the living, not the dead, for whatever outcome He willed. Norman was very pleased with this outcome because he knew something the others did not.

"Hello," he said quietly. Sam saw a look in his grandfather's blue eyes that was familiar but was stronger now. It was the look of wisdom, love, maybe faith, or maybe all these things. Norman moved his chair closer to the bed.

"Hi, Pop," Sam said groggily. He started to apologize for not coming to see him, but his grandfather gently cut him off.

"It's okay, Sam," he said.

"Thanks, Pop, for no lecture. Everyone else jumps on my every mistake and then saves them to use again, particularly Steve. But you . . . well, you have never done that. It's like you know something they don't."

"Everything is like it's supposed to be, Sam. If it's a secret, it's hiding in plain sight," he replied. "Simple as seeing God in everything."

"God in this? I guess I almost saw him face to face, but I don't know how He was involved in saving me from my stupidity," Sam said.

"I don't know about mistakes, Sam. God doesn't make mistakes. He's a lot closer to this than you know."

"What do you mean, Pop?"

"I have a feeling you'll figure it out very soon, Sam. It's not something I can explain. But there are some things I need to share with you tonight, just between you and me. After they had you stabilized, I went to the crash site Monday morning to see some things for myself. All the stories told today don't do justice to the picture I saw. No one could have walked away from that. Nothing but a crumpled yellow tin can upended in the dirt. No wings. No landing gear. That was all stripped off back in that tree line. It was wonderful. You could see God in this whole thing from beginning to end.

"I talked to the farmer. He was upset that the NTSB had stopped his planting and taped the whole field off, but he had quite a sense of humor. He wanted me to thank you for plowing up half the field for him."

They both laughed until Sam grimaced in pain. "Don't make me laugh, Pop." He grinned.

"Sorry," Norman said. "Couldn't help sharing that. He also wanted me to let you know he was grateful to be there for you, and then he handed me this. He found it on the dash. After he dragged you from the cockpit, he didn't want it to get stolen by some gold diggers. He thought it might be valuable. He was right in ways he didn't know."

Norman handed Sam an old, tarnished silver coin. Sam's eyes opened wide. It was only a few days ago since he had first seen that coin, but somehow he knew it was going to be following him for a long time. He took it with his good hand and examined it. It was different. It had changed again. On one side was a figure of a great white-haired man sitting on a throne. The other side was a figure of one man laying hands on a sick man.

Sam's mind went into overdrive. "Pop, do you know what this is? Is this what you meant that you could see God in this? I almost died. Are you saying He orchestrated this crash?" Sam laid the coin on the night table.

"Yes," said Norman.

Sam waited, expecting more of an answer. "What does that mean, Pop? All I know is I'm still here whether luck, serendipity, or divine intervention. I don't feel I deserve any special favor from God, but I sure don't know why he would try to kill me."

"God isn't much good at trying. Doing is His specialty. He's much nearer than you realize, Sam," said Norman. "He is not only with you. He is in you. In your heart and in your mouth."

Sam's groggy mind struggled to understand what his grandfather was trying to tell him. He and his grandfather had many conversations in the past. His words were so simple. Too simple, but they always rang true somehow. His words made something in the heart jump like a child kicking, a child yearning to be born.

"I believe you, Pop. I don't pretend to understand. I just don't know what's going on. What's with this coin? It's been plaguing me ever since Sunday. It's the weirdest thing. It won't go away. Maybe it has value as silver, but it's freaking me out. Have you ever heard of anything like this?"

Norman smiled. "Well, I've studied a few things about lost coins," he started.

"The lost coin?" Sam echoed. "Is that what you . . . they call it?"

Norman grinned. "Yes, that's what the mystics call it—the

lost coin."

"The mystics? Who are they?" he asked.

Norman smiled patiently. "They're just simple people. Like you and me. People whose hearts are tuned to God. They see God in all things. What some call evil and what some call good, it's all the same to them. They see with the single eye. That's all."

"Well, what does it mean to me? Why has this thing shown up now?"

"The first time the coin was mentioned in scripture was when Jesus was asked if it was right to pay taxes to Caesar. He said show me a coin. They brought him a denarius. 'Whose image and inscription are on it?' he asked. They responded, 'Caesar,' but they didn't notice on the opposite side of the coin, the tails side, was the image of a lamb. And they also didn't realize that the side with the lamb was the head, not the tail. The tax collectors who tried to spend it met with bad fortune.

"Eventually this coin was found by a righteous man, a mystic, who understood it could not be used for selfish gain but only for furtherance of the kingdom of God. Before he died, he handed it off to another, who in turn handed it to another and so on. It was continually paid forward, so to speak. If this is it, then God has a special plan for you. And based on the events of the last few days, it appears it has a mission for you."

"So what are you saying? Is it a good luck charm? A magical talisman? Something with super powers?" Sam asked.

"No." Norman laughed. "It's only a symbol. The only power it has is your faith in the power behind the symbol. It's a sign post showing you the way—your mission."

"What mission? Me? Wouldn't I be the last person God would choose?"

"The last will be first, Sam. Its real meaning is found in the parable of the lost coin. A woman had ten silver coins and lost one. She sweeps the house looking for it. When she finds it, she calls her friends and neighbors. 'I have found my lost coin,' she tells them. 'Rejoice with me.'"

"Pop, I've read that, but to be honest, I don't know what it means."

"It means, Sam, that God left all to find one lost coin. And that one will leave all to find others. You will come to understand."

Sam was silent. He mulled his grandfather's words. He suddenly became very tired. He wondered how his grandfather knew so much about the coin as he slipped into deep sleep without another word.

Norman sat there in the dim light looking at his grandson. The coin on the nightstand was gone. He felt an object in his pocket. He pulled out an old, tarnished silver coin. It was the same as it had been for many years. On the heads side was the likeness of the Son of Man. On the tails side was the image of a young Norman Season.

4

THE INTERROGATION

STEVE FINALLY MADE A showing, along with Sue. Sam was surprised. He wondered if it was his mother's doing. As they talked, the strain in their relationship hung thick in the room.

Steve took the chair in the corner while Sue sat close to the bed.

"How are you feeling?" Sue asked. "It looks painful."

"It's getting better," Sam replied. "I can feel improvement each day. I don't turn down any drugs." He tried to laugh but grimaced in pain. Sue stroked his arm.

"They say you'll be in for at least a month," Steve said. "Buddy, you really did it this time. Pretty lucky they say."

"I don't know what "this time" means," Sam replied, already feeling the heat. "It could have happened to anyone."

"Only someone that charged headlong into something they didn't know anything about," Steve retorted.

Sam's ears started to turn red. Steve had only two modes of talking, both of which Sam hated: The principal's lecture tone, which he was about to get, or the teacher's condescending tone.

"What's with this flying thing anyway? What's it going to do for you? It seems like you just graduated, finally got a worthwhile job, might be able to salvage some kind of a decent life after wasting it so far, and that you'd focus on that a while before getting all these wild notions. How about St. Paul's? Father David thinks you've abandoned the faith. He's been praying for you. What if you had died without the church? Maybe this excess energy that's suddenly come upon you could have been better used there serving the church."

Sam's pain was swallowed up by his anger. He tried to raise his head to get a direct bead on Steve. Sue could see his face starting to turn crimson and astutely intervened.

"I'm sure you can do it all," she said. "The prospect of flying an airplane is something that always excited me, but I never had the nerve."

"Since when?" asked Steve. "I didn't know that."

"Well, hon, there may be a few things you don't know about me. I might be a little more on the wild side than you give me credit for," she replied and winked at Sam.

"Whatever," he said, rolling his eyes. "Look, we have to go. I've got a meeting I need to be at. Good to see you. Get well."

Another meeting, thought Sam. *He needs to come up with something more original.*

"Besides, I understand you have some other visitors coming this morning. If you don't like my questions, I'm pretty sure you won't like theirs."

Sam knew he was talking about the NTSB. He supposed they had been to the crash site analyzing all the evidence. He could have saved them a trip. Pilot error. It was plain and simple. Maybe there was some alcohol involved, but only if they had proof.

"Thanks for coming," Sam said. "Thanks, Sue."

Steve wondered what Sam was thanking Sue for as he beckoned for her to come.

"You're welcome, Sam," Sue said. "When you get better you need to start making your mother's Sunday dinners. That will fix you right up."

"I know it. I will."

The NTSB was waiting. These people, Sam heard, were very acute and their questions directed toward specific types of answers. They would record the entire interview. They had already interviewed Sam's flight instructor, George Sherman.

Sherm was not allowed to have contact with Sam until the interview process was completed.

They had been out to the site of the crash and interviewed the farmer. The wreckage was extricated from the field. They could not find any issues with the structure, the power plant, or any navigation systems. Weather was not a factor that day, nor was traffic control. That only left the pilot.

It should have been one of their easier deductions, Sam thought. *Dumbass student pilot.*

After Steve and Sue left two agents knocked on the door.

"Come in," Sam said.

"Hi. Samuel Season?"

"Yes," he replied. "Call me Sam."

"Hi, I'm Sharie Morgan. I'm the lead investigator in this incident, and this is my colleague Jeff Smith. We're from the NTSB."

"I've been expecting your visit," Sam said.

"Do you feel like talking?" she asked. "I know you have severe injuries."

"I'm okay," he said.

"Great, Sam. We appreciate it. Just so you know, we will be recording this interview. Is that okay with you?"

"Yes," he replied.

They took the two chairs and pulled them up close to the bedside.

"To start, according to your log book, you have fifteen hours total with four of those hours solo. Is that correct?" she asked while Jeff took notes and operated the recorder.

"Yes."

"So, how were you feeling that day?"

"Well, okay. I had a few things on my mind, but . . . nothing that would have prevented me from being okay to fly."

"Any alcohol before the flight?" She maintained steady eye contact.

Sam knew he was made here. He was sure they took blood samples, but he knew it had to be close to zero by the time of the accident.

"The night before," he replied.

"Heavy?"

"Not exactly moderate," Sam said, losing eye contact. "But my mind was clear that afternoon."

"Okay," she said, dropping it, "and you were practicing a power takeoff stall when this happened? Correct?"

"Yes."

"So, please walk me through what happened."

"Well, I did it exactly as I was taught. Everything seemed to be working according to the textbook. I set the trim to takeoff, pushed the throttle to full power, kept nosing it up, adding more and more right rudder as the attitude increased until it stalled. I recovered perfectly. I was quite pleased with myself. Maybe smug. Then something happened. I literally just dropped from the sky, rotating in a spin. I . . . I guess I wasn't paying attention to my airspeed and, well . . . I suppose it's not a guess, I went into another stall and was taken off guard."

"Were you ever trained on how to recover from a stall or spin?"

"Sherm, I mean George Sherman, my instructor, demonstrated one time how to get out of a spin. He went through the whole thing. He stalled it, the nose dropped into a spin. He pushed on the right rudder to stop the rotation and pulled the nose up. Is seemed so easy when he did it. But when it happened to me, alone, it didn't work. The only reason I leveled off at all was doing the opposite."

"I see. Sam, we could not help but notice when we examined the plane that the throttle was still pushed all the way in. Do you think your body hit it on impact and pushed it in? Do you know how it would have gotten that way?"

Sam thought for a second. His eyes widened. The revelation struck him with a sickening feeling in his stomach.

"I guess I do know how it got that way. I never pulled the throttle back," Sam replied as his face turned red as a beet.

"Why not, if I may ask?"

"It happened so fast," Sam said embarrassedly. "I just reacted. In the wrong way apparently. Stupidity to be more accurate."

"Don't be too hard on yourself. I wouldn't call it stupidity. You would have needed a lot more training to say that. You survived. That doesn't happen often; actually it never happens under these circumstances. You only have seconds to correct and somehow, well . . . here you are. So, tell me. We've never seen this before. How did you level the plane off at full throttle and not simply crash nose first into the ground. Sorry to be so graphic, but that was what we would have expected."

Sam went through his last Hail Mary machinations; counter intuitively turning the plane in the direction of the spin and how it turned into a deep-diving spiral sounding like a dive-bomber over WWII Germany. He leveled off close to the ground with no time to gain altitude before he went bush hogging through that tree windbreak.

He had their attention. Jeff stopped taking notes. They both listened intently, heads tilted and jaws partially open, as they traded slight glances with one another. Sam detailed his one point landing, tobogganing into that freshly plowed field before upending into the double gainer with a twist, as Mo described it.

"That's quite a colorful way to describe a life-threatening crash," Sharie said. "Good you have a sense of humor. Now, before the crash, tell me one more time how you handled the controls."

Sam reiterated what happened, how he turned the plane into the direction of the spin and how he started to regain some control.

They asked more questions, but they sounded like the same ones just rephrased. When they were sure the story wouldn't change, they finished the interview.

"Well," Sharie said, "you are one lucky . . . well . . . I'm not sure if that is the correct way to categorize it, either lucky or something else. I'll be honest with you, Sam. I believe everything you've said, but it's hard. However, I have no alternative. Here you are. Evidence enough. Someone was apparently looking out for you. It had to be the way you described, so I will simply say I have seen something I have never seen before. And that is unusual in this job. But, then again, we don't get to interview everyone, if you know what I mean. All this will be reflected in our final report, which should come out in about thirty days. You can now have contact with Mr. George Sherman if you wish to discuss the incident and continue your career as a pilot."

"Well, I've had plenty of time to think about my career, and . . . maybe . . . I'm thinking maybe I'm more of a land lubber."

"That is not an unusual life choice change in these circumstances." She laughed. He held out his left hand to both of them. They exchanged handshakes and made their way out the door still bewildered.

Sam lay there, staring at the ceiling. *What a grueling day so far,* he thought. *Glad that's over with.* His thoughts turned to Mo. She would be in soon. She had become quite a flirt, and he enjoyed that. *Maybe she likes me,* he thought. He suspected she made more visits than protocol required. He waited eagerly for her visits.

Before he could finish his thought, Mo stepped in. Her smiling face always energized him, making him forget his pain. She was very petite, standing maybe about five foot two, less than a hundred pounds, he guessed. Her dark hair and big brown eyes with an aquiline nose that added just the right measure of character set off her pale face. But what really grabbed him was her seemingly constant enthusiasm for life. It was contagious. She was never without a witty quip and a smile. He couldn't help but admire her.

"How we feeling today, Captain?" She giggled.

"Not all that shipshape," he replied. "I'm thinking of resigning my commission."

"Tough day, huh? They were in here a long time."

"Yeah. They did their job, for sure. They left no detail uncovered," he said.

"Well, nothing wrong with staying an earthling." She laughed. "Get those feet planted firmly on the ground."

"I think you are having too much fun in my pain," Sam said. "Shouldn't you be more sympathetic? Isn't that what nurses are supposed to do?"

"Ha," she laughed. "I know you aren't in that much pain. I took care of that. Although that will be a'changing soon. Need to wean you off. But you ought to be delighted. To make it through something like that . . . wow! There's no doubt someone has plans for you."

Sam was perplexed at that statement. Who was this nebulous someone everyone kept referring to?

"I suppose," Sam said. "Whoever someone is. I'm not sure who or what that is. And . . . well, yeah . . . I do have plans. I just graduated, got my first real job. Yeah, I'd say I have plans."

Mo just smiled. "Well there are your plans and then there are "other" plans."

"What do you mean?" Sam asked.

"Oh, you'll figure it out."

Figure it out? Sam thought. First his grandfather says these cryptic things and then Mo. *How is it everyone seems to know something I don't? And all the strange things happening. The old man in the alley and that shape-shifting silver coin, which keeps getting lost and showing up at the weirdest times.*

Sam looked around and realized it was lost again. It really was the lost coin.

Mo looked at her watch. "Sorry, no time for any more clichés. Gotta make my rounds. I'll check back with you before my shift ends. By the way, I met John and Molly after they left. They sure are nice. They invited me over. Hope you don't mind."

"No, no, no," Sam said excitedly. "That's great. And think how well that will work. I'll be out of here in a few weeks and we can move to home care. See'n as how we're neighbors and all, you and me. What do you think of that?" He smiled sheepishly.

She grinned ear to ear. "That could be arranged, I believe . . . but it will cost you. I'll have to check the rules regarding nurse-patient relationships." She laughed one more time and was gone.

"I'm looking forward to it," Sam said to an empty room. All his inhibitions were gone. There was nothing intimidating about this beautiful girl. He was disarmed totally and completely—and very happy.

5

REFLECTIONS

FOUR WEEKS WAS A long time to be bound to a bed and reality shows. *Really?* Sam thought. *Who can watch this stuff? No wonder I love scotch.* He tried meditation. He prayed marathon prayers. But he never lasted that long. *How did the "real" religious people do it?* he wondered. Sam wondered what they had to say that took so long. *Were they doing the talking or was God? Or were they just braying like sheep? Long-winded, vain repetitions? It has to be pretty boring,* he thought, *for them and for God.*

But Sam was thankful for the time. It forced him to reflect—a mandatory exercise for those with near-death experiences. He was face-to-face with who he was, and he didn't like it. Most of his life was spent running, looking over his shoulder like a man being pursued by an invisible policeman. Now he was finally stopped, caught, and arrested. There was an eerie peace to it all.

Sam's life passed before him in a split second that fateful Sunday, but now it was laborious and slow—recounted in real time, second by second, minute by minute, day by day. He remembered the Sunday school stories he loved as a child. There was Jesus as a child teaching the masters. How great was that?

He believed then as only a child can do. Then real life crept in, little by little.

Junior high was the first revelation of cruelty. Outcast. Bullied. High school took it to another level with the hurt, the pain of not fitting in, and the silent treatment. But the finale was yet to come . . . adulthood. Life became adulterated all right, destroying the remains of childhood belief. It was dog-eat-dog dressed in their Sunday best with shiny, smiling faces. Christians welcomed you with one hand while stabbing you with the other. But now, none of it seemed to matter.

Now, the wind fell calm on angry sails. The anger effervesced. All the people in his life, all that had happened, whether considered good or evil, he knew was good—just as God had planned. Even his current, crippled estate was good. Sam met Mo, the beauty he never would have had the nerve to talk to before. Goose bumps trickled up his arm.

And he was coming to know his grandfather, who Sam always held in awe, on a deeper level. Norman had always taken a peculiar interest in Sam; something that did not go unnoticed by his brother, but now was more intense, like time was of the essence. Norman loved to talk scripture but in a casual, easy way. His gospel just flowed naturally from his heart. Sam didn't understand it all, but his heart jumped at what it knew was truth being revealed. Pop would just laugh at Sam's quizzical looks and pat him.

Sam's grandparents were always unconventional, an enigma to the "religious" churchgoers. Never talking church dogma, they only talked Christ, about being "other lovers," and life being easy. They just loved and it showed on their faces. "Forget the law," Pop said. "Live the spontaneous life like Christ did. Live Christ as you."

Most mentally rolled their eyes at their easy-come gospel and their indifference to church tradition. "Organized religion for the most part," he remembered Pop saying, "stunts your growth." Despite his grandparents unorthodox Christianity, it was clear his grandparents had something that made others around them envious.

They had the true Spirit, Sam believed, living a life of freedom—unencumbered by any law. It dumbfounded the religious majority, this total freedom from the law. Yes, they agreed, we are free from the law as the scripture says, saved by grace, but somehow we're still able to mix the two together, no questions asked. That was as successful, Pop would say, as combining oil and water.

His grandparents were probably no different than the Apostles, Sam figured, living on the fringe. But they weren't the only ones. Many showed up for small-group meetings in Norman's house. Sam didn't know where they came from but they were so different, so unpretentious. They walked confidently, so sure of themselves; not like others with their constant fear of being exposed. They were down-to-earth people from all walks of life—doctors and lawyers, janitors and garbage collectors, teachers and the unemployed—you name it. Like his grandfather, they called themselves *knowers*, their only boast being containers for Christ. They said they were Christ in their human forms. That made many uncomfortable, but they were so relaxed in their own skins you couldn't dispute they had something. They never judged others or themselves.

Sam wanted that. Norman's words were like music in Sam's heart, but his head trailed far behind. He wanted so to catch up. He didn't understand why he was so slow.

"I think you give me too much credit," he told his grandfather.

Norman smiled. "Patience, Sam. We're in no hurry. God has a plan for you. Hmmm . . . I think he has a plan to make an oak tree out of you. And God takes his time making an oak tree."

Sam let it go at that.

Sam had other visitors over his tenure at the hospital. Sue visited a few times. He never really had gotten to know her before. She was so sweet. He wondered what she saw in his brother and then felt bad for thinking that.

Peter McDonald, his boss of only a few months since he graduated, stopped in one day for a few minutes. Since Sam had been there such a short time, he was concerned they might decide to cut their losses and hire someone else. Peter assured him his current projects had been reassigned, and his job would be waiting for him. Sam thanked him for coming.

Sherm also stopped by to see him in the hospital after a couple of weeks. Sam felt as sorry for him as Sherm did for Sam. He was visibly upset when he entered the hospital room. Sam immediately apologized about the plane, but Sherm didn't even answer to that, almost tearing up.

"You don't need to apologize, Sam. I do," he said. "Whenever there is an incident, minor or major, that is a failing on my part, not yours."

They talked for an hour about the incident and even managed to laugh at a few things that had happened in his short fifteen hour tenure of flying. He told Sam about the NTSB investigation. They had interviewed him for several hours, drilling into the minutia of each minute of instruction, what he had said, what he didn't say, had he trained him in all the essentials, how to recover from a spin . . .Was Sam capable of being a pilot? Had he soloed too soon?

They questioned him about his credentials. Sherm was the same age as Sam, but he had several thousand hours and just earned his instructor certificate. He felt they were also questioning his ability as a pilot and an instructor. Sam had seen Sherm's skills. Though he didn't have anything to compare them against, he was certain they were second to none.

"It was grueling, as I'm sure you found out. They even asked me about your mental state." He laughed. "Like I'd be qualified to assess that. As far as ability, of course I thought you were ready. Otherwise I would not have issued a solo certificate when I did. And I still think you have the skills, Sam, to continue with your training. But that's up to you, of course. I would understand if you decided not to."

"I was going to say I'll have to think about that, Sherm, but I've had plenty of time in here to do that, of course. I still haven't made up my mind. Let me ask you. It seems like this would be a common situation any pilots might find themselves in. Why aren't we trained more on recovering from a spin? I know you did the one demonstration, but that was all."

"The truth is, Sam, it's not taught anymore. The reason? Too many students killed practicing that maneuver," Sherm said. "It was removed from the program, which is a mistake, obviously. Doesn't make sense, particularly given your example. What's funny . . . sorry . . . not funny, but it's not that difficult, you actually only made one mistake. If you had pulled back on the throttle, you would have had no problem. Look, it's up to you if you want to continue with the lessons or not. I wouldn't blame you. But if you can trust me one more time, I'll ask you to do one thing for me—if you're up to it. Let me take you up one more time and show you some things you never imagined about that craft. I guarantee it will be eye opening. No charge. Deal?"

Sam thought for a moment. "Deal." After Sherm left, he thought about it some more. His muscles tightened.

And of course John visited often, usually with Molly. "Long tall John," Sam would remark whenever he saw him coming. Sam loved John. He was his antithesis. John wasn't quite ready to shake his hippy college look and attitude, which is probably why he didn't have a job yet. His long hair always had that clean look, but it conflicted with the clean-shaven, iPad-carrying geeks doing the interviews. "They don't get it," John would say. He was right. He was bright, energetic but he didn't quite get it either—yet. He, like Sam, had to realize that life had phases. It was time to let some old things go and grab some new ones.

Sam envied John's free spirit. Maybe he wasn't Jesus, but his yoke was light and his burden was easy. Though college was over, he continued on with his wild abandon. Sam, on the other hand, worried about everything, even stuff he had no business worrying about. He remembered when he and John drove through a parking lot barrier at the Marriot and crashed a wedding, feasting on shrimp and hors d'oeuvres while the groom looked at them strangely without saying a word. They walked to the pool area and found it abandoned. Despite guests milling around the halls, John stripped and jumped in. He skinny-dipped a few laps with the most relaxed strokes and a laughing smile on his face. "Come on in," he yelled, "the water's fine." Sam looked around to see if anyone heard. He was chicken. John finally jumped out, grabbed a towel, dressed, and they walked out like they owned the place. Sam was as excited as though he had dared to brave the feat, too. He was, after all, an accomplice. They hopped back in the car, popped a couple beers, and laughed all the way down the road. John was his vicarious alter ego. There were some close calls, but they got away with it.

††

The next afternoon, John was there to pick him up. Sam didn't realize what a mother hen John was until he tried to get Sam into his compact car. Sam tried putting one leg in first. That didn't work. Then he sat and his leg wouldn't bend enough to swing in. Finally John lifted him into the car.

"Phew," John said. "You're still a mess. You look like the Mummy with that cast and sling. Ask me again to go for a plane ride with you. I dare ya."

"I feel like the Mummy," Sam agreed.

"Well, we'll get you home and get a drink in you, man. Then you'll feel right at home."

"I'll think about it," Sam said. "No alcohol for a month . . . It wasn't bad, actually. Clear mind. Clear eyes . . ."

"Gaawd, man," John piped up. "You ain't going straight on me, are you?"

"Easy. Just thinking about it. I'm off the hard stuff, I can tell you that. That's my penance for now."

"That's my boy." John laughed.

"Uh oh," Sam said as they pulled up to the apartment building.

"What?" asked John.

Sam pointed to the staircase. He hadn't thought about his walkup apartment until now, like you never think about an appendage until it hurts. John followed behind him as Sam navigated one rickety flight at a time.

"This is going to be interesting," Sam mumbled. "Maybe I should have taken my parents' offer to stay there until I shed all this medical paraphernalia." Then he wiped that idea out of his head. That was stupid. He smiled thinking about how close he was to his neighbor, Mo.

Sam finally managed himself into John's old easy chair. It was still yellow with red flowers. The blue oak leaf ashtray sat beside it. It was still full. It still stunk.

John grabbed two beers and handed one over to Sam. He took a sip. It tasted strange. He took a longer swallow. It wasn't bad, but he had to be careful with his medications.

He was a little light headed when the can was empty. Jumbled thoughts flooded back into his head. Thoughts of the crash, the so-called divine intervention, all the words his grandfather had shared in the last few weeks.

"Say, John, do you ever think about life after death?" Sam asked.

"Oh, dude." John groaned. "Don't get ghosty on me. Look . . . I think, I feel, therefore I am. We're just here for the now, my man."

"Yeah . . . I'm not so sure. I almost wasn't."

"Don't get too far out there, man," John countered. "Stuff happens. When it's your time, it's your time. It ain't your time . . . yet. That's all."

"So existential, man," Sam said as John went into the kitchen to grab a couple more beers.

"Look," he yelled from the kitchen with his head stuck in the refrigerator, "maybe there's a God. I don't know. But I do believe what I said. When it's your time, it's your time. I think you need to get back on that horse and ride it."

"We'll see," Sam said as his butt tightened up thinking about it.

"What did you say?" yelled John.

"I said I'll think about it," yelled Sam.

John appeared in front of him with two more beers. "What are you yelling for? Now . . . dinner. What'll it be? Hamburger Helper? Or Tuna Helper?"

My best friend just became my mother, Sam thought, looking at him.

"Welcome home," Sam said.

6

MO, HARRY, AND SAM

MO MADE HER HOUSE calls as promised. The highlight of Sam's day was her visits, which were most evenings. And, as promised, they came at a cost. "No free lunch," she said. If Sam thought John was a mother hen, he hadn't seen anything yet.

As his private nurse, Mo saved him the need to go to physical therapy. She brought it to him. Being lazy wasn't an option. As the casts came off, the exercises began. She pushed him hard. It was painful and it paid off. He started getting his mobility back. She was good at her job.

She also had a problem with their menu. "Tuna Helper!" she exclaimed. "Seriously? Disgusting. I didn't know they still made that stuff." She made no comment about the beer other than to caution about mixing it with his medications.

"Well, we don't eat Tuna Helper every day," Sam defended. "We have other stuff."

"Right," she said. "Hamburger Helper? I stand corrected."

Mo could cook. She started to prepare tasty meals: grilled fish, casseroles, pastas with plenty of vegetables and salads, which was foreign to the Sam and John household. Even John thought he would keep his mouth shut and go with the flow. Mo tending to Sam was working out pretty good. *We don't need Sam getting cured too soon,* he thought.

Molly started writing down the recipes. "Where did you learn to cook like that?" she asked.

"Down on the farm," she said. "We did a lot of cooking. Not much fancy eating out."

It was clear to John and Molly that Mo had fallen for Sam. It was clear Sam had fallen for Mo. But it was also clear to everyone that Sam was slow to catch on. He still couldn't believe this beautiful, outgoing girl could be interested in old introverted Sam. She had this free spirit, always bright and cheerful. That was the opposite of the shy worrier Sam. With his casts off, he worried she might not come around as much.

John and Molly looked at each other in disbelief. Finally Molly spelled it out for him.

"Sam, are you that dense? She's in love with you. She's not just here for your health, dumbo. If you're wondering why, you're not the only one. But you better make a move before you blow it."

Sam looked over at Mo who hadn't taken her eyes off him the whole evening. He recognized the look. It was the same one he had.

"A farm girl, huh?" he asked.

"Yep, born and bred." She giggled.

"I never would have thought, I mean . . . your sophistication . . . uhh . . . I mean not that farmers aren't . . . well, you know."

Mo laughed so loud it filled the room. "Here, let me take that shovel away from you before you dig a hole so deep you can't get out."

Sam laughed with a tinge of blush. John heehawed. Molly rolled her eyes.

After that night, all pretenses were gone. Their relationship quickened fast. Most of the evenings were spent at her apartment. She would cook and then they would talk—for hours. Despite being opposites, Sam soon found out they were a lot more the same than he imagined. They were seeking the same things. Her conversation always gravitated to her faith in Christ.

Sam shared his innermost feelings and fears. Something he had never done with anyone before. Somehow it seemed natural. No more hiding. He wanted to tell her, and he wanted to know all about her. He told her how Christ filled his thoughts constantly starting a few months before the accident, but he never felt part of the church-going crowd.

"The last time I felt connected to God was when I was twelve. A friend invited me to a revival. I didn't even know what that was. I felt the speaker was talking directly to me. When they gave the invitation, I went up. I remembered how different I felt. Even at that age, I could feel the weight being lifted. But it wasn't long before I was back in my own church, and the weight slowly returned with full measure. Church did little to relieve the burden."

"You're funny." Mo laughed. "For someone who didn't get much out of church, you sure seem to pull out quite a few scripture references."

"Oh, I've had a lot of time to study lately. And my grandfather is always quoting scripture. But you, you know so much, and you have never mentioned church. It's clear your faith is very deep and much more relaxed and confident than mine. You have something I envy."

"I have no problem with church," she said. "I've enjoyed more church sermons than you can imagine. I went to church every Sunday morning, every Sunday night, every time the doors were open. I had no choice, but I'm thankful for that. I learned a lot of scripture, which was very important in my life, but I too didn't really learn all that much about God. At the time I thought I did. There was a notion hidden in the background that with continued effort, you could be like Christ. Then something told me there was much more to God than trying to be good and not sin. I learned from others that the only person that can be like Christ is Christ. Really knowing Christ and knowing who we are in Christ is a personal journey, and you can't go there as a group. They will always hold you back. You have to go it alone. The Bible says extend the borders of your tents. If you live in a Baptist tent or a Catholic tent, you can't do that. Their pegs are driven in concrete. They can't be pulled and stretched. No, you have to want it and you have to go it alone and it can be lonely. We've known each other a short time, don't ask me how, but I know that is what you want. God is leading me—us—on a different path. You ask me what denomination. Think how ridiculous that is. There's no such thing as Methodist, Baptist, or Catholic. We're just Christians, the only kind that God sees."

Sam stared. "That was the best micro sermon I have ever heard. I'm willing to go it alone, but I may need help."

She smiled. "I know. We all do. And you're going to meet the help tonight."

"I am? I'll take your word for that. You sound like you're related to my grandfather," Sam said. "I think I'm looking forward to it. But tell me more. I love hearing your story."

Mo was pleased. "Like I said, I grew up in the church—a strict, fundamentalist Baptist church. And I love those people. Still do. They were as sincere as spring water. It met their needs. But after a while, it no longer met mine. The sermons just repeated themselves. They stopped short of the whole truth. We had one pastor who actually preached a teaching message I learned so much from. The one after him had nothing to say that quickened me, and he couldn't preach. Yet no one noticed the difference. They just kept taking notes. I wanted much more, and God revealed to me it was there for the taking—the total truth."

"I love your outlook," Sam said. "I just see the negative side, the hopeless side. All I see now is hypocrisy and self-righteous people going through the motions like robots. I look around and all I see is the Emperor in his new clothes, strutting around naked."

"There is plenty of that," Mo said, "but it doesn't have anything to do with us. Sometimes we look at things through the wrong end of the telescope. Besides, when it comes to hypocrisy, we all live in glass houses. Like my church brethren, I spent many years pretending I could live the Christian life, believing if I prayed enough, read the Bible enough, went to church enough, worked for Christ, I could get there. I guess I was one of the few that realized it doesn't work. It's a total lie. You can't work for Christ. You can't pay Him back. I devoured all the how-to books, the ten steps, and the twelve steps. There was no shortage of how-to experts to help me be a better person. Secular teachers.

Religious teachers. You name it. I tried to please my parents, my pastor, and my teachers. They all worked for a while, but in the end, they crashed and burned. That was when I ran into a person who made me realize that there is no such thing as self-improvement. The people you are referring to haven't, can't, or won't come to that conclusion. They are still under the delusion we can be good if we work at it."

"What do you mean we can't be good? Why is it a delusion?" Sam asked.

"Well, you'll learn more when you meet my friends. I got so frustrated with Christianity that, like you, I hated going to church. My dad forced me until I left for college. That was when I stopped going altogether. I didn't share that with him, of course. The only thing that saved me is the 21st century. A hundred years ago, they would have stoned me." Mo laughed. "I was so sick of scripture being quoted to me that was clouds and wind with no rain. It didn't quicken."

Sam laughed. "Wait a minute, isn't that quoting scripture?"

Mo blushed. "Well, yes, but rightly divided."

"What does it mean didn't quicken?" Sam asked.

"It falls flat. It's like taking uncharged paddles to jump-start your heart. Nothing happens. They just lay on your chest. You die."

"There is a picture worth a thousand words."

"Anyway, to make a long story short, I, like a lot of forced Christian children, finally cut loose. I got a little wild. It was nice. Freedom was like cool evening breeze—for a while anyway. But it took a while to come to know what real freedom was. Letting loose was good. At least it was honest, something new to most Christians. Many may think it was not so good, but it was necessary for me to learn true freedom to really know Christ. I had to plumb some depths, but God lifted me up. I met Harry. He introduced me to total truth." Mo stopped there with her smile and looked for Sam's reaction.

Sam tilted his head. "Total truth? That sounds ominous," he said. "You sure you're not related to my grandfather?"

"Oh, I'm pretty sure we are," she said.

Sam still wasn't sure. He wondered how he had missed all this. She did sound like his grandfather. It made sense, but it was so contrary to everything he had learned. Mo was so sincere. She didn't push anything. It was offered, that's all. He liked that.

"Are you ready to go?" she asked.

"Where?"

"To meet my friends. The ones I just told you about."

"Ohhhkaaay." He balked. "It's getting late, though. We have to work in the morning."

"You'll be fine," she said. "Let's go." She reached over and grabbed his hand, pulling him up from the chair.

Mo helped Sam hobble down the stairs to her car. She drove. They drove to the other side of town to another apartment building, not unlike their own. She was able to park right in front.

"What luck," she said. "Oops, the parking meter is expired. I don't have any change."

"I'll get it," Sam said, getting out first. He rummaged through his pants pockets. Empty again. He reached in his back pocket and pulled out something hard. It was the old, tarnished silver coin. He thought it was lost. He stared at it while Mo wondered what he was doing. He looked up and to his surprise the meter had two hours on it. This thing was really starting to scare him.

"Need change?" Mo asked.

"Not anymore," Sam replied. "Two hours enough?" Sam hadn't shared anything about the coin yet. He didn't want her to think he was crazy.

"I'm sure," she said. "We are really fortunate tonight. Harry is going to be here. He is so wonderful to listen to. So full of the Spirit."

"Full of something, I'm sure," said Sam.

Mo narrowed her eyes and glared. "Skeptic?"

"Hey, I'm here. I like it. It's got an elevator. You can be sure my next apartment will have one."

"Hmm, I hope that won't be the highlight of the night."

They rode up to the fourth floor and walked down the hall. It was a small apartment. When they entered Sam could see a half dozen people milling around. The pleasant smell of coffee filled the room. There were cookies on the counter and no one was shy about digging in. They weren't shy about anything. Mo navigated the room, hugging each person and introducing Sam. "Is this your boyfriend?" they would ask. Mo just smiled.

Sam usually tensed up meeting new people but quickly found himself at ease in this place. He had met these people before in his grandfather's house. They were unpretentious, unassuming, like long-lost friends.

What was it about these people, Sam wondered. They looked like other people, but they were different. Were these the ones who knew total truth, as Mo put it? Sam strained to figure it out. What was that look on their faces? Love? *That's corny,* he thought. Yet the sense would not leave him. He could see why Mo was so attracted to these people. This was what he was looking for.

If anyone was unassuming it was Harry. Harry was . . . well . . . old. He must have been about seventy-five, short, gray, balding, and thick around the middle. Harry sat in an overstuffed chair as others grabbed the remaining chairs or sat cross-legged on the floor in front. Before he spoke a word, you could feel love flow from this innocuous person.

There's something about those eyes, Sam thought. He had seen them before.

The chatter stopped. Harry started to speak. Sam thought it odd they didn't have a long prayer to open up the session.

"Tonight," Harry started, "per Mo's request, I am going to talk about the self-improvement myth."

He looked down and smiled at Sam. Sam was completely disarmed.

"To do that, we have to start at the beginning, before Genesis, and understand who God is so we can understand who we are. God, we know, is tripartite—three persons in one. In His essence, God is Spirit. But Spirit has no form or expression. He must express Himself through His Word, the second Person of the trinity. He spoke the world into existence. The third Person, the Holy Spirit, made it happen. So the Spirit, the Word, and the Holy Spirit, or Father-Son-Holy Spirit, make up the three offices required to make a whole. You can also see that the three persons represent the three capacities necessary for a person to function—thought-word-deed.

"When God made man in His image, He created him tripartite also: spirit, soul, and body. Spirit is that hidden part of man where his heart is, where he wills and knows things, where his true nature resides. Soul is the expression of the spirit to the outside world where thoughts and emotions reside, where we try to understand things. Our body is the action part. There you have man in the image of God with the same three requirements for a person to function: thought, word, deed. We think it. We say it. We do it.

"Now, our spirit is who we really are, but our spirit is different than God's. God's spirit has life in itself; ours does not. It is created to be a container only. The question is to contain what? In the beginning, it was meant to contain God. His Spirit would be joined to our spirit in a union. That is how it was until Adam and Eve disobeyed God. They were not soul conscious of their union with God, but when Satan tricked them they knew then that something had drastically changed. The Spirit of God had left and Satan entered, taking over control. They were conscious they were naked. Their eyes were opened. Yes, they now knew right from wrong, but it was then, and still is, a distorted view. Before, all things were good. Now, everything is divided. They were now under the control of Satan. That is why Jesus said in John 8:44 to the Pharisees, 'You are of your father the devil, and the desires of your father you will do. He was a murderer from the beginning, and abode not in the truth, because there is no truth in him. When he speaks a lie, he speaks of his own, for he is a liar, and the father of it.'

"That is very strong language," Harry continued. "He is saying that man is not in control and never has been. He is under the control of, and takes on the nature of, whomever he contains. If the spirit of Sin, then the desires of Satan he will do. He cannot improve Satan, no matter how hard he tries. When the Holy Spirit convicts us of sin and righteousness and we recognize our sin, then we can make a different choice of owner, but that is all. When we make the choice for Christ, He replaces the Sin spirit with Himself and we take on His nature. We talk about Christ in us, living in our hearts, being the Lord of our lives, but do we really understand the gravity of what we are saying? Do we know what Paul meant in Galatians 2:20 when he said, 'I am crucified with Christ: nevertheless I live; yet not I, but Christ lives in me?'

"It means that he, Paul, no longer lives. Christ lives. In him, as him. Are we making ourselves as God? Of course not. We are simply containers for the deity that always intended to live in us.

"What is the practical application for us? It means that we haven't changed. The only thing that has changed is whom we contain. Before, we contained Satan and his desires we had no choice but to do. Now we contain Christ and His desires work in us. Trying to be good is ridiculous. That is His job. We are one with God. First Corinthians 6:17 says, 'But he who is joined to the Lord becomes one spirit with him.' One Spirit!"

Sam strained to soak it all in. He had heard these words from his grandfather. Hearing them from another helped quicken them in his heart.

Harry said man is perfectly made. He just needs to recognize what his role is and why he was made. God made man to manifest and reflect His glory throughout the earth. Man is the receiver, the negative to the positive. He is made to work perfectly if he can just believe and get his hands off the controls.

That last part really puzzled Sam. *How do you do that?* he wondered. *Get your hands off the controls?*

"Okay, to wind it up, why does that mean self-improvement is impossible? Why can't we get better and be like Christ? Because the only person who can be like Christ is Christ, and we are already Christ in His various human forms. You couldn't do good before, and you can't do it now. As long as we live under the delusion that we are on our own to be good with hope of overcoming the sin in our lives, we will fail. Recognize who you are in Christ and rest in Him. You are just containers for Christ, to let him live His life out through you, as you."

He stopped and looked around. "I think that is enough for tonight. It's a lot to take in. Any questions?"

Sam raised his hand. "What about Adam and Eve? If it was so great being in union with God, why did they rebel?"

"Good question, Sam," Harry said, looking around. "I think everyone is a bit tired after all that. How about I save that for another night?" Harry smiled at Sam.

"Wow," Sam said, looking at his watch. "I think that is a good idea." Two hours had passed. He couldn't believe it.

The parking meter grabbed his thoughts. *Damn,* he thought. Then he remembered the coin. *No worry, Sam. God has this one.*

††

Mo had been quiet for the entire two hours. She was watching Sam's reaction. He was totally lost in the meeting, not even aware she was beside him.

"So, what did you think?" Mo asked as they got on the elevator.

"Crazy stuff. Crazy enough to be true. Why is this a secret? I don't know why it all made sense. It quickened," he added with a laugh.

"I'm so glad it quickened," Mo said. "That's God revealing to you secrets from the foundation of the world. I don't know why it seems so hard for most to accept. Maybe it's too simple and too easy. Even though the Bible makes it clear we have absolutely no righteousness, Satan does a good job keeping the Total Truth out of their hearts. Remember the parable of the seeds."

"It's a lot to mull over," Sam said, arriving at the car. The parking meter had one minute left. He reached in his pocket for the silver coin. Gone again.

7

I Can Fly

SAM WAS BACK AT work, and Pete MacDonald wasn't kidding—there was plenty of work. The company was expanding locally and around the globe. No worry about job security.

Sam enjoyed engineering. He followed in the footsteps of his grandfather while Steve had followed in his father's footsteps as an accountant. Sam's projects ranged from upgrading equipment to plant expansions. He particularly liked new installations. He was just assigned as a team member on a new project to expand polymer operations. He was working under the senior project manager to add a third line. This project was particularly challenging in that it required real-world application of what he had spent years learning. He was sitting at his desk running heat-transfer calculations to see if the existing chiller was going to be able to handle the load for the new process line. The phone rang.

"Hey, Sam, it's Sherm," said the voice.

Sam hesitated for a second. "Hey, Sherm. What's up?"

"It's been a while. I was thinking of you. Did you remember my offer? To take you up at my expense? Maybe it will bring closure to your experience, maybe not. But I thought you might like to understand what happened and, like I said, you might learn a few things about this vessel. I'm not pushing it. I can understand if you never crawled back into a plane, but I don't want you to be scared to. It's my fault if I didn't teach you that the first time."

A moment separated them. "Sam? You there? Can you hear me?"

"Yeah," Sam said, cracking his frozen thought. "No, I hear you. Actually, I thought about calling you. I guess I have mixed feelings about flying again. It's eagle versus chicken, I guess, and I've been waiting to see who was going to win."

Another moment of silence passed.

"You know what, Sherm?" he said finally. "Eagle wins. I'm going to take you up on your offer. I don't know if it will make a difference, but let's do it."

"Great. Ten o'clock Saturday?"

"I'll see you then. Bye." Sam hung up the phone.

Mo invited Sam over for dinner, which was becoming the norm. When he arrived, she was making quesadillas. The smell of sautéed chicken and onions filled the little apartment.

"Hmmm," he said, kissing her on the cheek. "You have definitely raised cuisine to a new level."

"Thanks, sweetie," she said. "And the bar was so high."

They both laughed. She filled two hot flour tortillas with the mixture, sprinkled some monterey-jack cheese on them and a spoonful of chilies, and brought the plates over to the kitchen table and sat down.

"How was your day?" she asked.

"Interesting," he replied. "Sherm called me today. Remember I told you. He was really upset about all that happened and wants to take me up for a free lesson. I guess to show me what I did wrong."

"Do you want to know?" she asked.

"In a way. I guess in one way I do and in another I wonder what difference it makes. I really don't intend to continue to get my license. Of course, this may change my mind. Sherm was adamant that even if I didn't complete the course, I should go up at least one more time just to be sure. John, of course, keeps saying I need to get back on that horse and ride. That's easy enough for him to say since he doesn't have any gravitational concerns walking around on earth. Maybe I should get him up on that horse. He might have a different perspective."

"I understand," she said. "I have a feeling, though, it might be good for you. I know it's been on your mind a lot."

"Yeah, it has. Anyway, I told him I'd be there. Ten o'clock Saturday morning."

††

It was Saturday morning before Sam knew it. He met Sherm at the terminal. Sam's stomach growled. It was cold. The leaves were off the trees now and a small layer of snow covered the ground.

I don't believe it, Sam thought walking out to the little red Cessna alongside Sherm. There he was, standing beside the machine that attempted his murder. Had he not learned his lesson? He wondered how he could be such an idiot. He thought Chicken was dead, but he was wrong. He was alive and well. *I hate to say I told you so,* Chicken whispered.

But here he was. He tried to lighten up.

"Well that's a nice plane, Sherm. Looks kinda new. I wonder who you have to thank for that?" Sam gave a nervous laugh.

"I wonder," Sherm said with a smile. "Good things come out of bad, I guess. Do you remember how to preflight?"

"Sure," Sam said. "I replayed that a thousand times in the hospital, from preflight to . . . well . . . whatever."

Sam walked around the plane and did all the checks. He had to admit it was a pretty plane. The cockpit was the same but looked more modern. He climbed into the left side. Sherm climbed into the right side. Sam popped open the window.

"Clear," he yelled with that familiar odd feeling because of no one, again, in sight to hear. He turned the key. A short sputter morphed into the sound of a one-ton bumblebee. He tensed.

He keyed the mike and was ready to radio the tower that seven-zero-four-hotel-tango was ready to takeoff but remembered that old seven-zero-four-hotel-tango was no more.

"Tower, this is eight-niner-seven-alpha-omega ready for

taxi," Sam corrected.

He looked over at Sherm and said, "Alpha and omega? Really? How apropos." Sherm laughed.

"Roger, eight-niner-seven-alpha-omega. You are cleared for taxi. Pull up to runway three zero and hold."

When he reached the runway, he finished his preflight. The engine was revved, the carburetor heat choked the engine; everything was ready to go. He switched to the tower frequency.

"Tower, this is eight-niner-seven-alpha-omega ready for takeoff."

"Roger, eight-niner-seven-alpha-omega," the same voice crackled over the speaker. "You are cleared for takeoff."

Sam checked his trim and turned onto the runway. His hand tightened on the throttle as he slowly pushed it in as far as it would go. He knew it was too late to back out now as the plane picked up speed. He looked over at Sherm. He was glad he was there.

He was at takeoff speed in an instant. He started the roll. As it left the ground, a crosswind from the right caught him off guard, jerking the plane to the left. For some reason the right crosswinds were more difficult to handle, but he corrected quickly and began his climb straight out from the runway. At four hundred feet he made a left bank and climbed to four thousand feet, a little higher elevation than he was before the accident. Sam was calmer now. He had to admit, it was still a beautiful sight. This time the little roads drew black lines in the white landscape as miniature cars moved like snails.

They tried some simple maneuvers. Sam got increasingly more comfortable. He was getting bolder knowing he had Sherm to handle any mishaps. He was even starting to enjoy it. *Take that, Chicken,* he told his imaginary tormentor.

"Okay, Sam. Ready?" Sherm asked.

"Ready as I ever will be," Sam replied, immediately stiffening up.

"Okay. Easy does it. This time we are going to do a power-takeoff stall, just like you did before, only we are not going to try and recover. We are going to let it stall and go into a nose dive."

"Okay. You're the boss." Sam set the trim to takeoff and nosed the plane up and up. The plane slowed more and more as

Sam increased the attitude. Images of his last flight flooded back to him. His stomach knotted up. He kept the little white ball in the middle with the right rudder. He could feel in his bones what was about to happen. Suddenly the nose dropped. As instructed, Sam did not try to recover. He let it fall. It nosed straight down and started to spin. Déjà vu.

Sherm touched Sam's tense shoulder. "It's okay, Sam," he said, pointing his finger at the throttle, "pull the throttle all the way back."

Sam wasted no time yanking it to idle.

"Now, don't touch anything," Sherm instructed. "Give it a little right rudder and keep your hands on the wheel to guide it."

The plane stopped spinning and began to level off on its own without any effort. Sam looked over at Sherm. He was shocked.

"Really!" Sam almost shouted as he reset the trim and gave it some gas. "You mean that was all there was to it? This thing flies itself?"

Sherm just smiled. "Almost, Sam. Let me explain what you did. First of all, this plane is designed to fly. It's a natural flyer. The only way it can't fly is if we make it not fly."

"Make it not fly?" Sam asked puzzled.

"Exactly. When you kept the throttle in and were pulling on the controls, you were in effect holding it in a stall, preventing it from flying. If you had taken your hands off all the controls, it probably would have done what comes naturally, flying."

"Amazing," Sam said. "All along I thought I was flying the plane and lo and behold, I wasn't flying it at all. It was flying itself. You're saying all I have to do is make small adjustments and point it in the right direction?"

"That's about it. The plane is going to follow the laws of aerodynamics if the operator aligns himself with them. If he fights them, it doesn't work. The only thing I can figure about what saved you, other than divine intervention, was that when you turned the ailerons in the direction of the spin, at least you stopped fighting it. That was apparently enough alignment to come out of the spin into that spiral you described and defeat death."

Agree with your adversary quickly in the way came to Sam's mind as Sherm talked. He kept mulling what he had just learned. It was such a simple concept. *Simple?* That was a term he and Mo had been discussing a lot recently. Sometimes it was too simple to see.

Sam thanked Sherm for the lesson. "I don't know if I'll continue," he said, "but you really opened my eyes. Thank you."

"You're welcome, Sam. Anytime. I'm glad you decided to take at least one more trip."

††

Sam couldn't wait to get back and tell Mo what he had learned. That evening they stayed home and he cooked for Mo. Something, of course, that she had taught him. Tacos.

As he was making dinner he told her all about it. She listened intently.

"So, what did you really learn, Sam?" she asked. "You look like you had some kind of revelation."

"I think so," he said. "You remember when Harry was talking about us being only a vessel, made to contain someone? How we do not have a nature of our own, let alone two natures? He says it's a delusion to believe we are independent and can operate independently. We take on the nature of the deity we contain and are operated by. That's either the false god Satan or the true God, and we have no choice but to express the nature of whoever that person is."

"Yes," she said.

"So, that is all true. But only if we allow, or "let", as Harry would say, that person have complete control. With Satan, it's not a problem. Before we know Christ, we are in perfect alignment with him. We share the delusion of independence and he reinforces that delusion even though he is running the show. He makes us believe it is us. There is no conflict until we are convicted of sin. When we receive Christ, though, it's different. We are saved but we carry over Satan's delusion of independence, that we operate ourselves with a little help from God. What that means is we have the option of disrupting the natural order of the design. He allows us to play with the controls and fiddle with the knobs, or at least lets us believe we can. That dooms us to failure every time. It's a lesson he lovingly repeats ad infinitum until we finally learn that we couldn't operate ourselves by the Law before we believe, and we still cannot operate by the Law after we believe. We continue in failure until we learn to trust him alone at the controls to operate us, the vessel, as we were intended.

"What I learned today is there are not just immutable laws of physics in the universe, there are immutable spiritual laws. You can fight them if you want, but they always win. Take the plane as a metaphor. Say I am the plane. The cockpit is my spirit. It's perfectly made, designed to do what it does, just as man is. Nothing wrong with it. The pilot determines how it operates. The pilot knows what he is doing and guides the plane according to his will. When aligned with all the laws of aerodynamics there is no problem. But if it's not aligned with those laws, it falls from the sky.

"If our cockpit contains God and we are in alignment with His will, everything works perfectly. If not: disaster. Anytime the plane decides it can fly itself, or we decide to climb into the cockpit ourselves, God lets us so we can prove to ourselves it can't be done. The result is always the same. We crash and burn. The plane is just the vessel, the container in need of a pilot. Man is just the vessel, the container in need of an operator. In my ignorance, I took a perfectly good vessel and forced it into a stall until it all but killed me. We do the same thing in our spiritual lives. When we take control and start jerking and pulling at the controls because we can't wait on God, we force ourselves into a spiritual stall. Wait, the Bible says, on the Lord."

"Wow," she said. "It's amazing how quickly you absorbed these truths. It takes most people years."

"Well, I think I do have the idea, but the application is still hazy. I wouldn't jump to any conclusions. My head has it but it's confused as usual. Actually, it hurts."

"Maybe," she said. "However long it takes, I think God has great plans for you."

8

THE GOOD, THE BAD, AND THE PIOUS

IT WAS OBVIOUS TO everyone that Sam and Mo were a done deal. It was just a matter of time, they all said, when they saw those starry eyes. They were seldom seen one without the other. Mo had a glow on her face. Sam was determined to please her.

Sam would have gladly gone like an ox to the slaughter if Mo hadn't drawn a clear line on his amorous advances. She loved the physical contact, the caresses, the hugs, the kisses, but when it went beyond love, she put up her hand. She would say, "It's not time. I don't feel any differently than you do, but what we have is far more than physical attraction. We need to wait."

Sam obeyed. He always did. He was putty in her hands.

Armed with Harry's total truth and power, Sam set on a path to finally clean up his act once and for all. He was going to do it for Mo. He decided to stop drinking, much to John's chagrin.

"Oh, God," John said, "not again."

"Yes," Sam replied. "Again, and for the last time."

John knew he had nothing to worry about. His old drinking buddy swore off booze many times before but always came back, especially on bachelor nights.

Sam's failure to curb his drinking made him sheepish at times around Mo, but she never said anything. It was like she understood something and just waited patiently. For what, Sam wasn't sure. She didn't judge him, unlike others.

Despite her failure to judge, Sam didn't shirk from taking on that responsibility himself. The fact that he couldn't shake off his drinking when he wasn't with Mo bothered him. He checked his profile in the mirror and was dissatisfied with the look. Need a flatter stomach, he believed. Need to clean up my mouth. As hard as he tried, he always seemed to come up short.

John thought he was crazy. "Hey, man," John chided, "you just have to be yourself. Let it all hang out. You can't be something you're not. She'll have to take you for what you are. To be a blob or not to be a blob, that question is answered. All you can do is be you." John laughed hysterically at his joke. Sam's ears turned red.

Sam's pride burned from John's teasing, but he knew in a weird way that John was right. He was saying the same thing as Harry, only in a hedonistic way. John, of course, was totally oblivious to his genius. To his credit, as opposed to many Christians, he didn't pretend to be something he wasn't.

Sam wished he could be more like Mo; he wished he had her inner strength and resolve. He came to trust her, sharing his deepest tribulations.

"I really don't understand," he said. "I just want to live the Christian life. I know I can't do it. Only Christ can. But He isn't doing it either."

"Sweetie," she said, "patience. You said it yourself. God allows you to repeat the same lesson over ad infinitum until you get it. What's that movie you like so much? *Groundhog Day*? That's where you are and where you'll stay until you stop trying. Trust and believe. That's a tall glass of water to drink."

"Get my hands off the controls," Sam replied. "Be the plane, not the pilot. He has it under control."

"You said it," she reminded him. "That's what we are. Vessels. Made to contain the pilot."

"I know. I'm not used to that much understanding. It's not something I have a lot of experience with. Which reminds me. There is one perfect person in this world who does it all right and you are going to meet him tomorrow."

"Oh, really," she said, "and who might that be?"

"Well, actually, he's the sideshow. I really mean we have been invited to Sunday dinner at Mom's. Actually, we always had a standing invitation, but now she says enough is enough. She only met you in passing at the hospital and wants to properly, as she put it, meet you."

"Oh," Mo said. "Well . . . I'll have to figure out what to take . . . what to wear."

Sam laughed. "You don't need to take anything. And remember? You just have to be yourself."

"Right," she said as she disappeared into her bedroom closet. He could hear hangers sliding this way and that. It was a few minutes when she came back out with two dresses.

"Which one do you like the best?" she asked, holding up a red dress and a blue dress.

"I like the red one," Sam said.

"Why?"

"If there are going to be follow-up questions, honey, I'm not going to comment."

That was the first evil look he had seen her give. She closed the bedroom door behind her. In two minutes she came out in the blue dress.

"Perfect," he said.

She smiled. "Now," she said, "who is this righteous person I'm going to meet?"

Sam grimaced. "My brother, Steve. The good son."

"Ooooo. I can't wait."

††

Sam drove. Mo was excited. Every time Sam looked over at her she was pulling down the visor mirror, checking and reapplying something. Sam wasn't sure what.

"You're so cute when you're nervous." He laughed.

He got his second evil look.

He was looking forward to introducing her to the family. She was the one. He defied Steve to make some sarcastic comment.

As they got closer she asked, "How do I look?" She asked again with a half-smile as they got closer.

Sam knew this had better be a good answer. "Beautiful," he replied. "Perfect."

"I don't believe you," she said with a grimace and pulled out her lipstick one more time.

"Time for touch ups is over." He laughed as he pulled into the dooryard. She flipped the visor back up and started to straighten her dress.

Sam pulled in behind Steve's shiny black BMW. An old familiar feeling in his stomach quenched his excitement. *No time to drop your guard,* he told himself as he rebooted for fighting mode. Mo noticed the change.

"I know you met them in the hospital," Sam said. "You'll like . . . most . . . of them. Relax."

"Maybe you better," she said, rubbing his back. "Wow! Whose car is that?" she asked.

"That little gem belongs to brother Steve," replied Sam unenthusiastically. He hated to admit it was a beautiful car.

"Great," Mo said, "I am looking forward to meeting your evil nemesis."

Sam had shared some of his experiences with his elder brother. She listened very patiently. She didn't remember him at the hospital. The only comment she made was that he's on a path of his own like the rest of us. Sam agreed silently . . . a path to Hell.

"Funny. Looks like you will," he replied. "Look at this thing. He must have waxed it before church this morning. That is the biggest, shiniest, blackest black I have ever seen. It reminds me of the song the "Long Black Train." And look at those chrome wheels. I wonder how long it took to polish those things. Don't they just blind you? Talk about over the top."

"Sounds more like jealousy than evil," she remarked.

"Maybe," he acquiesced. "Anyone would be of Mr. Perfect. You'll see."

Sam tucked his shirt in. *Maybe she's right,* he thought. *Maybe he was just an over- achiever whose only problem was he had to let you know. Of course, maybe he had another problem—trampling over anyone that got in his way.* Sam tried to shuck off the bad thoughts. He practiced a smile.

"Nervous?" he asked.

"Of course. Let's go," she said, marching toward the door. "Come on."

Sam was more nervous than Mo. "Wait up there, girl," he cried after her. "No fire."

Sam moved ahead of her and opened up the kitchen door. Mo could see the room was filled with people talking, laughing, and moving about. Everyone was in the kitchen except for Steve who was talking on the phone in the living room. Sam's mother and Sue were engrossed in some culinary decision being made over the stove. His father was engaged in a conversation with Pop at the kitchen table. With the chatter, no one noticed they were there until the door slammed behind them. Sue turned and was the first to see them.

"Ohhhh," she exclaimed with a huge smile, bringing attention to the newcomers. "So this is the one who stole Sam's heart." She rushed to be the first to kiss Mo on both cheeks.

"I love that dress," she said. Mo immediately felt at ease.

The family rose politely and moved toward the couple with big smiles taking turns for introduction, or reintroductions to those who knew her from the hospital. Steve was still immersed in his phone conversation, oblivious to those around him.

"You're so beautiful," Debbie said as she hugged Mo. Mo handed her a gift, a scented candle.

"Oh, you shouldn't have done that," she said with obvious delight.

Joe came over. "Good to see you again," he said and gave her a hug. He winked at Sam. Sam blushed.

Pop was next, gently kissing her on both cheeks. "We are so glad to have you with us."

"Please, have a seat," Sam's mother said. "Everything happens at the kitchen table in this house."

"The same in our house," Mo said.

Sam's mom gave him a big hug. "Stranger," she said. "You live an hour away and we see you twice a year. Except when you try to kill yourself. Then we get to see you quite often." Everyone laughed.

"No excuse, Mom," he replied. "I'll do better. I promise."

With the amenities behind them, Mo became the center of attention. She was flooded with questions. Where did she come from? What did her family do? What college did she go to?

"Farm," she said. "Born and raised. My dad raised a little of this and grew a little of that. We had some pigs, chickens, a few cows. Nothing big."

"And you went to the university to get a degree in nursing?" Sue asked.

"Yes. That's always been a passion of mine. It started with the animals." She blushed. "I thought of being a veterinarian once, but I knew my real passion was to help people."

"So, this is the beauty that finally humbled my little brother," said Steve, interrupting her story with his big voice and wide smile, bursting into the kitchen like he owned it. Mo stood as Steve hugged her.

He looked her over. "I approve. Beats me what you see in him but hey, who am I to say?" He laughed with a sideways glance at Sam.

Sam's ears turned pink. Mo blushed. It was clear Sam was primed for a retort, but Mo sunk her fingernail into his palm. He reluctantly let it go.

"Good to see you too, brother," Sam said.

"Dinner is ready," announced Debbie. "We have pasta with marinara sauce, meatballs, salad, and . . . all kinds of things."

She reserved two chairs for Sam and Mo next to her and placed Steve at the other end.

"Steven, do you want to do the prayer?" she asked.

"Of course, Mom," Steve replied with a smile. Steve started and his parents chimed in.

"Give us grateful hearts, our Father, for all thy mercies, and make us mindful of the needs of others; through Jesus Christ our Lord. Amen."

"Thank you, Steven," Debbie said and started passing the salad around. She reached for the wine bottle.

"Mo, wine?" she asked.

"Yes, please. Thank you."

The wine was passed around the table. When it came to Sam, Steve said, "Try to not overdo it, Sam. All things in moderation."

Sam's ears turned red, the sign for Mo to take a hold of his hand. Now he remembered why he was such a stranger to family gatherings.

"I'll try, Steve. I'll try. Maybe it's time for you to get some kids of your own to practice your condescending tone on. God help him, or her." He poured himself a big glass.

Uh oh, Mo thought. *Game on.* Steve's face tightened up. The table braced.

"So, Mo," Steve said, "I understand you two met in the hospital when Sam was recuperating from his . . . well, mishap. Isn't that some kind of like doctor-patient conflict of interest?"

Mo hesitated thinking how to answer.

"I'm just kidding, Mo." Steve laughed. Everyone exhaled with smiles and light laughter.

"Oh, I know," she said. "Actually it's more of a Good Samaritan relationship. We're neighbors. We actually met the day of Sam's accident . . . sort of. He was sipping coffee on his veranda and so was I. I have to admit it was a pretty cursory introduction. When he saw me staring at him, he fled. I said, 'Pleased to meet you. Oh, thank you, I'm fine.' I was sure that he meant to say all those things."

Everyone laughed. They'd already heard about their first contact and they knew Sam.

"So, Mo, tell us more," asked Debbie. "Sam has kept you as a mystery woman, all to himself. It's time to share."

"Well, I hail from upstate. Like I said, my dad was a farmer. Guess like a lot of kids on those farms, I couldn't wait to get out of that one-horse town. I knew early that I wanted to be a nurse. When I was small, I would line up all my dolls and check their vitals, which were pretty bad by the way." They laughed.

"Anyway, that is always what I wanted to do and so I went to the university, graduated, got my RN license, and here I am."

"How long have you been at this hospital?" asked Joe.

"Three years now. I really like it here. People are so caring and professional."

"Sam says you are a lady of faith," said Steve. "Maybe you can get 'ole Sam back in church where he belongs. What church do you belong to?"

"Well, I am, but I can't say I'm any better about church attendance. We meet with other Christians and do Bible studies. Sam is really involved and we're both learning so much. As to church, I'm still a member of the Southern Baptist church in my hometown, but we don't really affiliate with any denomination. We're just plain old Christians. The generic kind."

Steve's face went blank thinking about holy rollers. For once he was speechless.

"I suppose that is better than nothing," Steve responded, "but real work for the Lord begins and ends in the local church. You have to be very careful with these fringe groups, Jesus freaks, and their New Age mumbo-jumbo."

"Easy, Steve," interjected Pop who had been silent up until then. "There may be only one Lord and only one way to that Lord but there are many squiggly paths that take you there. I wouldn't go so far as to say the church, as you define it, is the only suitable workplace for his flock. In fact, it can be pretty stifling."

"Maybe, Pop," Steve replied, backing off. "I'm just saying, man will be judged by his works, and Sam needs to learn that the . . . uh . . . lifestyle he is in at the moment could end up yielding a lot of burnt wood and stubble."

Steve respected his grandfather and knew better than to challenge him. Though they often differed in beliefs, he was no match for his wisdom.

"Well, there will no doubt be the smell of fire throughout heaven when that time comes," Pop agreed, "but you might just be surprised what you see when the smoke settles."

Sam and Mo just sat silently listening to this dialogue. Sam was relieved that Pop was cooling Steve's diatribe.

"I'm just saying, Pop, works are important. I put blood and sweat in our church. I, for one, don't intend to be a garbage man in the Kingdom of God."

"I don't know how many openings there will be, Steve. I'm glad you are so passionate for the Lord. I hope it works out for you. But I would be careful to judge. What man thinks is pleasing to the Lord and what actually is are many times two different things."

Steve sat quiet. His grandfather had a confidence and poise that was difficult to challenge. And Steve wasn't really sure what he was talking about.

"Back to dinner, I say," interrupted Sue. "Mom, I don't know how you make this sauce. It's wonderful, as usual. You have to get us the recipe."

"I agree," said Mo. "I'd like to have it, too."

Debbie smiled. "Of course. Now, Sam, when Mo makes this for you, you can say it's just like Mom used to make."

After dinner there was coffee and cake and casual conversation. Steve was quieter than usual.

"I sure like your family," Mo said on the ride home. "They're so genuine."

"Most of them," Sam agreed.

"Well, there might be one that needs a little work," Mo said. "I wouldn't give up on him yet."

Sam looked at her. He felt the coin in his pocket and pulled it out without letting her see it. It had a likeness of a robed Pharisee with broad phylacteries and long fringes on one side and a man in sackcloth and ashes on the other. He wondered what it meant and tucked it back in his pocket.

9

WILL YOU?

SIX MONTHS HAD PASSED since Sam's "mishap," as Steve called it. He had been back on the job for three months. John had finally landed an entry-level job at a consulting engineering firm in town where he and Sam had interned during summer breaks. Things were going well for both of them.

Sam decided it was time to get rid of his college junker and go for a new car. He took Mo and tramped through several car lots, finally settling on a bright-red Camaro. It wasn't a BMW, but he was proud of it. His parents and Sue thought it was wonderful. Steve said it was an okay starter car.

He waxed it the first weekend to take Mo out. Things were getting very serious. Mo already knew. She was just waiting for him. Sam, on the other hand, was ready but still unsure of himself. He worried she might say no. Six months wasn't a long time.

Molly couldn't have possibly rolled her eyes any further inside her head when she got wind of that notion.

"John, you need to take that boy aside and have a talk with him. He's very sweet . . . and very dense," Molly said.

John and Molly's relationship seemed to work for them. It was clear that they loved each other, but neither felt the need to make it legal. When half of all marriages fail with a so-called commitment, how could he judge them? But that was not for Sam and definitely not for Mo. There was something about it that just didn't seem right. There was no commitment. He couldn't defend the atrocious success rate of marriage, but he wondered what the failure rate was for non-married couples.

John noticed the change in Sam. He might sit there and have a beer with John, but his mind was somewhere else. And John knew where that somewhere else was. He hated to see his buddy split, but he knew it had to be.

Sam picked up Mo Saturday evening for dinner and a movie. His whole day was spent shopping for a ring and preoccupied thinking about a life with Mo. He had the ring. It was a three-quarter carat solitaire. The attractive blond saleswoman convinced him this was the best buy for his money. The only question now was did he have the courage? He was about to find out.

"Where have you been all day?" Mo asked. "I've been trying to call you."

"Oh . . . shopping," he mumbled.

"Shopping." She laughed. "You shopping? We haven't known each other very long, but one thing I'm sure about, you don't shop, except at twenty-five miles per hour."

Then she got quiet. She started to think. *Hmmm, what would he be shopping for? Could it be?*

She got quiet as they drove, which was unusual. For Sam to be quiet was not unusual. Neither said much until they got to the restaurant. Mo just stared ahead mulling over his comment.

Sam handed the keys to the valet. The little valet's cowboy eyes worried Sam as his brand new car disappeared out of sight, but his attention was quickly diverted to the big brown eyes waiting to be escorted into the restaurant.

"Oh," she said. "This is very nice. Special occasion that I am not aware of?"

"Uh . . . yes," he replied. "Exactly."

"I'm excited. When are you going to tell me what it is?"

"Hmmm . . . pretty soon."

Sam tipped the maître d discreetly as he ushered them to their table, a private one in the corner. They ordered a bottle of wine and started to relax with some small talk.

Mo talked, but Sam wasn't hearing. He just looked at her and nodded his head from time to time. In the movies, the question was always popped at the end of dinner, but he was more impulsive. He wanted to get it over with, but he didn't want to spoil the moment either. His hands shook slightly as he lifted his glass of wine and took a rather large draught of his Merlot. Mo noticed and was nervous for him.

"Ya, know, Mo," Sam started.

Her nose wrinkled. It was a reflexive reaction whenever she heard the grating ya-know-Mo rhyme, a signal to Sam.

"Sorry," he said. "What I mean is, well . . . we haven't known each other a really long time but . . . you know I love you."

"I love you too," she blurted out. "Sorry . . . you were saying?"

She sat there staring at him with a smile as broad as the ocean, waiting for him to continue.

"Well . . . I was wondering . . . that if you felt the same . . . I realize we may be rushing, but . . . will you . . .?" He started to slide out of his chair to get down on his knee but never made it.

"Yes, yes." She jumped out of her chair and almost knocked him down as she planted the most voluptuous kiss on his lips as he struggled for the ring box tangled in his pocket.

" . . . Marry me?" he said, finally getting his knee to the floor.

The clatter of chairs drew the attention of the other diners. They all stopped eating at once and clapped.

"I thought I already answered that question," she teased.

"I guess so," he said, red-faced and finally extricating the box from his pocket. He awkwardly cracked it open, revealing a rainbow of color.

Her jaw dropped. She tried not to scream. "That is the most beautiful ring I have ever seen," she gushed.

As he slipped it on her slender finger, her gaze was more on him than the ring.

"Did you pick it out yourself? How did you know my ring size?"

"I did," Sam replied proudly. "Molly figured out your ring size." He was very pleased with himself.

Dinner continued in slow motion as she exchanged glances between Sam and the ring. Sam couldn't believe this wonderful woman wanted him. The blush on her cheeks was more than the wine. The escargot, salad, poached salmon in dill sauce, crème brulee, and espresso would be delicious memories of an evening not to be forgotten.

The movie tickets were forgotten. Rather than go back to either apartment, they decided to drive to an old-fashioned parking spot full of teenagers to talk and watch the full moon rise over the lake.

"Well, you know what the next step is, I guess," she said.

"Your parents?" he guessed, hoping he was wrong. "The dreaded undressing of the groom?"

"Uh huh," she replied. "It won't be that bad. My mother will fall in love with you. Dad? Well we might have to soften him up a bit, but don't worry. I can handle him. I'm still his little girl."

"Are they going to consider us unequally yoked?" Sam asked, concerned. "Do Episcopalians measure up to the standards of Southern Baptists?"

"Well, he already thinks I'm an un-churched backslider, so he may think marrying an Episcopalian is an upgrade." She laughed. "He's having a little trouble with my form of Christianity, but he'll have to get over it. Love conquers all."

"I'll follow your lead," he said.

They talked more intimately than they ever had. Sam shared things about his family that he had kept bottled up. That meant talking more about his brother.

"It was clear since I can remember," Sam said, "that Steve wanted to be an only child, the center of attention, and I, little ole me, foiled his plans by being born. Steve had no shortage of creative ways of letting me know that. When he was in college it really got bad. I dreaded him coming home. He would order me around. If I balked, he would intimidate and sometimes hit me. He dared me to tell Mom and Dad. One day he sucker punched me in the stomach for taking the last cookie."

"There certainly was some cloud hanging over your mom's kitchen. I can understand your feelings. But like I said, love conquers all. You will get over it."

"You like that saying," Sam said. "I like the way you put

the emphasis on will. It'll take some time. He never missed an opportunity to drive it in deep. When I left college, he unofficially renamed me Quitter. Hey, Quitter, you'll never amount to anything. Hey, Quitter, what are you going to quit today? I don't understand why I was a threat. He was ambitious, as you could see. He's smart, good looking, athletic. He seems to have it all but it's not enough. He has an unquenchable craving for more, even if it's someone else's."

"I hate him," Sam said finally.

Mo took his hand. "No, you don't, Sam," she said.

"I don't? Sure feels like it."

"You may feel like you do, but they're just feelings. You are not your feelings. Feelings are a faculty of the soul. They are as variable as the wind. They come and go. We are spirit remember? Spirit is invariable. We all have people in our lives that rub us the wrong way, or we may actually have feelings of hate. But that is all they are. Feelings. Real love is not a feeling. It comes from our spirit center where we are one with Christ. Because you are in Christ, Christ will love him through you regardless of how you feel."

"That's an interesting concept," he replied. "It sounds good, but it doesn't "quicken" yet."

"It will. There's a lot to know, and you're a quick study. Look, we all carry around baggage. Satan also doesn't lose any opportunity to point those out."

"I'm sure," he agreed. "Just seems my family and I have more than our share."

"Hey, we all have secrets and baggage. I hope you don't think you know everything about me. You may have to bear with some of my stories, and you haven't met my family yet." She laughed.

"Well, I'm looking forward to all of that. I want to know all about you."

"Oh, you will."

10

THE TWO BECOME ONE FLESH

SAM PICKED MO UP at nine for breakfast before their meeting. He thought he would introduce her to *La Grande Bouche*. Mo had looked very comfortable walking in, smiling at Guido and Joe, whose rough exteriors dissolved into something that almost looked like gentleness. Sam stared in unbelief.

"Wow," she said, "what a neat little place."

"That tells me a lot about you." He laughed. "I wasn't sure how you would take my greasy spoon."

"Hah," she laughed. "It looks mighty tasty. You forget I grew up in the country. Nothing fancy."

"What will you have, ma'am?" asked Joe, walking up to the table. "Any questions?"

Ma'am? Questions? Sam was dumbfounded. *Is this Joe, the breakfast Nazi?*

"Hmmm, scrambled eggs, sausage, biscuits and gravy," she replied.

"Thank you, ma'am," he said taking her menu.

"Wudda you want?" he asked turning to Sam.

"The same," Sam said, wondering about Joe's split personality.

"Guido," he yelled, "scrape two, log roll, heart attack on rack. Due."

"Is that what I ordered?" Sam joked.

"I hope so," she said.

"This is pretty good," he said. "I don't know what's better. Those big brown eyes of yours or the smell of sizzling bacon."

"Tough choice, I imagine." She smirked.

"No contest. Sorry about unloading on you last night," Sam said. "It should have been a bit more intimate evening. The wine I guess."

"It was intimate, Sam," she replied. "I want to know all about you. You're mine now. We're one."

"One, huh?" he asked. "Why do I have a feeling I'm about to get another revelation?"

"You bet." She laughed. "And it's a very important one. Who knows? It might be a good topic this morning."

"Don't we know what the sermon . . . I mean topic, is going to be beforehand?"

"You're funny," she said. "There are no canned sermons or planned agenda. That's what's so beautiful about it. It all comes from the heart, the spirit, right when you need it. Spontaneous."

"That's interesting."

"Hey," she said, "this isn't bad for city gravy. Not good, but not bad. You'll get the real deal pretty soon."

"I have a feeling I know what that means. A real country breakfast in the country?"

"Uh huh." She winked.

After they finished breakfast, they drove across town to another apartment where Harry and the gang were meeting.

"I don't know why, but I always have this odd feeling meeting in all these different homes," Sam said. "It's so different from the Sunday church routine, kind of exciting and refreshing. I wonder if this is how the apostles felt; radicals meeting in different places to avoid being detected by the religious authorities."

"I know what you mean," she said. "I feel the same way. The original Gospel was so simple. No Law. Just Christ. Total Freedom. That was radical enough to brand them outlaws. It's not much different today. Most teaching mixes grace and the law so subtly back together you can't distinguish between the two. They just wag their heads at us. They can't believe it's that easy. But they do envy our freedom."

"Well, I guess we can go home now," Sam said with heavy breath after trudging to the third floor. "I've had my sermon for the week."

"You're funny," she said. "I know you. You can't get enough."

Sam couldn't argue. She was right. They knocked on a shabby looking door. Warmth greeted them.

With no time to waste, Mo said loudly, "Guess what, everybody?"

Martha looked up with her sagacious eyes and said, "Let me guess. You're getting married."

"Wow," exclaimed Mo. "How did you guess that so quickly?"

"Duh," was all she had to say.

Sam's ears turned red.

Everyone merged on them, hugging Mo and admiring her ring. It took Sam a while to understand it wasn't the size of the ring they were impressed with but what it represented. The men came around shaking his hand. The ladies had no problem hugging stiff Sam. He liked it.

Mo looked at Sam and blushed. "Sorry," she said. "Guess that wasn't exactly lady-like, but what can I say. We are!"

Sam never liked being the center of attention, but he was really enjoying this for Mo. He had never seen her let it all hang out like this. He was excited for her.

After things calmed down, everyone grabbed their coffee or tea, maybe a pastry, and sat. Harry sunk his frame into an easy chair.

"Thanks for coming," Harry said. "Looks like a lot of excitement this morning. Okay, what do you all want to talk about this morning?"

There was a bit of silence. Harry looked over at the grinning Mo. It was somehow known that Mo would select the day's topic.

"I think, Harry, if the group doesn't mind," she said, looking around, "that our engagement might be a great segue to talk about what marriage is really all about, what it means spiritually. You know, our union with Christ and why God said 'the two shall become one flesh.'"

Sam nodded. "I'd really like to know more about that."

"Excellent topic," Harry began. "Biblical marriage is another earthly picture of our union, our spiritual marriage, to Christ."

"Sorry, Harry, to be so dumb, but what do you mean our spiritual marriage to Christ?" Sam asked.

"There are no dumb questions, Sam," Harry said. "Our earthly marriage is how God reveals something much greater, a heavenly truth—a spiritual marriage. Two becoming one flesh is a picture of two spirits becoming one spirit. Most don't realize, but we have always been in a spiritual union. In the beginning, we, through Adam and Eve, were married to God. We were one with Him. When they ate of the apple, they rejected God and were tricked into a marriage union with Satan.

"That is the miserable dilemma that all mankind has to start with. I say miserable, but the world at large has no idea that they are in this marriage or that it is all that bad. They buy into Satan's delusion of independence and that they can be good people on their own. Others realize that is impossible and earnestly crave a solution. But it's not so simple. We can't do it ourselves. Someone else has to do it for us. God provides that way.

"According to God's immutable Law, neither the earthly nor the spiritual union can be undone as long as we live. There is only one way out. Paul explains how in Romans 7—how through the Law we can be freed from the Law. Remember, he is again speaking in earthly terms of spiritual things. He says as long as our husband lives, we cannot be separated or divorced to marry another. But if our husband dies, then we are free to marry another. There it is—your way out—death! All you have to do is die and you are freed from your bad marriage and free to marry another—Christ."

"Death?" Sam exclaimed. "You're starting to lose me. How do you die to live?"

Harry softly smiled. "This is the good news. Christ did it for us. When you believe that Christ died for us, died for our sin, by hanging on that cross, then you died that day also. You ask me how? I don't know. It's a spiritual mystery, but it's true. Jesus did it for us as us, before you and I were born. We were there.

"Once we believe, we are free to enter into a spiritual union with Christ. That is why He is called the bridegroom and the church the bride. We become one with Him. First Corinthians

6:17 says, 'But he who is joined to the Lord becomes one spirit with him.' One! Not two!"

Harry paused and looked around the room. Silent eyes were glued on him. "Any questions . . . Sam?"

"I like it, Harry. My heart says yes. It quickens, as Mo would say. But something holds me back. I hear, but, as you say, maybe I don't have ears to hear."

"Well, it should ring true, Sam, since all I am doing is quoting scripture. These verses say what they mean and they mean what they say. The Holy Spirit is working in you to reveal all truth, but only when you are ready for it. Don't worry whether you totally understand it now. It will come. You have ears to hear for sure. Otherwise you wouldn't be here.

"I know I sound like a one-stringed fiddle, but let me repeat Galatians 2:20, 'I am crucified with Christ and I live, yet not I, but Christ liveth.' What does that mean to you?"

"Another mystery," Sam replied. "It sounds so good. But to be truthful, it just doesn't work. It does for a while but before the day is out, I get tired, I get angry at trivial things, and I get grumpy, actually more than grumpy sometimes. It's just a mess. I can't control my tongue. I can't control anything. I wonder sometimes if I'm not possessed. Just yesterday a guy cut me off on the freeway and I pulled up alongside of him and cursed him a funeral."

Sam sighed and looked up in surprise when several in the group laughed.

Jerry chimed in, "There's nothing wrong with you, Sam. You're not possessed. Everything is happening exactly as it is supposed to. The more you try, the more you fail."

"That's right," said Harry, laughing. "Thank you for sharing that. There is not a person in this room who hasn't experienced the same thing. Hurry up and get to the end of yourself. That is exactly what God wants you to do. When Galatians 2:20 sinks from your head to your heart, you'll ask yourself, was it really that easy? Galatians 2:20 says you are not the one living this life. It is a replaced life. You no longer live. But Christ lives it. I know it sounds like double talk, but don't give up. God will open your heart and mind to the truth. You are TRYING. Stop it! The three hardest letters in the English language are L-E-T, let. Let the power of Christ live His life through you, as you, to work it out. When you try, you are really saying I don't believe. And essentially, that is the only sin—unbelief."

"I do get it," Sam said. "You're definitely right. Letting go of independence, real or not, is not easy." His flying metaphor came to mind, and he realized he was simply climbing back up into the cockpit where he didn't belong.

Harry looked around once more. "I can see I've said enough for this morning by the looks. This is plenty to mull over in your hearts."

"I'll say," said Sam. He looked over at Mo who never said much at the meetings, just nodding, smiling, and soaking it in. It was like she already knew things that the rest had not yet learned. She never pushed it. She was so patient.

"Don't worry, Sam," she comforted. "God has great plans for you. That is why you are mine."

Sam wondered. He had a feeling that was why she was his. He felt the coin again in his pocket. He pulled it out enough to see. On one side was the image of a bride and on the flip side an image of a bridegroom. One coin. Two sides. But one. Sam hadn't told Mo about the coin yet. He was sure she would think he was crazy, and he was also sure he couldn't produce it on demand. It disappeared in his hand. Lost again.

11

Baptized By Father

SAM'S FATHER HAD JOINED the Episcopal Church when he married his mother, who had been a member. Being the son of Norman Season, Joe grew up rather itinerant. Joining the church gave him stability. He liked the ceremony, the tradition, and the structure. Now Sam was starting to question some of the traditions, like baptism. He realized that though infant baptism might picture something beautiful in the future, it had not yet been his choice or his faith. With all that he had learned, it began to weigh heavily on his mind. He shared these feelings with Mo that he would like to be baptized.

"That's wonderful, Sam," she squealed. "It's so wonderful to watch God working in you like this. Baptism is not necessary for salvation, but it is a commandment that, yes again, symbolizes our union with Christ."

"Why am I not surprised?" he said. "Harry said you could pick any chapter or verse and see God's ultimate plan over and over."

"He's right." She nodded. "Some think it's a washing away of sins but it's much more than that."

Mo pulled out her Bible. "Let's take a look again at Romans 7. Baptism symbolizes our death, burial, and resurrection in Christ. Remember, Harry said that when Christ died, we died. When Christ was buried, we were buried. When Christ was raised, we were raised. Once we believe, we partake of that. We were there somehow, mysteriously, spiritually, when Christ was crucified, buried, and resurrected. He did it "as" us. Baptism symbolizes the death we talked about in Romans that frees us from our bad marriage so we can marry another. Once dead, the false spirit leaves us. Then we are raised in newness of life free to marry another—Christ."

Sam just stared. "You make it so simple," Sam said. "Too simple. Too easy. Maybe that's why I am having so much trouble making it work. Too good to be true?"

Mo laughed. "It is that simple. You don't have to make it work. That's God's job. That's the good news. Good meaning, as Jesus said, 'my yoke is easy and my burden is light.' You have to remember that we are raised from little children to be independent, to be self-sufficient, to perform. Christianity is contrary to the world because it is not performance based. It is not like your work life where if you don't perform there are consequences. But in all things, even in your work life, it is Christ that does the performing in you as you."

"As me." Sam jumped. "You guys keep saying that. What does that mean? I keep hearing that. Now I'm wondering what I'm getting into!"

Mo had the smile that defused any anxiety. "Thinking cult, eh?" she joked. "Don't worry; it will all make sense. Just as he died *as* us, He also lives *as* us. That's the deal. But it hardly means we disappear. We are two yet one. We are more alive than ever."

"Well, if you say so," he said. "Okay, let's do it. I'm ready to be baptized."

"Wonderful!" Mo rejoiced. "Now to figure out who to do it. I guess we could go back to my home church. Next weekend was our plan to go break the news to my parents anyway. We could meet the pastor. He will probably want you to join the church, but he's not as dogmatic as the previous one, much to my father's dismay."

"Right." Sam remembered. A little knot started to form in his stomach. "Let's see if that is possible."

"Great," Mo said. "I'll call Mom. She'll be pleased. I haven't told you much yet about my family, but you'll find out soon enough."

"What about them?" Sam asked with eyebrows raised.

"We'll wait until we are on the road." Mo laughed. "Until the point of no return and then I'll divulge all." She giggled again. "It's not that bad."

"Also . . . hon . . ." she added, "you should invite your parents for the baptism."

Sam had forgotten about them in the excitement. He hadn't really given it much thought and now he wondered how they would take it. They were staunch Episcopalians. Would they take it as an affront? Pop will be delighted. He knew Steve would just have a smart remark, except he didn't care what Steve thought.

Mo talked to the pastor herself. She was surprised at his openness. No, he didn't have to join the church. He would be happy to baptize any believer. After hearing her tell Sam's story, he was very pleased that he felt so strongly about following the Lord in full baptism. He would have to talk personally to Sam to hear his testimony first to be sure of his commitment to Christ.

Sam's parents were a little confused but said they would be there. For Pop, there was no question. He was excited. Steve had other commitments.

"I thought we were already Christians," Steve said. "What is that doofus doing now?"

The road trip began. Mo was excited and Sam nervous as they headed north in his new car to her family's farm. Her parents knew by now this was it and what this trip was about. Mo said they both were excited to meet him.

"But," she said, "expect some scrutiny."

Sam looked over at her.

"Okay, I said I would give the tell-all, so here it is."

Mo spent the three hours telling Sam all about her family and her upbringing. She was an only child, raised in a very strict, very fundamentalist, very Christian home. She had curfews, chaperones, dress codes, conduct codes . . . actually, her entire life was code driven. They monitored her behavior constantly, never spared the rod, and basically controlled every aspect of her life. At least the aspects they knew about. She was a red-blooded teenager, and she never missed an opportunity to break out of the cell when possible to hang with her friends and do the things they did. As she got older and the possibility of college grew closer, she began to resent her parents.

"Actually," she said, "I began to hate them. I felt guilty about my hateful thoughts. I thought they were totally messing up my life. Everything I did was wrong. They acted like they didn't trust me. As soon as I was eighteen all I could think about was getting away."

Her parents wanted to send her to the local community college and have her live at home, but she convinced them that it was not suited for her. She wanted to be a nurse. She wanted a full bachelor's degree and maybe study for an advanced degree later. That meant she would have to go to the university. That convinced them. They were not poor, but the cost of sending her away would put a strain on their finances. She was so pleased when they finally relented, both to become the nurse she always wanted to be and . . . of course, to finally escape the prison.

"I have to be honest, Sam," she said. "I was no angel. In fact, I went wild. If alcohol had never passed my lips prior to then the dam was broken my first semester. I wanted a taste of all the forbidden fruit. And I came pretty close. I was and am in no position to judge anyone. Sin reigned freely and, for a while, I liked it. But the thing that started to put things into perspective . . ."

She hesitated wondering whether to proceed, but only for a second. She knew she could say anything to Sam, even though they had only known each other for six months, she knew Sam's heart and that is where they were joined. She shared her secrets.

"It didn't go well," she confessed. "There was an incident late in my freshman year. It was at a frat party. I had overindulged. Let me rephrase. I was drunk. There was this one frat brother. He was good looking and drunk himself . . . It went too far. He tried to rape me. I punched and kicked him and got away. I knew then that whether or not my parents went about it perfectly, they did it all out of love."

"So," said Sam," the moral of this story is don't mess with Mo." He laughed.

"I can laugh it about it now," Mo said. "Most would look at that as ghastly, but it was an important life lesson. My parents would never understand. I know that guy meant it for evil, but God meant if for good."

"How so?" asked the puzzled Sam.

"Sweetie, there is nothing that ever happens to us that God is not involved with. The Bible says all things work together for good to those who love God. He says what He means and means what He says. Most religious Christians would scoff, but God was in that room. He led me there. He wasn't just allowing, as some would say. He was taking me there, to teach me something, to reach the end of my independence, my arrogance, and myself. Don't think being brought up in a fundamentalist home didn't teach me to have healthy helpings of guilt, and I did for a while. But then I realized that I had no reason to feel guilty. If it's all true, then my sins are all forgiven: Past, present, and future. All I need to do is confess, which I did. Not in sackcloth and ashes. Just acknowledged that my life was going in the wrong direction, a direction I had no control over. That is when I met someone who really started to make it real to me, to explain what Christianity is really all about. That is when I met Harry."

"Turn up this road," she said. Three hours had passed like a second. The two-story white clapboard house was straight ahead. Sam started to tighten up. Mo reached over and touched his hand. The warmth soothed his nervousness.

"Any last minute advice?" asked Sam.

"Well, Mom's no problem. You'll love her. But Dad . . . well . . . I should have brought this up before, but he is kind of old fashioned. It would go well if . . . well if you could ask him for my hand in marriage." Mo looked at him with those big, brown begging eyes.

"Whaaat?" Sam panicked. "And you're asking me now?"

"Sorry," she said with a puppy dog look. "Just think about it. I love you." She kissed him on the cheek.

"I love you too," he said, wondering how he was going to approach the subject with her father.

Mary Rice, Mo's mother, was standing on the wraparound porch. She spotted the trail of tan dust rising from the long driveway tracking their approach. She was smiling ear-to-ear and waving dramatically as he stopped the car.

"She's easy," Mo said, smiling. "It's the other one. No drinking, no swearing, and . . . well you quit smoking. That's good."

He gave a nervous laugh. "Thanks for the pep talk."

"Praise the Lord, praise the Lord," she said, walking swiftly to Mo's side of the car and pulling her to her with a huge mother-daughter hug. "It is so good to see you."

"Ohhh, I see. And this is the One, I guess," she said, studying Sam who was standing on the other side and wanting to stay there.

He didn't have to move. Mary was on his side in a second hugging him also. "Come in, come in, come in, we are so excited. Let's get some iced tea. Mike is over in the barn. He's been haying all day, but I'm sure he saw that trail of dust, too. He'll be over in just a minute."

Sam walked into the house through the kitchen. That, said Mo, was where everything happened: All the debate, all the eating, of course, and all the paddling, too. It looked like a typical farmhouse with all of its white-painted cabinets. The dining room held a lonely table and a hutch filled with crystal and keepsakes. The living room was warm looking and comfortable. An old TV was the central point of the room. There were three unheated bedrooms upstairs. Sam took Mo's bag to her childhood room and his to the spare.

As he came back down the narrow wooden steps, Mike had already come in from the barn and was standing there with a half-smile and his hand extended way out. Sam quickly reached out to receive an extremely firm grip that shook, it seemed for minutes, as Mike looked directly into Sam's eyes. Mike was slightly taller than Sam but he seemed much larger. His hands were warm and calloused and huge.

"Sam," Mike started, "it's so good to meet you. I have been getting the scoop secondhand, mostly from Mary," he said looking over at Mo with faux disapproval, "who does all the talking to Mo."

"Well, I hope it's good. What you heard . . . I mean," Sam said.

"Oh, nothing bad." He laughed. "But then again, I'll be the judge. Now that I can get it firsthand."

"Oh, stop it, Mike," interjected Mary, firing her eyes into his forehead. "Don't worry, Sam. He's not that scary. Take my word for it. I know. Everyone sit down out here on the porch. I've got plenty of iced tea ready to go. Lemon?"

"Yes, please," Sam said. "Thank you."

Mo hadn't said her father had a sense of humor, dry though it was. That was refreshing.

They all sat around the table in the warm afternoon sun, refilling glasses of iced tea. The first hour was mostly between Mo and her parents catching up.

"Yes," she said, "I know. I've been a stranger. But you know I don't have that much time off, working all kinds of shifts."

"Easy on her, Mike," Mary said, rushing to her defense. "She has more important things to do now than to spend her free time with old fogeys like us."

"Now, Mom, not true. It's just . . . well, been hectic. Lots of things to do, lots of things to think about."

"Sam, I understand you're new out of college with a new job?" asked Mike, changing the direction of the conversation.

"Yes . . . yes, sir," Sam said. "I have an engineering position with a local manufacturer. I work on capital projects. I am really enjoying it."

"That sounds good," Mike said. "And church. Where do you attend church?"

"Mike," Mary cautioned giving him a look.

"I'm just trying to learn a little about our future son-in-law, honey. I mean, I guess that's in the cards, eh Mo?"

"Well," Sam blurted, "first I . . . uhh . . . I mean with your blessing? I guess, I mean . . . I am asking for your daughter's hand, sir."

Mike just stared at Sam without saying a word.

"Stop it." Mary laughed. "You're killing the child."

Mike laughed and rose up and hugged Sam. "Of course, Sam, of course." This clearly pleased Mike who immediately softened his stance.

Mo smiled warmly at Sam and her father.

"Well, to answer your question, sir . . ."

"Don't call me sir, Sam." Mike laughed. "I work for a living."

"Err . . . ok . . . sir," he continued as they all laughed. "Anyway, I was raised in the Episcopalian church. That is where our family attends. I am finding out now, mostly from Mo, that the church membership is one thing, but a true relationship with Christ is really what it means to be a Christian. Anyway, I was never baptized, at least not in a way I think it was meant to be. I just have a strong feeling I need to do it right. So this is a special weekend. I get to meet those that will be my future family and obey what I believe the Lord is leading me to do."

Mike certainly had his opinions about the better-than-thou Episcopalians, but held back on making any comments. He liked much of what he heard.

"Well, you have to do what the Lord leads you to do," Mike agreed. "I'm very glad you have chosen our church to make that public profession of faith. I know Mo has been deeply involved in some quasi-Christian group. Oops. Mo, sorry. I see that look. I mean at least she is involved with some Christian group. Don't know if I can swallow everything she says, but she always backs it up with scripture. Anyway, we are excited, and I am pleased to have you as our first and only son. The son my wife never gave me."

Mike ducked as Mary hurled a magazine at him. They all laughed.

12

AND WATER

JOE, DEBBIE, AND NORMAN Season were ready to go by seven-thirty. They had a two-and-a-half hour drive to get to Ebenezer Baptist Church. They would attend Sam's baptism, meet his future in-laws, and return to Murrysville that afternoon. It was a beautiful spring morning and this drive would take them off the beaten path through some very scenic areas of the state. Steve declined the invitation, saying he had Sunday church duties that were more important. This baptism thing was nonsense, he told them. Sam had already been baptized.

Pop sat up front with Joe. "You know, Pop, I think Steve is a little harsh at times, but I have to admit that I don't really get it either. We raised Sam in the church. He was baptized as an infant. He was confirmed. I know he seemed to drift away after high school but that's normal for young people to feel their way. He's a good person. That is how we raised him. Why does he think that was not enough?"

"Son, those things are all good," Norman replied. "Sam is not rejecting your faith. He's come of age and is making it his own faith, not the faith of Episcopalians or any denomination.

Just the faith of Christ. It's heart driven. Sam is compelled. He can't help it."

"But why does he not want our church?" Joe asked.

"Sam is more of an explorer. For you, the church gave support and structure that I couldn't. Sam wants to test the love of God beyond the limits of tradition. God has each person exactly where he wants them at each moment in time. Sam just needs to be somewhere else right now."

Joe looked over at his Dad. Debbie leaned forward to hear this conversation.

"What do you mean beyond the limits?" he asked.

"Traditional thinking is limited by the consensus of its leaders. That cuts out a lot of false teaching, but it also leaves out a lot of truth because the level of understanding never rises above the lowest common denominator. The Holy Spirit says I have a lot more to feed you if you will listen. Sam hears that and knows there is a wonderful world out there that expands far beyond what we can even imagine. To expand your knowledge of God, you have to go it alone."

"I hear you, Dad," Joe replied, "but I still don't know. This family has tried its best to do the right thing in every situation. Sure, we fail sometimes, but we keep trying. We try to follow the teachings of Christ and His philosophy: love your neighbor, do unto others as you would have done unto yourself and so on. Maybe I'm simpleminded. I just try to be a good person. What more is there?"

"There's a lot more, Joe. You know Jesus asked, 'Why do you call me good? There is none good but God,'" Norman said, looking at his son. "What do you think that means? If He isn't willing to call Himself good, how can we?"

Joe looked very puzzled. "I guess that's a good question, Dad. I don't know. Explain."

"Baptism is one way to explain it," Pop said.

"How so?"

"Some look at baptism as the washing away of sins. But sin is not our problem."

"It's not?" Joe asked. "What is?"

"No. The problem isn't sins. It's *Sin* with a capital S."

Joe tilted his head and looked at his father over his sunglasses.

"Sins, Sin? What's the difference? Sounds like a word game to me."

"Keep your eyes on the road," Norman joked. "We are neither good nor bad. We have no nature of our own. The sinner commits sins only because of who he is. Before we accept Christ as our Lord, we are married to Mr. Sin, Satan, and we express the nature of our husband as his slaves. We have to rid ourselves of Mr. Sin with the capital S. Baptism pictures how we end that illicit marriage relationship through death and become free to marry another, Christ. Then we express His nature. There is your goodness. Your only goodness is Christ in you."

"Okay, Dad." Joe sighed. "It's getting deep again. You always have good things to say. Let me think about all this, and we will continue the discussion another time."

"Fair enough," Norman replied.

As the Rices rolled into the church parking lot, the Season's car came in right behind them. The timing was perfect.

They all piled out of the cars. "Mom, Dad, Pop, thanks for coming," Sam said. "Let me introduce Mo's parents, Mike and Mary Rice."

There were smiles, handshakes, and a few hugs as they greeted each other and meandered slowly into the small, white steeple building.

"Let's go meet the pastor," Mike said to Sam. "I'm a bit surprised he's doing this for a non-member. He's young and new, definitely much more liberal than the last pastor we had, or for my taste for that matter. No offense. Our old pastor wouldn't have done it if you weren't committed to the local New Testament church. But I'm glad he's doing it, Sam. I see a real sincerity and belief in what you want to do. Of course, there is one condition, Sam. You have to convince the pastor also in order for him to do it in good conscience."

"Thank you, sir," Sam said. "I understand and I am sincere."

Joe looked around at the simple sanctuary. There were pews for maybe a hundred people. No stain glass windows. No altar. No incense. The pulpit was a wooden lectern mounted on a sapling tree trunk. He looked at the darkened baptistery above the choir loft. *Immersion?* He shook his head in wonder.

Mike walked through the aisles with Sam and Mo as parishioners sauntered in. He shook hands with each like they were long lost brothers and sisters. He finally made his way to a tall young man down front. He stood about six foot six inches and must have weighed two hundred forty pounds. He looked to be about Sam's age. His smile was as broad as his shoulders as he gregariously greeted each person clasping their hands in his.

"Sam, Pastor John Jones," said Mike.

"Nice to meet you, Sam. Good to see you, Mo," said Pastor Jones looking down at the two of them.

Sam stared. He was a little taken back at his size and youth. His hand was twice the size of Sam's.

"You can call me Little John," John said with a laugh, putting them at ease. "Everyone else does. Or so I'm told."

Sam laughed nervously. "Pleased to meet you, Pastor."

"Come, let's have a little talk first, Sam," said John and walked him into a tiny office behind the pulpit. "Mo, you can come too."

The office was austere. It had a desk, wooden swivel chair, and three old, cushioned chairs facing the desk. One side was a wall-to-wall bookcase overflowing with books. Sam tried to pick out some of the titles but he was not familiar with any of them.

"Just a short chat, Sam," started the young pastor, "to make sure you are aware of what will be happening today and what it means. I am always excited when we have a baptism. It's kind of like your birthday, the day you become a child of God. Not that this is the actual time of your birth. You become a member of the Kingdom at the time you truly receive Christ as Lord and Savior and invite him into your heart. Baptism sort of makes it official and settles it once and for all. Well, usually. There have been a few who seemed to want to make double sure. I do want to make it clear that this is something being done in obedience to the Lord and has nothing to do with salvation. Do you understand all this?"

"Yes, sir," Sam replied.

"Sam, do you understand that this means dying to your old self and being raised in the newness of life. Do you realize you are making a commitment to the Lord to follow Him, to resist sin, to do your best to live a life that honors and glorifies Christ?"

"I do," replied Sam. He looked over at Mo with a question on his face. This didn't sound exactly right. He would if he could, but he had come to know that only Christ could live like Christ.

She nodded in agreement.

"Excellent, Sam," said John. "I am looking forward to baptizing you. Let me introduce you to Jim, our music leader. He will set you up, and I will meet you in the baptistery later."

Jim, a balding man in his early sixties with a small potbelly and a big smile, took him up the steps to the baptistery and explained the procedure. It was very simple. Sam put on some swim trunks and covered up with a gown and waited.

The music was traditional Baptist songs that Joe and Debbie had never heard: "The Old Rugged Cross" and "Nothing but the Blood." There were a few more songs dealing with the blood. Joe and Mary listened intently, straining to see how this was different than their church. It was certainly more informal. The music was more spontaneous, but Joe couldn't see much difference in the people. Their faces didn't reflect any more joy than his own church.

After three songs, the music stopped and the baptistery lit up. It was situated up above the pulpit. All eyes focused on the pastor who was already standing in the pool with his Bible.

"This is a glorious day," he said. "Today, we have a new believer. One who has received Christ as his Lord and Savior, and today he is making his public profession of faith by following the Lord's command in baptism."

Sam stepped into the pool from the other side. The smile on his face was nothing to compare to the smile in his heart. That provoked an even bigger smile on the pastor's face.

"Sam, as a public profession of your faith, have you taken Jesus Christ as your Lord and Savior?"

"I have," Sam replied loud enough for the back row to hear.

"Then, Sam," said the pastor, putting a handkerchief to his nose and supporting his back, "I baptize you in the name of the Father, the Son, and the Holy Spirit, buried with him in baptism . . ."

The tomb of silent darkness welcomed him, wrapping its cold tentacles around him. There was no one there but him alone for what seemed like several minutes. He could see the death and burial in his spirit. It was wonderful. Something pulled him upward. He arose to light and warmth to hear, " . . .and raised in newness of life."

His body vibrated with an inexplicable feeling as he emerged, revealing a face radiating a simple smile. The congregation clapped and shouted "alleluias" and "praise the Lord."

"Thank you," he said to the pastor.

Little John was pleased as he stared at Sam's eyes. He loved that look.

Sam dragged the heavy wet gown up the baptistery steps to the dressing room. He dried off and sat there, satisfied. He reached for his pants and felt the now familiar coin in the pocket. It was clear by now the Lost Coin showed up whenever it willed, not when he willed. He pulled it out. On one side was the image of two men being baptized. One was like the Son of Man. How he knew that, Sam had no idea. On the other side was the image of one ordinary man rising from the water. His face was as bright as the sun and a white dove was descending on his shoulder.

"Yes," he said to himself, "that's right." He put the coin back in his pocket to disappear until the next time.

Sam returned in time for the sermon. Everyone was quiet as he sat down beside Mo and the rest of the family. The pastor mounted the stage. He started to preach with an open Bible in one hand as he paced the stage quoting it but never reading from it. His voice started out slow and low then picked up speed, vacillating between stroking and admonition. The congregation would relax to his soothing speech and then jump as he squarely questioned their commitment to the Lord.

"Are you working for the Lord?" he asked. "Or are you falling at the foot of the cross every day or falling prey to worldly sins? Counting your worth? Ready to tear down your barns and build bigger ones? Or do you pray every day? Read your Bible? Witness?" He went on for forty-five minutes before starting to coast to a stop.

Joe vaguely remembered sermons like this from his youth with his father. They were in stark contrast to the ones of St. Paul's that focused on how good people should treat one another; how to be a better person. *Self-improvement and education. That's the difference,* he thought. His church focused on the positive. This one on the negative, on how bad people can be. Sin was running rampant and the only way to escape hellfire was to fall on your knees and beg Christ to come into your heart. Now. No other hope. Joe wasn't sure. It seemed like the good people of St. Paul's were doing pretty well. But it did peck at his conscience.

He paused and looked around the room. It was like he was peering into the souls of each and every one, and they felt it. They were sure he knew what they had done the day before and dropped their heads in prayer. Sam looked over at his parents. They were fidgeting and dropping their heads, also. Sam said a little prayer for them.

The pastor made one final appeal to lost sinners and then gave the invitation. "Don't delay," he cried. "This might be your last chance."

"Just As I Am" was sung with several refrains as the pastor stood up front waiting to welcome sinners into the Kingdom of God. Many went up to the front to pray but there were no new converts.

They were dismissed through the one exit door. No one could escape without a handshake or a hug and a word of encouragement from Little John.

As the congregation left, Joe heard one saying to another, "Mighty good sermon. Boy he really let us have it that time."

Joe thought how odd that a flogging apparently made them feel good. Now he was more confused.

The Rices invited the Seasons back to the farm for refreshments. Mary had her homemade lemonade, sandwiches, potato salad, fresh corn, beans, and apple pie for desert. Sam had difficulty not letting his tongue hang out.

"I'm marrying you for your mother, Mo, just so you know." They all laughed.

"Flattery will get you anything you want, Sam," Mary said, quite pleased with her future son-in-law.

The warm afternoon was almost expired. Everyone had to get back on the road. Sam and Mo both had to work the next day. They did their hugs, handshakes, and goodbyes and piled into their two cars, raising a tandem trail of dust down the dirt road. Joe was mostly quiet on the drive back, trying to find a common ground between the disparate messages. *Who was right,* he wondered? Norman let him mull it over.

Sam and Mo drove for an hour without saying anything. "It was a good day," Sam said quietly, breaking the silence as the afternoon light started to dim.

"Yes . . . it was," Mo agreed, gently squeezing his hand.

13

DIVIDING ASUNDER

THE WEDDING WAS SCHEDULED. It was going to be a backyard wedding in late September on the Rice's farm. That would be a year, almost to the day, from Sam's flight through the shadow of death and, of course, when he opened his eyes and saw his Mo standing over him.

Little John was asked to perform the nuptials to which he agreed, despite the fact they had not darkened the doors of Ebenezer Baptist Church since the baptism. It was, of course, contingent upon another talk with Mo and Sam prior to the ceremony and another opportunity for John to instruct them in the way they should go. Like the baptism, he wanted to make sure they knew what marriage was about, the commitment they were making to each other, and how it was their obligation to love, honor, obey, and live for Christ, to live like Christ would have them live.

Sam really liked Little John. He was sincere and genuine in his beliefs, but his constant attention on sin while preaching grace was a dichotomy. John seemed to focus on the outside of the cup rather than the source of the problem—the heart.

But Sam couldn't be too critical of the Baptists since he wasn't exactly producing any better results. Of course, that was the problem he was told—focusing on results. The only difference between him and Little John's flock, Sam figured, was he was trying to let go and they were trying to hang on.

Despite the setbacks, Sam was not giving up. Sam read and reread Romans chapters 6, 7, and 8. He thought he understood. He was dead to sin. Paul talked about sin that dwells in him. "What was the answer," Paul asked rhetorically. Simple—Jesus Christ! Sam totally believed that, but why was he locked up in chapter 7? He wanted to do good, but found it impossible. *Why is the world still having its way with me? If I'm dead to sin, why do I keep sinning? Why can't I do the things I want?*

As sweet as Mo was, Sam knew that angelic face could turn dark in a flash. The difference was she never dwelled on it. She apologized and moved on like it never happened. Sam, on the other hand, festered. *What is it in us that must have its pound of flesh?*

Mo just smiled and said, "Honey, honey, honey. What you feel is no different than what any of us feel. Satan whispers in everyone's ear, you're not the only one, but he's a liar."

Sam looked surprised. "But, you . . . you always seem so confident . . . so comfortable in your own skin. You can't be like me."

"Oh, yes, I can," she replied. "We all can. We all are. We are all made the same way. Humans of like passions. There is nothing known to man that all have not felt. It's all in God's purpose."

"So you're saying sin is normal and natural? Anger, hate, fear, depression?" Sam asked. "I thought we were dead to sin."

"Well it's natural for those who reject Christ," she said. "They just cloak it in self-righteousness, but not for those in Christ. You are confusing feelings with sin. Feelings and temptations are not sin. We don't operate from our feelings. We operate from our spirit center, which is Christ and never varies. That is why you desire and will to do good for others, and it tortures you so when it appears you want to go in the opposite direction. This is where the two-nature myth comes from.

"People confuse these negative pulls with the so-called second nature. Our feelings, both positive and negative, are normal and natural. Evil thoughts, sexual thoughts, jealousy, hatred, depression, and so on; these are all things everyone has. If we respond to them, then yes, we can sin, but we don't have to. The truth is, like you said, we are dead to sin. That is a fact. You have to believe that. But you have to know that sin is not dead to us."

Sam's eyes lit up. "Sin is not dead to us," he mumbled to himself. She could see it struck a nerve.

"Satan is not called the Prince of Power of the Air for nothing. This is his world, but like Jesus said, 'he has nothing in me,' and neither does he have anything in us. But he lives and does have his tentacles twirled around our body and soul. If we are fooled into believing we have to respond to his negative pulls, then he has tricked us into sinning with guilt riding on its coattails. Then he piles it on the more we listen. He's the master Accuser of the Brethren. The only real sin is unbelief. When we sin, we confess it and we're done. We are the only ones keeping it alive by nursing our stillborn baby of self-righteousness. Until we let go of any vestige of self-righteousness, we will never appreciate the gift of His righteousness that dwells in us. And that is the most difficult "letting" you and I will ever have to endure."

"Wow, hon, you are good. It's sinking in."

"The key is to remember who you are in Christ. He replaces you. Galatians 2:20, remember? It is no longer I who lives, but Christ."

"I remember," Sam said. "I keep trying to apply that."

"Ah ha!" exclaimed Mo, pointing her finger. "Therein lies the problem. Stop *trying*! Reckon it to be so. Let it be so. Call those things that be not into existence as though they were."

"I remember, again," Sam said. "L-E-T. It's tougher than I thought it would be to do . . . or not do, I guess. I'll do better . . . errr . . . be better? Guess I'm still confused."

"Don't worry about it. It'll come," Mo said patiently. "We can talk more about it tonight with Harry. He does a great job of explaining the difference between soul and spirit. Right now, I'm famished. Let's eat and then we'll drive over to meet the group and have dessert!"

††

Mo and Sam didn't have much time off or much money, so they decided on a short honeymoon in New York. With their savings and a little help from Sam's parents and grandfather, they would soon have enough for a down payment on a three-bedroom house in the suburbs. They found a one story with an unfinished basement. They prayed that God would hold it long enough for them to make a contract. Mo admitted that might be a little selfish, but she couldn't help it. They got more and more excited as they talked about how it would be, how it would be furnished and decorated. Sam would finish the basement. Of course, there would be a nursery, color yet to be determined. Mo had a dreamy look on her face.

That night with the group, when Harry asked what they wanted to talk about, Mo's hand went up again. Harry laughed. "Ok, Mo. What is it tonight?"

She shared all the things they had been discussing that day. "How about covering for Sam the differences between spirit and soul?" Everyone nodded in agreement.

"Absolutely, my dear," said Harry. "It's not so simple. That is what Paul meant in Hebrews 4:12 when he said, 'For the word of God is living and active, sharper than any two-edged sword, piercing to the division of soul and of spirit, of joints and of marrow, and discerning the thoughts and intentions of the heart.' Many think they are the same thing, but they are two separate and distinct parts. To be able to distinguish between the two takes the word of God.

"Our spirit is who we are, the essence of our being. It has no feelings. It is simply the *container* for another spirit—God. It is where love dwells and where we will and know things. It is invariable, just like God is invariable, the same yesterday, today, and tomorrow. It's where our true nature resides, the nature of Love, of God. It's the mind of Christ.

"So, what is the problem? Well, it's mistaking soul for spirit. The soul is where we have emotions, where we feel things, and try to understand the world around us. It's the clothing and expression of the spirit but it is also hard-wired to the outside world. On one side we hear the still, small voice of God. On the other side the loud and obnoxious voice of the world. Because it is variable, one day we are on top of the world and the next in deep depression. Satan uses this confusion to make us believe our feelings are who we are and that we must respond. No feelings in themselves are evil. Used in the positive way they were meant to be, they are for others. Respond in the negative, and then it is for self and sin.

"For example, Sam mentioned stress with all that is going on in his life. Stress is not a bad thing. It has its place. It makes us pay attention. Too much stress is not good. It can affect our health, our attitudes, or exacerbate negative feelings. The problem is how we respond. When they are stretched out from their normal intent and we are tricked, they are used for self and the result is sin. Someone insults us. We feel bad, hurt, and feel like striking back. We may respond, but we don't have to. We just love that person who spitefully uses us."

"This makes sense, Harry. But I don't get this we don't have to respond stuff. What does that mean?" Sam asked.

"Good question, Sam," replied Harry. "The answer is not easily imparted except by revelation. It takes the word of God and simple belief that it is so. The only one real sin in this world is unbelief. It all comes back to believing Galatians 2:20. Believing that the two spirits are one. Believing that you and Christ are one person, that Christ living in you as you has replaced your life. Just like Jesus said if you have seen me you have seen the Father, if I have seen you I have seen Christ. It is Christ that does the works."

Sam walked out oblivious to all around him. All these new ideas were settling in. He kept comparing them with Little John. They wanted the same thing, to be like Christ. Jesus said it was easy. John said it was hard. He knew the hard way didn't work, so it had to be something else. *Only Christ can be like Christ,* he repeated to himself. *I am Christ in my human form.*

A light went off in Sam's spirit at that moment. He couldn't verbalize it, but he knew. He just knew. He was now a knower.

As they approached the car, Sam felt the coin in his pocket and pulled it out under the streetlight. On one side was the image of the Son of Man, Christ. On the other side was an image of himself! Two sides of the same coin!

"What's that?" asked Mo.

14

I WILL

"LOOK," HE SAID, "YOU'LL get paid! Don't call me at work again!" Steve Season slammed the phone down.

It was a super storm of financial ruin and Steve was desperately trying to stop the hemorrhaging. The bets gone badly over the weekend made it worse.

The arithmetic wasn't working out. The mortgage he took out was to the hilt of what he could afford and the new interest rate just kicked in. It seemed like the right thing to do at the time. Now Steve was underwater on the mortgage to boot.

Steve's new tactics at work had backfired. Dick Masterson, the employee he laid off, filed suit claiming age discrimination. The case was dragging on, putting him in a dim light with upper management who didn't like conflict.

MacNeil and MacNeil was a small firm in a small city and could not afford the negative press or the financial loss. They knew that if this went to a jury trial, they would lose. Steve was told they would be better off to throw themselves off a cliff than put this in front of a sympathetic jury tired of indefensible employees being beat up by the big, bad, greedy corporations, particularly one terminated near retirement age. They were trying to negotiate a settlement, but it was going to be expensive. Dick wasn't going to roll over.

The large bonus Steve anticipated for his first year as CFO was put on hold, which meant it was gone. There was no annual increase as the company cited he had not been in the job long enough to merit one. Further advances were not likely until the litigation was resolved, and perhaps the damage was irreparable. He was now viewed as an overly ambitious cowboy, naive and inexperienced in the ways of business.

To top it off, Sue just informed him she was pregnant with their first child. It was news that otherwise might have been happily received if not for the timing.

Things were looking grim, and the stress was wearing on him more each day. He put his head in his hands as he pictured his four-bedroom brick colonial in one of the most prestigious areas of town. Three-car garage. White picket fence. He was very proud of his house and his cars. The thought of losing any of it depressed him. This was what it was all about he thought. Success. Any other belief was a lot of horseshit as far as Steve was concerned. Everyone wanted more. If anyone said anything to the contrary, they were liars. He wasn't going to lose it.

He looked over his expenses for the millionth time. No, he wouldn't consider trading his BMW. Maybe Sue's car. She didn't need anything fancy. But that wouldn't come close to bridging the gap. He was proud of being the breadwinner, but maybe she could go back to teaching full time. *Damn,* he thought. The pregnancy killed that idea.

The church came to mind. He had solved their money problems through some creative accounting techniques that brought in federal money to the church school. He also took Tim McCreary up on his idea of reducing some staff, but not what Tim envisioned. He let some of the teachers go, increasing class size, but kept the administration. Tim criticized the decision, but Steve told him that the church school was not part of the Financial Committee's charter and not to worry about it. That didn't stop him from snooping around. Steve planned on deriving some personal income from those operations as long as he could keep McCreary at bay.

He knew that eventually there would be a significant inheritance from Norman's estate, but that did him no good now. From eavesdropping on Norman and his father, he knew they agreed to leave it all to the boys. Steve expected that he would receive most of it considering all he had done for him over the years. He painted the house, built him a deck, mowed his grass, and basically took care of Norman's needs as he got older. Sam didn't deserve anything. He would get the details from Norman's lawyer, a friend of Steve's who he recommended to his grandfather.

He wasn't sure how much it was worth, but he knew that developers were very interested in it. The house itself had only three bedrooms and one story, but it was twelve acres and situated in a very desirable area of town almost completely built out with strip malls and condos. Norman said he would stay there as long as he was ambulatory. Maybe he would get it sooner, but he had no control over when this financial windfall might happen.

It was late. His head throbbed as he drove home. He had no good answers. *Where's God now?* he thought as he rolled into the driveway. *Where is He when you need Him? I've done everything right. I've worked my ass off, played by the rules. Been a good person. Worked for God. Put plenty of sweat in at the church and for the family. What do I get in return? Where is the payoff? I deserve something. Damn!*

Sue was in the bedroom freshening up. She had a meatloaf ready to reheat since she never knew exactly what time he would be home. Lately, she hadn't been looking forward to his homecoming. Steve had been very short and irritable, criticizing her cooking and cleaning. She knew he was stressed out, but she did not know why. He kept it all to himself. She was unaware of their financial situation. The last thing on her mind was that money was a problem. After all, she was married to a CPA.

Her only outlet lately was substitute teaching. She really enjoyed getting out of the house. Teaching literature, reading, and creative writing to ninth graders was fun. As freshmen, they hadn't figured out how to game the system, yet. They were still enjoyable and malleable.

She heard the car in the driveway and headed toward the

kitchen. *I wonder what remark I'll get over heated up leftovers,* she thought.

Steve walked in the door without saying a word.

"Hi, honey," Sue said as she walked over to give him a kiss. She managed a peck on the cheek as he brushed by.

"Bad day?" she asked.

"This is a day the Lord hath made," Steve said sarcastically, "let us rejoice in it. Right!"

"Steve. You are going to have to tell me what is troubling you. To be honest, I am beginning to dread this time each day. What is the matter?"

"Just a few issues at work," Steve replied in a softer tone. He didn't want her to get too suspicious of how bad things were. "Nothing to worry about. What's this?" Steve asked looking at what appeared to be an engraved invitation on the coffee table.

"Sam and Mo's wedding invitation," Sue said excitedly. "Just four weeks away."

"Hmm, exciting," Steve said. "Where is the little shit going to do the deed?"

"Steve, give your brother a break. What has he done to you? I don't understand this. To answer your question, they plan on having the wedding on Mo's family's farm."

"Ohhhh." Steve laughed. "E-I-E-I-O, with an oink oink here, and moo moo there." Steve couldn't stop laughing. "You've made my day."

"Oh, stop it, Steve. I don't know what your problem is," Sue said. "I think it sounds lovely."

"Right, whatever," Steve said. "What's for dinner? That might get me more excited."

"Meatloaf. I have to put it in the microwave. It'll be just a couple minutes."

"Wonderful," Steve said, rolling his eyes as he walked into his den to deposit his briefcase.

"If I knew when you were coming home, I would have something freshly prepared," she snapped after him. He made no reply.

Sue tried to engage Steve in more conversation during dinner, but Steve was somewhere else. She didn't understand why he wasn't as excited as she was about their upcoming parenthood.

"I'll be getting a sonogram Tuesday, Steve," she said. "They'll be able to tell the sex of our baby. Are you excited? Don't you want to know?"

"Of course, Sue," he said.

"Do you have a preference?" she asked.

"Of course not, babe," he lied. He wanted a boy.

Finishing dinner he said, "Oh, I should have mentioned. I need to meet with Abe Shapiro tonight to talk over some business. I was going to meet him at the Pig and Pickle for drinks."

"Tonight?" she asked.

"Well, he's busy. We have an issue at work and I wanted to meet with him privately to discuss it," he replied.

"Okay. Don't be too late," she said, as the depressing thought of another night alone gripped her.

"I won't," Steve said hurrying out the door.

Abe was a private lawyer on retainer for the MacNeil company. He was a personal friend of Steve's who had recommended him for the general counsel job. Abe was handling the Masterson lawsuit, and Steve hoped to get some information on the expected outcome. He also handled all the Seasons' family affairs; including Norman's last will and testament. Abe was listed as the executor of the estate. He planned on finding out the details of the will, as well.

Steve drove to the Pig and Pickle, a small but busy bar off the beaten path where things were a little more discreet. Abe was seated at the bar. Steve beelined over, ignoring a yearning smile from the pretty barmaid.

"Hi, Abe," greeted Steve. "Good to see you."

"Same here," Abe returned. "How are things with you and the family? I heard you might be with child."

"True, true," Steve said. "We're excited. The family is doing fine to answer your question."

Steve ordered a drink as they made some small talk. It was clear there was some catching up to do. Abe had a significant head start.

"Abe, I know it's confidential, but can you tell me how this suit with Masterson is coming along?"

"It's not looking good, Steve," he said. "Unfortunately they have created reasonable doubt about the motives to let him go over a younger person, albeit qualified. Masterson's EEOC suit indicates that an anonymous person employed by the company was witness to some comments by you that might have been . . . let's say . . . misinterpreted as prejudicial."

"Bullshit, Abe!" Steve erupted. He ordered another drink.

"Easy, Steve," assured Abe. "Don't take this stuff personal. If this were to go to jury, the testimony would be damning. But this person isn't as anonymous as she wishes she were. We may be able to work with her to make her understand that your comments were benign and had nothing to do with age discrimination. Put our own doubt in her mind. We can't afford a jury trial, particularly if she testifies in his favor. Just the innuendo would drive a nail in this coffin. We know that with or without her testimony, though, it is not likely a jury of his peers is going to side with the evil company. The company usually has the upper hand when it comes to the law, but that means nothing in front of a jury. Corporations are fair game these days. We have to negotiate a settlement, and we will. If we can sideline this so-called witness, it will go better and that will be the end of it."

"Not really." Steve groaned. Abe knew what he meant.

They had a few more drinks with more small talk, which eventually led to the Seasons' family affairs.

"I guess Pop has his affairs all in order," said Steve, changing the subject. "Guess he gives that more thought as the hourglass winds down."

"Oh yeah. All up to date. Really straightforward. Split fifty-fifty between you and Sam," he blurted. "It will be easy."

"Fifty-fifty!" Steve bellowed. The tables near him turned their heads. He quieted down and just stared at himself in the mirror for a moment. "That can't be right," he mumbled. "After all I've done for him, and he is giving that worthless little doofus . . . he gets the same? Goddamnit!"

Abe knew he had messed up. "Well . . . uh . . . easy, Steve. That was what he wanted to do. I shouldn't have told you that. I apologize."

"Don't apologize," Steve said. "I should know. It's my right to know, and it's not right what he is doing. It's not right. Something has to be done about that. Is this all locked in?"

"Well . . . nothing is ever exactly locked in, Steve," he replied. "That's the great thing about the law. There's always room for interpretation."

"I hope so," he said. "We will talk more after I have time to digest this."

He abruptly got up off his seat without saying another word to Abe. His wobbled out the door unable to process what he just heard.

15

THE CONFESSION

SAM WAS CAUGHT. MO put out her hand and he sheepishly handed her the coin. *At least she can't think I am totally nuts,* thought Sam. He had the evidence right there under the streetlight. Sam let her examine it without saying anything.

"What . . . what is this?" Mo asked. "How did you get your picture on it? And who is this on the other side. It looks like Jesus, if I knew what He looked like. Is this silver?"

"Yes, it's silver," Sam replied. "I have been meaning to discuss this with you. I call it the Lost Coin. It keeps appearing and disappearing."

"Appearing and disappearing?"

"Well . . . yes . . . sort of. That is why I haven't said anything until now. It isn't in my possession all that often." She stared at Sam with curiosity. "Look . . . here is the whole story. The truth. I can't help it if you don't believe me but it is. Remember the morning we met . . . sort of . . . but not really, out on our verandas?"

She nodded.

"The day of the great flight? Well, when I left the apartment that morning to get breakfast, I took a shortcut through the alley. You know, the one a block over from our apartments. It was dark, but halfway through there was this old man who stood there waiting. I thought he was a beggar. He put out his hand as if asking for some money and I brushed him off. He grabbed my arm and tried to hand me this coin. I tried to just move on but he dropped it in my pocket and walked away. And he knew my name! I didn't know him from Adam. Since then it keeps showing up. Sometimes it shows up when I am in need and all of a sudden my need is supplied without any effort. Other times, like now, it shows up like a milestone or pointer or guidepost to confirm some revelation that I received. Like tonight. Somehow, and I can't really verbalize it, Harry's words when he quoted Galatians 2:20 this time . . . it quickened. I could see it. In my Spirit. I could see the union. How the two are one. Then the coin popped up in my pocket revealing these two images. Christ and me. Two sides of the same coin."

Mo just stared at Sam, then the coin, then Sam, then the coin. "Ohhkaaayyy," she said. "I believe you." And handed him back the coin.

"That's it?" Sam asked. "That's all you have to say? You believe?"

"Yes," she replied. "Why wouldn't I believe you? It's right there in your hand. Sam, I don't know if you realize what I see. I see more than a coin. And I hope you believe me. God has great things planned for you. I should say us. We were meant to be."

"Okay," he said. "You amaze me. This was a big night. Let's go home."

Sam walked Mo to her apartment door and kissed her goodnight. The love he felt for her was pounding in his breast.

Sam started up the old rickety steps to his apartment. He knew there wouldn't be too many more trips. John was halfway through a six-pack with Molly, watching a football game on TV.

"Hey, man," John said. "How's the groom to be? Beer?"

"Sure," Sam said, snapping it out of the air. He popped it open. He thought about how disappointed Little John would be if he knew. It was on the sin list. Nevertheless, he couldn't kick it. *I'll be Episcopalian tonight,* he thought. *No sin there.*

"Game any good?" Sam asked.

"No. Time to change the channel. This is embarrassing.

Forty-two to six, fourth quarter," he replied.

"Just as well," Sam said. "Got a lot of things to do tomorrow. You practicing up the best man stuff? Knowing you, you better practice."

"Right." John laughed. "All I have to do is show up."

"And?" Sam asked, smiling.

"Oh, yeah . . . show up with the ring, of course," John replied.

"Better drink up, buddy," Sam said. "Won't be any beer at this wedding. Won't be anything remotely like alcohol."

"So you said. Unbelievable." Then John started singing, "In heaven there ain't no beer, that's why we drink it here . . ."

"I can't believe there is actually someone out there cornier than me." Sam laughed. "I'm calling it a night. Oh, yeah. You and Molly."

"What about Molly?" John said, lifting his head.

"I'm in the room, guys. I can hear you," Molly said.

"Oh, nothing, really," Sam said. "We need to keep in mind who we will be with at the wedding is all. Remember, many of them are deeply religious. They look at things differently than we do sometimes. Things like living out of wedlock. Now, I am not saying to not be who you are or lie about your beliefs. Those are up to you. We just don't have to advertise any information that might offend them."

"Ohhhh," said John. "Play the hypocrites. You bet, Sam, we can do that. We'll probably fit right in."

"Well, ole buddy, we all probably will. It would be hypocritical to say otherwise."

John and Molly blushed.

"We'll make you proud. But we ain't wearing any fake wedding bands," John said, punching him in the shoulder and laughing.

"You're a good man, John Case. Good night. Good night, Molly."

"Good night," they chorused.

††

Sam pulled off his pants. The coin, of course, was gone. His mind whirled with an overload of information. Thinking about the coin. Thinking about Harry's teaching. Thinking mostly about what Mo said: God has great things planned for you. For us. What did she mean? How did she know?

He mulled over Mo's comments and optimism. Things were going well for them. They had their house picked out. She was enjoying her job. She loved doing for others. His job was on a nice track.

After a year, he had been promoted to senior project engineer. It was unusual to be promoted so quickly. They were headed for the American Dream. *What more could they want? Isn't this God's plan? What else could there be?*

Suddenly his thoughts darkened and veered toward his brother. *Put that in your pipe, Steve, and smoke it,* he said to himself. He quickly shook off the negative thoughts. *Satan just playing with my soul feelings. Maybe I can't love Steve but Christ in me can.*

16

WELCOME TO AMERICA

JOSE HERNANDEZ LOOKED AT the clock as he hoisted one more bale of cotton to load into the opening machine. He cut the bands and jerked his hand out of the way just in time as the machine traversed the line of bales gobbling up fibers to send down the line to the carding machine. It was cold in the drafty old 1920's brick building. There was just enough heat to keep the equipment running, but Jose was still working up a sweat. Jose grabbed a towel and wiped the wet cotton dust from his neck. It was nearing eleven. He would be paid tonight. His wife, Maria, would be waiting at home for him with hot empanadas, tortillas, and black beans. His two young sons, Juan and Jorge, would be bundled together in the single bed next to their bed in the one-bedroom Bronx efficiency.

The minute hand grew closer. He started sweeping up the tailings, which stirred up a cloud of white and grey dust that hung in the air. The dust-collection system provided little relief. He had never seen maintenance working on it in his three months on the job. OSHA, it was said, never darkened the doorways of the musty old factory.

As the whistle blew, he smacked his black pants and shirt to knock off as much white dust as he could. Then he headed for payroll. Everyone was lined up. On the table was a stack of white envelopes with handwritten names.

Most of the names called were Hispanic, and they were illegal like him. They were from every known South American and Latin country and Mexico. They shared their stories at breaks and lunch but were silent when the boss man was around. They kept their mouths shut knowing there was a line behind them ready to take their place. If anyone slacked off noticeably at all, they were immediately shown the door with an envelope and docked-off pay to cover the inconvenience. Those remaining just had to withstand verbal goads and flogging. If they could have used whips, they would have.

He had made a few friends, perhaps confidants, but he mostly kept to himself. He kept his "nose clean" and his "mouth shut" as instructed. The foreman was spending less time monitoring him—a good sign.

"Jose Hernandez," yelled the boss. Jose stepped up and received his pay.

"Gracias, Señor," he said.

No reply as the boss man yelled another name, "Jorge Rodriguez."

Jose stuffed the envelope in his back pocket and grabbed his lunch pail. He would count it once he got outside.

He put on his thin, brown jacket and stepped out in the cold. He stopped under the lighted sign on the dingy, brown three-story building with half its windows broke out. It read, *Patini Bros., Brooklyn, NY*. Underneath that it read *Quality Denim* and underneath that it said *Safety First*. Moving under the parking lot light he pulled the envelope out and started counting the money. Short again. He was not surprised. A burning sensation engulfed him for a moment. There was no time-and-a-half for overtime, and they had a habit of docking employees randomly, citing a break or lunch that exceeded the time limit. There was no documentation. No one said anything. U.S. labor laws did not apply here. Not for illegals. And they all knew it.

But he was still grateful for the job and to be in the U.S. He quickly remembered what he left in Honduras. Murder, mayhem, drug lords, and no work at all except to collaborate with Maria and Maria decided to risk it all to escape. It took every cent they had to pay traffickers to get them up through Mexico and into the U.S. They dodged federales to the Rio Grande and then U.S. Border Patrol Agents after that. Making it up to New York was not difficult. They had a network of friends and family to help them find work and an apartment. They were invisible to the white middle class hordes they waded through in the busy city streets.

Jose walked to the bus station to ride to the subway. It was a short ride. He would have walked it if it were daylight, but not this late. Stepping off the bus, he looked both ways and behind him as he made it down the steps to the subway platform. The train was running late. There were a couple others waiting at the other end of the platform. One uniformed police officer, looking like he was sleep walking, made one pass along the platform and disappeared up the exit at the other end where the other two late-night riders were huddled.

No sooner was the policeman out of sight when a tall, gaunt white man stood in front of him pointing a gun at his face. His eyes were wide and glassy, obviously on some drugs. His blond hair was long, scraggly, and dirty. His wild, almost spooky, blue eyes added more strangeness to his appearance. He stood at least six foot six, towering over Jose's five foot six, thin frame. Jose's hands were shaking. He knew what the man wanted, but he had no idea what he was capable of. People were shot all the time for a few dollars in the New York boroughs.

"Money," he yelled, shaking his pistol in Jose's face. "Hand it over." Jose knew these addicts often preyed on illegals. They were vulnerable, often carrying cash because they had no credit cards or identification. "Make it quick," he said as he shoved the gun closer to his face.

Jose stared as the man was getting more agitated. Rather than think about his life, he thought about the landlord who would be by for the rent in the morning. This was his second mugging since being in New York, but this time he knew he couldn't afford to part with his money. He and Maria lived paycheck to paycheck to say the least. His slumlord had no pity for those who couldn't pay and proved it time and again by putting whole families out in the middle of the night with their belongings scattered in the alley.

"Señor, please, I have a family . . ." was all Jose could get out before he was laying on the deck, bleeding from the face, pistol-whipped. The robber had his hand in Jose's pockets fishing for the envelope he knew was on him somewhere. Successfully extracting the loot from Jose's back pocket, the thief turned to run when he noticed the gold cross hanging around Jose's neck. His mother gave it to him while she was on her deathbed and because of its value more sentimental than anything Jose never flaunted it. Now it was exposed, popping out of his loose shirt when he hit the deck.

"No, Señor, please," he pleaded once more. The robber reached down and jerked it off his neck, stomped him in the chest and turned to go again. Jose grabbed his right foot as he started to run tripping him. The emaciated man got up and fired a shot, grazing Jose's cheek. He rolled over in the fetal position. The druggy was gone up the exit in a flash.

Jose was sick. It wasn't the pain. His thoughts were consumed with what he would do next. He had to have the money for the landlord. Otherwise his whole family would be thrown out on the street. He unwound himself and looked around to see that his attacker was gone. The two other subway patrons had moved toward the exit at the other end and just stared in his direction, offering no aid.

The train was arriving. He hung his head down and pulled out his handkerchief to stop the flow of blood. He knew that he was helpless. There was no point filing this with the police. They weren't the most responsive when in concerned illegals, and if he did, he could be deported.

Jose sopped up the blood the best he could and kept pressure on the cuts. As he started to board the train, holding his head down to hide his wounds, he saw a wallet laying on the platform. Looking around him, he stooped and picked it up and shoved it in his jacket pocket. He moved over to the most remote seat. There were few on board that time of night. It was clear he was hurt, holding his chest. They stared at him but said nothing. A middle-aged woman in curlers and a headscarf and wearing an old, grey coat, threadbare at the sleeves, looked but quickly turned her head away when Jose made eye contact. Jose sat quietly. His contorted face telling the tale as his mind oscillated between his physical pain and his new set of problems, the pain being the least of the two. *What will I do?* he fretted. *What will Maria say? How will I pay the rent? Where will we go?* He had promised Maria a better life.

The train made several stops. At his stop, he sat there still dazed. The doors opened and started to close when he realized he had to get off. He jumped up and quickly squeezed through the closing doors, still thinking about what he would do and what he would say to his wife.

Under the first streetlight, he pulled the wallet out from his jacket pocket. Opening it, he pulled out a driver's license. Maybe he would return the wallet. He looked at the picture. It was the thief. It was his wallet. That was his picture. It fell out of his pants when Jose tripped him. He could turn him in, he thought. He had his identity and his address. But that would do him no good. That wouldn't get his money back. Money is what he needed. Not justice. There were no credit cards, but there was some cash. Jose's eyes opened wide. Maybe there was justice after all. He pulled out some bills and counted seventy-five dollars. Not much, but maybe enough to pacify the landlord in the morning. He would have to see what they had stashed in the kitchen. Maybe he could get an advance at work. Forget that, he thought. That wouldn't happen. He would have to get his money back. Somehow. He kept the driver's license and cash and dropped the wallet in the dumpster next to his apartment building.

Jose entered the tenement building through the rear and walked up the back stairs. The landlord was illegally subletting the apartment and one of the stipulations was for non-white, low-income tenants to refrain from using the front entrance. He made his way to the fourth floor and inserted his key into the door. Taking a deep breath, he washed away the pain from his face and stepped in. He hoped to make it to the bathroom to clean up before Maria could see the blood, but that was basically impossible in a one-bedroom apartment, unless she had dozed off. No such luck.

"Honey, you're late," she said not looking up. It was nearly one. "I'll heat up your dinner." She turned to give him a kiss. Her sleepy eyes opened wide as she pursed her lips.

"What . . . what happened? You're covered in blood! Don't tell me . . . you were mugged . . . again? How did this happen?"

"It's not that bad, Maria," he said calmly. "It just looks bad. A couple cuts. Let me clean up and then we can have dinner. I'll tell you all about it."

"I want to know now!" she demanded.

"In a second," he replied. "I need to feel human first. Easy. Don't wake up the kids."

He walked into the bathroom and scooped up some water to wash his face. The cuts were deeper than he thought and still oozing blood. He washed his face with soap and water and stuck some bandages on the worst places. There would be scars.

Maria placed a plate in front of him. "Well?"

"Yes, I was mugged. Someone on drugs. He had a gun," he said.

Now he had her attention. "What? I hope you just handed over to him what he wanted."

"Not exactly," Jose said, looking down at his food. "I just got paid. It was all we had. The landlord will be by in the morning. If he doesn't get his money, well . . . you know what that means."

"You resisted?"

"Shhhhh," Jose said, "you'll wake the boys. Yes . . . I tried to appeal to his sense of decency, but he was full of drugs. Out of his mind."

"You tried to fight him? Are you a fool? Crazy? It's better to be eating out of dumpsters than have you shot and killed. He didn't shoot at you, did he? What if you had been killed? I guess then it would be just me and two small boys eating out of dumpsters."

"You're right," he agreed. "Calm down. It's all right. I made a mistake. I should have just handed it over. No, he didn't shoot," he lied.

"Well, it looks like he did a good job working you over." She sighed.

"Let's eat," he pleaded.

They ate their meal in silence, wondering where this new life was going to take them. Maria headed for bed. She had to get the boys off to school early in the morning and get to her job cleaning hotel rooms by nine. Maybe she could get an advance.

The bedroom was dimly lit so the kids could sleep. Above the cast iron headboard was a large crucifix. *Where are Jesus and Mary now,* she wondered.

Jose sat on the yellow and green twill couch to gather his thoughts. He checked the money can. There was three hundred forty, plus the seventy-five. All they had. *That should be enough,* he thought, *to get us by until we can get the rest of the rent. But where would that come from?* He pulled the driver's license out and perused it. *You bastard,* he thought. *You need to pay.* He looked at the address and wondered if it was still valid. Lower Manhattan. He could find that.

17

THE TWO BECOME ONE

IT WAS A SATURDAY in late September. The amphitheater was ablaze with yellows, reds, and oranges of oak, maple, aspen, and ash, intermingled with the greens of fir and spruce. The occasional spike of white birch punctuated the impressionist's canvas. A radiating yellow sun that had no clouds to interfere, nothing but an azure sky as a canopy, mollified the cool air.

Mo was in her room getting ready. Her mother was talking about her responsibilities, how her life would change, what her duties would be, what she should do, what she should not do. Mo wasn't listening. She wondered where God would take her, not where her mother thought she should go.

Out the window, she could see a few early birds showing up. Sam and his family were driving up that morning. The chairs and tables were set. The smell of freshly mowed grass was nostalgic, triggering memories of growing up on the farm. Images flooded her head. Her dad pushing her higher and higher in that old tire tied to the front yard oak tree. Sunday afternoons reading a book in the hammock and the irresistible nap that ensued. It was a strict upbringing, she thought, but oh so wonderful in retrospect.

Her father had set up an arbor in the rear and a pulpit; both built the week before in the barn. The altar was stained and finished in a clear urethane gloss. The arbor was painted a high-gloss white. Her mother and friends had interwoven every kind of flower throughout the latticework.

Tears started to well up in her eyes. "Honey, honey," her mother said, moving forward and hugging her.

"I love you, Mom." She sniffled.

"I know, sweetie, I know," she comforted. She hugged tighter. Mo hugged tighter.

"Back to business," she said, wiping her eyes and gaining her composure. They continued with the makeup.

"Are you sure?" her mother asked.

"I am," Mo said, making firm eye contact with her mother's.

"I know," she replied. "I know love when I see it. It's . . . well . . . we weren't sure why you picked someone that wasn't . . . at least initially, a Christian. You know what the Bible says."

"About being unequally yoked?" Mo said, her eyes flashing. "Yes, Mother, I know! Maybe faith has more to do with what can't be seen than what can . . . "

"Understood," Mary said. "Not to be brought up again."

Mo peered out the window to cool down. She could see Little John getting out of his car. He had the same dark Sunday suit on as the last time she saw him. His pants always came up a little short on those long, lanky legs. As he stood up, he pulled on his jacket sleeves hoping to stretch them, but alas, they bounced back. He had a blue and red striped tie with a blue and green checkered shirt. His black shoes looked like they didn't have many more shines left in them. With hand extended and a smile as wide as the sky exposing two huge rows of white teeth, he met Mike in the middle of the yard and patted him on the back. Mike reciprocated with a big smile in return.

A simple man, she thought, *and a simple wedding.* The Seasons, she knew, had hoped for something more elaborate. Joe had offered to pay for the wedding in the city in the Episcopalian Church. But she owed this to her parents. Maybe they weren't rich when it came to money, but they were rich where it counted. She looked out at the wedding cloister, the arbor and the altar glistening in the bright sun, surrounded by the best painted canvas God had to offer. It was beautiful. Priceless. No money on earth could have bought this day.

Mo snapped out of her trance, one of several that day. The little squall with her mother was forgotten. She took a look in the mirror. Her eyes widened in fear. "Mom, thanks for the help with the foundation and the hair. I think Suzy and I can take it from here," she said, gently pushing her arm away. Her mother put the brush down on the table.

"Okay," she said. "Just trying to help. There's Suzy now. Maybe I can . . ."

"We've got it covered, Mom," she said. *Thank God for Suzy,* she thought. *She can fix this.*

She opened the door. "Suzy," she yelled, "in here," and mouthed silently so only Suzy could see, "h-e-l-p."

Suzy tried not to laugh as she squeezed past Mary into the room. "Hi, Mrs. Rice. Exciting day, huh?"

"Hi, Suzy," Mary replied. "I get it. I can see that this is not where my gifts lie, so I'll leave you two alone for a while, but you don't have that much time," she warned.

Mo and Suzy giggled quietly after her mother left. "Let's get this stuff off your face, honey, and start over. Not salvageable."

"Mom never was one for makeup," Mo said.

Mo drifted off again as Suzy worked her magic. Suzy was always there for her, even when she had left for college and ignored her.

"What's the matter, hon?" Suzy asked. "Is this a funeral or a wedding?"

Mo leaned over and kissed her on the cheek. "Nothing, Suze, nothing. Forgive me."

"Forgive what?"

"Forgive everything."

Suzy just shook her head bewildered.

More and more people were starting to arrive. "Hurry, Suze," she begged. "Everybody's showing up. Why there's Kenny Smith. Looks like he has a girlfriend with him. Good for him."

"She's the runner-up, kiddo." Suzy laughed. "Just in case you didn't know, he's still in love with you."

Mo knew.

††

The Seasons started to show up in their three-car motorcade. Sam was solo. They would be heading for New York that evening for their short honeymoon. Joe, Debbie, and Pop came in another car. Steve and Sue came with Father David separately so they could leave right after the ceremony. He had pressing business to attend to.

Steve stepped erectly out of his BMW. He was wearing a three piece, crisply pressed blue pinstripe suit, pant legs down to the heels, shirtsleeves extending one inch out from the jacket sleeves. A bright-red tie split his white shirt. He straightened his perfectly tied tie in the side mirror. Sue, dressed to the nines, came around the other side sporting the latest fashions and four-inch Christian Louboutin heels. She looked spooked as she realized the venue was grass. As they sunk into the soil, she grabbed Steve's arm. Steve just looked at her.

Steve perused the field of people meandering around the backyard. *Interesting mishmash,* he thought, raising an eyebrow. *How could there be so many in ill-fitting suits with mismatched ties and shirts in one place,* he wondered. Some wore casual clothes and at least one wore overalls. *Really?* He shook his head.

"Hope we don't step in a cow pie," he whispered to Sue. Sue immediately started scanning the grass. She held tight to Steve, walking on the balls of her feet, ignoring people around her as she focused on her destination, the chairs ahead of them. Her sole objective was to sit before she fell down.

Father David was in the traditional black suit and white collar. He was a little unsteady on his feet as he plowed into the masses. He had no problem mingling and introducing himself. He quickly found Pastor John who he assumed was his comrade in the trade.

Steve placed Sue in the last row of chairs. There were three older ladies standing near in deep discussion about something. They slipped into whispers as they kept peering at Molly who was wearing a blue and pink pastel skirt about eight inches above the knee. The only part of their little conference they could pick up was something about no wedding ring and the word disgusting.

Steve looked over at Molly and did a double take. *What's the problem?* he thought as he stared and enjoyed those long, lean, curvy legs.

Mary came over and introduced herself to Sue and they started up a conversation. Sue was relieved to have someone to talk to.

Steve saw Pastor John for the first time moving about clasping everyone's hand in both of his. *Unbelievable,* he thought. *Did he have to have his hair combed straight back like those preachers on TV? That little shit has stepped in it now. I tried to warn him but he just doesn't get it. He should be grateful I even showed up for this shindig. Little bastard didn't even ask me to be the best man. To hell with him,* he thought. *He's just a pimple on my rear.*

Steve continued walking around studying the gathering. He walked by two men who were discussing tithing. The argument was whether one should tithe on gross or net. He found John and Molly. They were in conversation with one of their college friends comparing after college notes.

"Well, John, you got the program memorized?" Sam asked.

"Well, let me see. Pull out a ring when it's time," he said. "I don't know why you didn't get a trained monkey. At least you wouldn't have to pay him."

"I've got a monkey," Sam said, "just not trained, and he ain't gett'n paid."

The borrowed church chairs were getting full. In addition to Sam and Mo's college and work friends, the entire Baptist church was invited and it appeared that most of them came. There were friends that Mo had grown up with and played with. There were their parents. Many had grey hair now and were sporting canes, but she remembered most of them. They were always so kind when she visited their homes. She snapped out of her trance again. It was time. Showtime!

The music started and Mo stepped out the backdoor. Everyone stared. Her father was waiting. Sam was at the altar. His penguin-style tuxedo accentuated his handsome face and neatly combed dark hair. The waltz up the grassy aisle was as if in slow motion. Mo's ten-year-old cousin dripped red and white rose petals behind her. She could see all her friends, old and new, out the side of her eyes with perfect recognition. Their smiles warmed her. She could see her entire life up until that moment.

Suddenly the music stopped. Her father let go of her hand. Pastor John said something. She just nodded absently, not having any idea what he said. John went through the traditional passages. Sam stared at Mo. Mo stared at Sam. Little John felt lonely. He wondered if anyone was there besides him when they were there going through the rehearsal.

"Do you?" He asked a second time, leaning into her face.

A day of trances. *Let me enjoy one more,* she thought. *Let this be frozen in time.*

"I do," she said and leaned over and kissed Sam with a long kiss.

"You may kiss the bride," Pastor John said as the entire congregation roared.

Formality lost, the country folk resorted to old time hugs and congratulatory kisses. The city folks waited reservedly in line to congratulate the couple. The kids skipped all of it and found a shortcut through and around the adults to tables laden with finger sandwiches, fried chicken, salads, side dishes, and, most importantly, the desserts.

Steve kept looking at his watch as he moved forward in what could not really be construed as a line. *Heathens,* he thought. *No class. Time to go.* He and Sue finally made it up to the couple.

"Congratulations, Sambo," Steve said unenthusiastically as he leaned over to peck Mo's cheek while checking at his watch one more time. "Wish we could stay, but I have some business back in town."

"Understood," said Sam, shaking his hand as Steve's eyes strayed toward where his car was.

Sue gave real hugs to both, nascent tears in the corners of her eyes. "So happy for you two," she said, reminiscing of such a time not so many years ago when she was just as full of hope and faith. How she wished she could reel back that time in her life. She wondered if there had ever been a time in her life when she was as happy as they.

"Let's go, hon," Steve said, turning and moving toward the car.

"Wait," she cried sternly, reaching out and grabbing his arm for support so she could hobble across the short grass without falling down or sinking her heels. They stopped to thank their hosts, Mike and Mary, and made a short goodbye to his mother and father.

Steve walked up to his BMW and ran his finger through a layer of dust. "Damn," he said. "Dammit. Let's get out of Hooterville." Sue looked at Steve and sighed. Steve headed out the dirt and gravel road. He looked in the rear view mirror at the dust trail rising up behind him.

"Damn," he mumbled, shaking his head and stepping on the gas. "And damn Sam."

Sue gave him a disgusted sideways look.

Pop sat patiently at a table alone waiting for everyone else to finish their congratulatory salutations. Soon Sam and Mo would be leaving for New York City. They had already changed. The bags were in the trunk of his Camaro. They would drive part way, spending their honeymoon night in an old romantic hotel that Pop had spent his honeymoon in sixty years ago. Pop's face went from peaceful to an amusing smile as he watched John and his buddies trash the car. *Leave the mischief to John,* Pop thought. He was marking up the windows with hearts and arrows, tying cans to the rear and was doling out what looked like a fifty-pound bag of rice amongst all the revelers.

Pop felt someone behind him gently take hold of his shoulder. It was Mo. With an immense smile she hugged him so hard he couldn't breathe. "Easy, honey, easy." He laughed.

"Pop," Sam interjected, leaning over to hug him, "thanks for everything." Pop had financed this honeymoon: The first night in a nostalgic, romantic hotel off the beaten path and the honeymoon suite overlooking Times Square.

"My pleasure," he replied. "You two don't know how happy I am for you. I see in you what Ann and I had for almost sixty years." His eyes started getting weepy as he continued. "Sorry," he said with sadness.

"It's okay, Pop," Sam said, rubbing his shoulder. "We all miss her. You don't know how much it means to us to have your blessing."

"You do," he agreed. "I know that God has great things in mind for both of you. Just go and believe. Know that you are under his wings."

"Thanks, Pop," Sam said. "We love you. I guess we're off. Looks like John can't do much more damage."

John, glad that he no longer had to dodge the questions about how long he and Molly were married, was relieved when the happy couple finally approached the car. Sam and Mo ran the gauntlet, rice dripping from their clothes as he placed her in the car, a few handfuls thrown in for good measure.

"Thanks, buddy," Sam said, rolling up the windows for protection. The cans dragging behind quickly stirred up the road and the car disappeared in a fog of dust and twilight.

Sam and Mo said nothing for an hour as they slowly reminisced the day, reliving every morsel of what could only be considered perfect. After coming back down to earth, they just looked at one another, silently contemplating the future ahead and their first night together.

Using the directions from Pop, they pulled off the interstate and eventually down a dirt road. *What has Pop done?* he thought as it snaked through the dark corridor of tall pines. Mo looked over at Sam.

"Believe," he said and laughed. They saw a sign for the hotel. Straight ahead, it said. *What other way was there?* he wondered.

The road opened up and before them stood what looked more like a huge, old mansion. The small parking lot was full. *Good sign,* thought Mo.

The lobby had an old oak counter that looked a mile long. An elderly lady behind the desk smiled. "You must be the Seasons," she said. "We have been expecting you. Please sign here."

The warmth of the old mansion set Sam and Mo at ease. *Leave it to Pop,* Sam thought as he signed the book.

"You are in our honeymoon suite. Very private and very quiet. It was reserved six months ago by another Mr. Season."

Sam and Mo looked at each other with raised eyebrows. How could Pop have reserved it six months ago, they wondered. They hadn't even set the wedding date. *Believe,* they telepathed to each other.

"We have a full breakfast from six on in the dining room.

Sorry we don't have an elevator, but Charlie will take your bags up."

Sam looked down for his bags, but Charlie was already heading up the stairs with them.

He held her hand as they climbed the two flights of old wooden stairs. Charlie had already placed their bags, turned down the bed, and was nowhere to be seen. The wallpaper and the painting over the bed looked familiar. He had seen it somewhere. It was the painting that made him realize that this was Pop's very room sixty years ago. Pop had a picture on his dresser that had been there since he could remember. Nothing had changed. The wallpaper was made up of blue, white, and red flowers in fields of green with hummingbirds sucking nectar as butterflies swarmed overhead. Over the headboard was a painting of the wedding feast of the Lamb. A set table laden with fruits and meats and silver centerpieces extended on into infinity. The words underneath read: *Come, For All Things Are Ready*.

They slowly moved around the room, just soaking in the sight of each other. Without any words spoken, she went into the bathroom to freshen up and change. Sam started to undress and waited in anticipation. He had thought about this moment for a long time. He knew it would be wonderful. She had made him wait, and he was glad. When she came out of the bathroom in her negligee, he stared in wonderment. He had not expected this. Her beauty was beyond the physical. The love at that moment was indescribable. She was his. And he was hers.

She slipped between the sheets and lay sideways, staring at him as they were nose to nose. Those big brown eyes mesmerized him. He was totally within her control. She smiled. He smiled. He slowly placed his hand around her, soaking in her beauty. They embraced. The smiles turned into laughter.

18

THE QUICK AND THE DEAD

SAM FELL INTO A deep sleep like none he had ever experienced. He found himself in a fifth dimension. It was not heaven. It was not hell or purgatory. He was immersed in space. Floating . . . floating . . . ascending . . . ascending . . . descending . . . transparent. He could see himself, but he couldn't. He was, but he wasn't. He was spirit. Pure spirit. He saw himself as he really was, things that no man had ever seen. It was love. Pure love. He was immersed in love, immersed in a sea of light, in many shades of pure light. There was no mythical bright light. It was a comforting light, soothing to the soul and spirit.

He realized he was swimming in an ocean of spirit, the true eye of man and of God. He thought of the verse, "Who of men knows the things of the man, except the spirit of the man that is in him? So also no one knows the things of God except the Spirit of God." Was he beginning to understand the spirit of man and its connection to the Spirit of God? If so, there were no mortal words to articulate it. This was where the essence of man dwelt and the abode of the secrets of God.

He sensed many, many others around him. Their presence was comforting. He could feel their love. If there were any malevolent spirits, he could not sense them. They were swallowed up in the light. Rendered null and void. Impotent. Powerless.

The presences he felt were like drops in an ocean. The ocean was God and the drops were one with God. God was they and much, much more. More than the spirit of man could know.

Sam's eyes popped open. The clarity of the dream overwhelmed him. He looked at the clock. It was just after one at night. He eased out of bed and walked over to the window overlooking Times Square. It was true. It was the city that never sleeps. Peeling back the drapes he could see people still bustling about. People were going in all directions, oblivious to those around them. *There it is,* he thought. *There is my dream. There is the manifestation.*

He looked over at Mo lying in bed. The city lights leaking through the drapes accentuated the silhouette of her naked body. She looked so peaceful in her sleep. He wondered what dream was dancing through her head.

"Hey, lover," he heard in a low voice.

Apparently none, he realized happily as she beckoned him back to bed.

Jose Hernandez's shift had ended two hours ago and he knew his wife, Maria, would wonder and worry that he was late. He got off on Delancey and Essex Streets on the Lower East Side. That would put him within walking distance of Marco Santini's home according to the address on thief's driver's license. Jose had heard of that neighborhood. It had a reputation for muggings and drugs. Stay out of it, he had heard. Undaunted, he maneuvered his way down the dark streets to the address on the license, avoiding eye contact with anyone he saw. After waiting for half an hour in an alley right across from his apartment building, Marco finally showed up. He walked by Jose without recognizing him. Jose's mouth dropped when he saw the gold cross hanging around Marco's neck. His body filled with rage. He started after him but something pulled him back. His breathing was hard as he calmed himself. *No,* he thought. *Got to do this right.* He felt the switchblade in his pocket. It was at the ready. *That son of a bitch isn't going to take the food out*

my family's mouth, and that heathen certainly isn't going to parade my mother's gold cross.

Jose didn't have to wait long before Marco exited his building and headed out on foot. He could see the bulge of Marco's pistol stuck in the back of his blue jeans hidden by the tail of his shirt. Marco hopped on a bus to head uptown. Jose hopped on the same bus and sat across from him. Jose had his hand on his knife just in case Marco attacked. *Amazing,* thought Jose. *He doesn't recognize me.* Jose had expected Marco to show up at the subway station in Brooklyn to find his wallet. *Surely,* Jose thought, *this guy must know that he has been identified.* Now it was clear. This guy cared so little for his victims, he didn't even bother to worry about who they were or what they looked like. *This will be easier than I thought.*

Marco got off the bus near Times Square. Jose followed Marco as he navigated dark allies clearly on a mission. Marco never turned around to see if anyone was following him. Finally, Marco stopped at a corner. Two men appeared out of nowhere. An exchange was made. They quickly separated with no words spoken.

Jose wished he had confronted him before he spent the money on drugs. *What would he do with drugs,* Jose thought. Click! With his blade open he moved up behind Marco who was now on the move. Jose's heart was pounding and his hands were shaking. As tall as this guy was, he would have to jump him from behind in a headlock and put the knife to his throat. From his previous encounter, Jose knew Marco was wiry and could easily squirm out of his grasp, but Jose's anger just hardened his resolve. He crept quickly up behind him and was within five feet when a patrol car rounded the corner. Marco turned, pushed Jose out of the way and made a run for it. The police hit the lights and siren as Marco disappeared down the nearest alley. They drove right by Jose without stopping. Relieved, he quickly and silently disappeared down a different alley, waiting for the heat to die down.

Jose had missed his chance, but now he knew Marco's routine. He looked around to get his bearings. He was close to the theater district now. He headed for the nearest subway station and started working on his story for Maria. It was almost two-thirty when he got home. She would be asleep. Maybe he could sneak in without waking anyone.

He took his shoes off in the hallway before entering, slowly turning the key in the lock. Maria was in bed. The kids were asleep. She left a cold plate on the table for Jose. He was hungry. Quietly sliding out the chair, he lifted the fork and knife and started eating. Maria's eyes opened as she watched him from the other room. She closed them and pretended to be asleep. *No point,* she thought, *in waking the entire household and neighbors this late.*

Jose removed his dirty clothes and silently made his way to his side of the bed. No shower tonight. He looked up at the crucifix over the headboard and quickly dropped his eyes. *So far, so good,* he thought, easing into bed beside her. She opened her eyes again just staring at the wall. There would be little sleep for her that night. Jose was already picturing how he would take care of Marco the next night.

Maria waited for him to fall asleep. The moments seemed like hours, but finally he was snoring. She slid out of bed and started to go through his clothes that were piled on the sofa. In the right pocket, she pulled out a worn driver's license and the switchblade. The name Marco Santini meant nothing to her, but her whole body shook envisioning what this was all about. The switchblade. This was the knife he promised to get rid of once they made it through Mexico. It would just mean trouble, she had told him. Why did he not do what he promised? Placing both items back in his pants, she slipped back into bed as he continued to snore. Her mind manufactured all kinds of scenarios, none of them good. Sleep would be hard coming this night.

Maria planned all night what she would say to her husband the next morning but didn't get the chance. He snored through breakfast. He snored through her shower. He was still sleeping as she got Jorge off to school and left Juan with a neighbor. The Honduran community took turns looking after each other's kids. She left for work. She would wait up for him tonight, even if he was late, and get to the bottom of what was going on.

Jose slept almost to noon. His shift would start in a couple hours. He ate the leftovers from the morning's breakfast and rummaged through the refrigerator for something to take for lunch. The only thing left was some refried beans and rice.

After showering, he found some fresh clothes Maria had laid out. He put them on and then went over to his other pants to clean out the pockets. He pulled the knife and driver's license out. *Didn't I leave these in the right pants pocket?* he wondered. Then he knew! She was wise to something going on. He would have to finish this quickly. Tonight and be done with it before she suspected more.

Jose fondled the knife in their living room. Click. Fold. Click. Fold. *A gun would be better,* he thought. *Level the playing field.* He could get one. He knew where, but those hombres were probably worse than the one he was dealing with. *No, the blade will have to do.*

As in a fog, Jose robotically headed to the subway to get from the Bronx to Brooklyn. He noticed no one as he boarded. His mind kept replaying how it would all go down. He would track him on his way to buy more drugs. Marco would be flush with cash from mugging someone, no doubt. He would have to make his move this time before he spent it. Wait until he was in one of those dark allies he was so fond of and jump him. Put the knife to his throat and demand his money back and rip that cross off his neck just like it was ripped off his neck. If he pulled the gun, he might have to stick him. He didn't want to kill him, but if he had to, he would.

Thoughts flashed back to the trek from Honduras to the United States: The drug cartels, the slavery, the rapes, the murders, and the corrupt *federales*. There wasn't much he hadn't seen. This was nothing compared to the evil he had experienced.

One of his co-workers boarded the train in Manhattan. "Hey, amigo. Qué pasa?" he said to Jose. Jose didn't hear.

"Hey, man, qué pasa?" he said louder, repeating himself.

Jose looked up and recognized Ricardo staring at him waving his hand in front of Jose's face.

"Uh, no mucho. Cómo estás?" asked Jose as he continued to stare at the floor of the car.

"Estoy bien," replied Ricardo as he sat down beside him with a puzzled look.

The train made its monotonous stops, as Jose remained

engrossed in his nefarious thoughts.

"Jose! Jose! You getting off man?" Ricardo yelled, as he was halfway out of the doors. "This is our stop!"

Jose finally broke his trance and jumped up toward the closing doors, which grabbed the back of his jacket. He frantically jerked on it releasing it from the railcar's grip and silently followed Ricardo toward the mill. Ricardo made no more attempt for dialogue.

Focus! Focus! Jose kept saying to himself. This equipment was dangerous. This place was dangerous. An inattentive slip and a finger, hand, or foot would be lost. He had to give a foot assist to a bale of cotton as the opening machine made its way down the line. He pulled his foot away just in time. *Focus!* he kept repeating.

This night seemed longer than any before. The foreman looked at him suspiciously. He was making mistakes.

At the breaks he stayed off to himself, staring at the dirty cinderblock walls. The other workers looked over at him wondering what his problem was. Finally the whistle blew. Relief, fear, and determination consumed him. Now, again, it was time to focus. With no adios, he headed straight for the subway and boarded. His destination: Manhattan.

Jose set up his surveillance in the same alley across from Marco's apartment building. Like clockwork, he glided by Jose at the same time as the night before. *This is like hunting,* he thought, remembering how they hunted deer back in Honduras. *Creatures of habit. Always taking the same paths at the same time every night.*

Like the night before, he came back out and headed north toward the bus station. Jose wondered why he always made this stop at his apartment before going for the drugs. Maybe he was counting the loot from his latest mugging. He could see Marco's hands shaking. He needed a fix for sure. He seemed to be moving a little faster.

Like the night before, Marco hopped the bus heading to Times Square. Jose got on right behind him. Marco sat up front. Jose walked by him and seated himself toward the rear of the bus. His heart raced when he saw Marco's darting eyes make contact with him. Jose could see something different in his look. Marco had knocked him over last night but he didn't think he paid any attention to whom he was knocking over. Jose dropped his head.

When they came to the same stop as the previous night, Jose expected Marco to exit, but he didn't. Marco gave a furtive glance over at Jose and remained seated. At the next stop, Marco got up to get off. He looked over his shoulder at Jose. Jose hesitated, fearing Marco was suspicious. Marco was halfway down the street when Jose got up out of his seat and yelled at the driver to open the door, this was his stop. The driver yelled back, "Make up your mind," and reluctantly opened the door for Jose to get off.

Jose quickened his pace to catch up to Marco, trying not to arouse any suspicion from others walking the street. He was sure he was heading back to the same place to buy the drugs. He saw Marco's shadow turn down a different ally but in the same direction as the Theater District. Maybe he wasn't as predictable as he thought but not far off. Jose turned down the same ally. Marco was not in sight, but it was dark and Jose was sure he was close. He blindly forged ahead not giving up on his mission.

Sam and Mo had spent the entire day sightseeing and experiencing the cafes around New York: the top of the Empire State Building, the 9/11 Museum, The Natural History Museum, the Metropolitan Museum of Art. They were relieved to finally give their feet a break, relaxing at the Lion King on Broadway at the Minskoff Theater. Afterwards they dined at Lattanzi's on 46th Street and then took a slow stroll through the Theater District. The warm blush of the wine protected them against the brisk fall air. They would end a perfect evening unwinding with a bottle of champagne in the seclusion of their honeymoon suite. There was no hurry. They sauntered slowly arm in arm, saying little, just enjoying the moment. Mo kept looking up at Sam as they walked. Sam was away in one of his daydreams, thinking of his future with Mo. He looked down at her and smiled. Words were totally inadequate. They didn't notice people slipping into allies like cockroaches. They were oblivious to the world.

††

Jose was right. Marco wasn't very far in front of him. He hadn't made it very far when Marco jumped out from behind a dumpster and kicked him square in the stomach. With the wind knocked out of him, Jose hit the ground.

Marco cursed wildly. He had the gun in his hands and his hands were shaking more than before. His eyes were wild and glassy. "Who the hell are you? What do you want? And who do you think you are following me?" Suddenly his eyes squinted in recognition. "Wait . . . I remember you. Last night . . . last week in Brooklyn. You'd better kiss the Mother Mary tonight amigo, cause yer gonna meet her face-to-face tonight."

Jose whipped out his blade. His hands were shaking as bad as Marco's, but there was no turning back.

"The only thing I gonna kiss, gringo, is the stolen cross on your neck," Jose yelled as he jumped up and lunged at Marco, slashing blindly with his knife. With heart pumping to bursting level, Jose cut Marco on his left wrist and tried to grab the gun in his right hand. It was surreal, like someone else was struggling with this man in this alley, not him. His head felt numb as they wrestled awkwardly for the gun.

Jose tried to push the gun up in the air away from him, but Marco was much stronger than he thought. Marco pulled it down between them. It went off. Jose's ear rang and he felt the pain as the bullet penetrated his shoulder. Jose grimaced and fell backwards as the wiry Marco pushed him away. With gun pointed directly at Jose's head, he abruptly walked up to him and kicked him in the ribs. He moved in closer to stomp him in the head, but Jose rolled quickly out of the way and was back up and in Marco's face in a flash. Marco was bleeding profusely. He must have severed the artery in his wrist.

Marco grabbed his left arm to stem the bleeding with his gun hand. Seemingly more vulnerable now, Jose made another attempt to wrest it from him, but Marco quickly jerked himself away and kicked Jose to the ground again. This time he started firing blindly in the direction of Jose. Jose turned and started running down the alley, holding pressure on his shoulder to stem the bleeding. Jose was hit again, this time in the back. He felt the bullet penetrate deeply into his lung. Immediately he started coughing up blood as he ran, his heart pumping more and more blood from his chest and mouth.

Marco fired again, emptying his gun in Jose's direction although he could not see his target. It was too dark and he was too far away. He dropped the gun, grabbed his arm, and ran toward the other end of the ally.

Sam and Mo heard the shots as they came up on the mouth of the ally, but it was too late. The bullet came out of nowhere and hit Mo right in the heart. She made a slight sound as the wind was knocked out of her. She looked at Sam, her face paled with surprise as she felt the bullet bury itself deep in her body. Her legs went limp. She hit the ground, slipping out of Sam's arm. Blood was everywhere. She lay on the ground, her face turning white. Sam dropped to his knees in shock. He stared at his love, lying on the ground motionless—dead! He didn't notice a short Hispanic man crawling out of the ally covered in blood. He didn't notice the crowd congregating around him. No sound came out of his mouth. His face had no expression.

19

THE LION AND THE LAMB

NORMAN SAT ON HIS wrap-around porch. It was late afternoon. The ephemeral Indian summer had arrived, as days were getting shorter. The light, cool breeze wafted the smell of fresh-cut grass across his nostrils. He sipped his black coffee and fastened one more button on his hunter-green cardigan as he watched the sun go down. The snow would be flying soon.

His Bible lay beside him. He spent more time in prayer now and less time wondering about the final outcome of his life. He had learned the meaning of praying without ceasing. It was easy, natural. It was just being in Christ and knowing it.

Last night had been a little different, though. He awoke with a start in the early morning hours and was suddenly put on his knees, praying from something greater than him. He had been mulling it over all day while Steve hummed around the house on the tractor mower. He was at ease. He knew that whatever it was, Christ was in control and needed all hands on deck.

Norman reflected on his life, mostly unknown to all except his beloved wife, Ann. They had no idea of the life they had lived. It wasn't for the telling. There were so many things that no one would believe.

There was the time in Africa. He was on business locating a site for a new plant. Some locals had convinced him to go on a safari despite news of a man-eating lion on the loose. Setting up camp, that very lion came out at twilight. It bounded toward the camp to attack a young boy. Norman stepped in front of the boy and held out his hand. Boldness possessed him, he knew not from where. The lion skidded to a stop and stared for a few moments. Then there was enough time for the guide to center it in his sights and shoot. The lion lay dead.

Another time in Korea, he was again looking for a new plant site. A group of men approached him with a panel van loaded to the hilt with Bibles. The springs were sagging. They handed him the keys saying he would know what to do and just walked off. He didn't, but he got in the van anyway and started driving. It was so heavy in the rear he could hardly steer it. He drove it straight up to a North Korean checkpoint. They immediately opened the gates no questions asked. It was like they could not see him. He came to a little village and ran out of gas. It was dark and there were no lights. Suddenly a group of men and women came out with lanterns and embraced him. They thanked him over and over in Korean, but he understood every word, conversing with them in a language he didn't know.

Yes, it had been a very interesting life. Ann was the only one who knew. She was the prayer warrior who understood it all. Sharing these things with the uninitiated had no value, he knew.

His son Joe was a righteous man, but he never had that level of understanding. Sam might be the exception. Maybe it skipped a generation. He saw the spark in him after the plane crash. They recognized each other on a spiritual level.

Steve was a different story. Yes, he had to admit, Sam was his favorite. But he had to agree that Steve was the dutiful one, but there was something about the favors he sensed were not free. Steve's eyes roamed the place, sizing it up, measuring its worth. *This old, white clapboard house is a home, not a piece of meat,* Norman thought. He knew it would have to be sold some day, but it was more than cold, hard cash.

True, Sam didn't seem to contribute much in terms of labor, but he was always there when it meant the most. Sam had a rare quality. He questioned the status quo and the so-called core values that America touted, the so-called American Dream. Sam wondered what everyone was gushing about. To him, things had no other place in life than to be a means to an end, tools for living—not living for.

Steve, on the other hand, was consumed by money, glitz, and glamour. He was after prestige, to be seen not as an ordinary person, but someone better than the others—a somebody. Unfortunately, it was never enough. He spent it all and then more. The void inside him couldn't be filled. Norman prayed for Steve constantly.

Now he had decisions to make. He sighed as he looked at the portrait of him and Ann that he kept on the porch. Should he stay in the home or sell? If he stayed, how long should he? He had owned that house for fifty years. He called his twelve acres a gentleman's farm. A small barn was turned into a furniture workshop. Two end tables for Sam and Mo were ready for staining and varnish.

He had thought about giving the house to Sam, but he knew that would cause a big stir with Steve. *It wouldn't work now anyway,* he thought. He had loaned them the down payment and they were ready to close. They hadn't asked for money. He just knew young people needed some help getting started, just like he did.

No one knew what his place was actually worth. It had little value as a gentleman's farm, but it had great value to the developers who after fifty years had finally made it out as far as Norman's address; for a price he had never dreamed of—three million dollars. They wanted to build another shopping center. *Just what we need,* thought Norman, *another shopping center.* Maybe this was the best.

The cooler air prompted Norman to go inside. The sky was turning a hard blue as the sun began to set. He walked to his private study where he had spent so many hours reading, praying, and making plans. He sat in the creaky office chair. The scarred up old oak desk had seen better days. He smiled as he fingered Sam's carved initials on the top of the desk, triggering memories when he caught the youngster mounted on all fours with a Swiss Army knife digging away.

"Hey," he remembered yelling at Sam in anger, "what in the world are you doing? That's my desk!"

Sam started crying. Norman looked down at his pathetic and

guilty villain and the anger effervesced. "Here," Norman said, "this is how you do it," and he took Sam's small hand with the knife and helped him finish the last letter. Now he just glowed at the sight of the initials.

Norman pulled his Last Will and Testament out from the lap drawer. It was split fifty-fifty between the boys. If for some reason one of the boys would pass on, all would go to the lone survivor. He considered revising it and making Sam the executor, replacing Abe Shapiro who Steve had recommended after realizing Norman would not name him the executor. As Norman dealt more with Shapiro, he kept sensing something untrustworthy. There was something about his hungry eyes, the same look as in Steve's eyes.

Maybe that is what attracted the two together. Steve was a taker. He never missed an opportunity to take advantage, even as a child. He rolled into the driveway with a tricycle when he was five, a bicycle when he was six. There were all these mysterious things showing up in his room. No one knew where it all came form. He always had an answer that sort of made sense but not altogether. When Sam was born, Steve had a new target. It was a few years before Sam had anything Steve wanted, but when the time came, Sam was easy picking.

Yes, he was sure. Letting Shapiro have the power of attorney would be handing it over to Steve. He should have known better.

Norman rumpled up some old newspaper and slowly bent over the hearth of the stone fireplace. He stacked some kindling and hickory in his symmetrical engineering habit. The concoction flared brilliantly for a few moments and then began to simmer, exuding that smoky, hickory aroma he loved.

He reached into his pocket and pulled out a silver coin. It was old and tarnished like Sam's. It had a lion on one side and a lamb on the other. *Ahhh,* he thought, *my favorite. Be wise as serpents, Sam and Mo, and gentle as doves.*

The sun was setting. In the twilight he could see headlights coming up the long driveway. He rose to the window and peered out. It was a new red Camaro.

It was Sam and Mo. They both got out of the car and walked hand in hand toward the porch as Norman opened the door. He could see in their faces they had a story to tell.

20

ALL THINGS ARE POSSIBLE

SAM FELL TO HIS knees and bent over his beloved in unbelief. His mind raced. *How could this be happening,* he thought. *How could God do this?* He felt for a pulse. None. His hands and coat were covered with blood as he hugged the lifeless body. But he had no tears and gave no scream. Bystanders started to circle him and the body, covering their mouths in awe and shock, making muted noises.

Suddenly, calmness came over him like nothing he had ever experienced. It was a feeling of spirit, totally separate from the soul. Everything was all right, exactly right. "Don't judge from appearances," a still, small voice said to him. "See the power of God."

Sam felt transparent again, invisible, possessed but in control, knowing exactly what to do, what to say, but not understanding why or how. A surreal confidence took over. His heart calmed to a steady rate.

Kneeling over her lifeless body, he placed his hand on her heart. He prayed out loud for those around him to hear: "Thank you, Father, that you are the God of the living, not the dead." He said no more.

Mo's eyes opened. Color immediately returned to her face. The evidence of the shooting remained except for the hole in her chest. The wound was gone.

"Why is everyone staring?" she asked, pushing herself into a sitting position. "Why am I sitting on the sidewalk?"

She looked at the blood on the sidewalk and the hole in her coat and her dress covered in blood. Suddenly her mouth and her eyes opened wide! She remembered! She looked up at Sam in disbelief. Sam took her arm. She slowly rose and stood in front of him, wrapping her arms tightly around him. "Thank you," she whispered.

"Guess God has some great works left for you too," he whispered back, joyfully kissing her on the cheek.

Then he noticed Jose on the ground at the mouth of the ally bleeding profusely. He slowly walked over as if nothing had happened. Bending over him, he asked, "Do you believe?"

"Si, Señor, si! I believe in the Father, the Son, and the Holy Ghost," he replied as tears rolled down his pain-riddled face.

"So be it unto you," Sam said authoritatively and placed his hands on Jose's wounds. They disappeared immediately.

Jose's eyes lit up in unbelief as the pain evaporated. He pointed down the alley. "Señor, a thief, he stole my money, he . . . a bad man," he stuttered in an awkward attempt to explain to Sam what had happened.

"No need to explain," Sam said in a soft voice.

"But this gringo a robber . . . killer, hurt my family," Jose said appealing to Sam. Revenge in his heart had not waned. "What about him?"

"What about him?" Sam said with finality. "What is it to you what he does or where he goes? Leave that to God. Go home to your family and trust in God the way you did when you were a child in Honduras."

Jose stared up at him. How did he know about my childhood? It was a time so long ago he barely remembered. It was good then. God was good then. He believed everything. But he was a child. Now he was grown up. Now he wasn't so sure. He thought about what he had just seen. God had saved him, given him a second chance, but the thief was getting away, too. He was confused. Who was this man?

"See that you tell no one about this," Sam whispered in his ear as he got up to walk away.

"Si, Señor," Jose said, "gracias." Jose slowly walked away, taking the ally to avoid the crowd. The fear and hate he had been spent so much time building dissipated with each step.

The crowd grew larger. 9-1-1 had been called. Sirens were wailing from the next block over.

Those who were the closest asked, "Did you see that?"

Others replied, "See what? He just picked her up. She must have fallen."

"No," one man argued. "She was shot! Right in the heart! Dead! I saw it! Didn't you hear the shots?"

"Oh come on, man," another countered, "maybe she was grazed or knocked out. There she is right there, walking."

They all turned to look. There was no one there. While they were debating, Sam placed his coat around Mo and they walked right down the street. The people were so consumed with what they thought they had seen that they paid no attention to the couple as they disappeared from sight.

Both, bewildered by what had just happened, worked their way up to Times Square. No one paid attention to the blood all over their clothes. It was as if they were invisible. They walked right through the lobby. The doorman, the agent, no one noticed or remarked. They got back to their room and sat down and just stared at each other.

"What just happened?" they asked in unison. They laughed a giddy laugh, not knowing why.

Sam felt the coin in his pocket and pulled it out. "This is the only explanation I have," he said.

The coin only had one side. *How could that be,* he wondered. He passed it over to Mo.

"I think I see," she said.

The next day they checked out as if nothing had happened and drove straight through to Norman's house. He was the only one who might understand.

Norman listened as Sam and Mo recounted the miraculous events of the previous night.

Sam looked at Norman's attentive eyes. "Do you believe us, Pop?" Sam asked.

"I do, of course," Norman replied with a slight smile. "Why would I not?"

"I don't know," Sam said. "It's all so crazy. I know Jesus said we would do works greater than his, but I have never heard of such a thing. And . . . well . . . me! Look at me! I'm no savior, no great spiritual warrior, how could that be . . . me being used for such a work? Working miracles? Really? I'm totally confused."

Mo looked over at Norman with a knowing look on her face.

"Sam, these things go on all the time," Norman said and paused for a few moments before starting. "You call them miracles. I call them natural manifestations of God. Let me ask you, Sam, where do you think these things happen? On TV for everyone to see? When they come up on stage and throw their crutches down and jump up out of their wheelchairs? Do you really think God works in a theatrical way? Through charismatic preachers on TV with their gaggles of followers? No. He works quietly, without show. Those that need to see will see.

"Are his real servants sinless? No! He looks for simple people, Sam. Empty vessels, those who have inclined their heart to him. The meek. Those that have presented their bodies a living sacrifice to Him. You won't recognize them except through the spirit. They don't stick out to the world. God knows and that is all that counts. They don't seek honor from men, only God."

"I understand, Pop, but me? I'm not just a sinner . . . I mean it's not that I was a sinner. I still sin. Why would God use this vessel?"

"David was quite the sinner," Pop replied, "yet he was the apple of God's eye. Why? Because he was contrite and his heart was repentant. There are none of us immune to the pull of the flesh—even David. This fictional spiritual ninja you imagine doesn't exist. He uses you. He uses Mo. He uses me. Ordinary people."

"I know. It's just that . . . well, it seems Satan, or something, still has a power over me, and I can't seem to defeat it. Like Paul, I find myself doing things I don't want to do and finding it hard to do the things I want to do. If I can't control my own behavior, I just don't understand why God would use me in such a way. I imagine this hypothetical spiritual ninja would not be perfect, but certainly . . . let's say . . . further along the path than me."

Pop chuckled. "Really, Sam. The only problem you have, Sam, is your belief in a power other than God. You are too sin conscious. Be God conscious. You have everything you need. You are fooled by appearances and believing in an opposing force that has no power over you other than what you, yourself, give it. There is only one power in the universe because there is only one Person, and that is God."

"But what about Satan? What about evil?" Sam asked. "Are you saying evil is not real?"

"It is as real as you want to believe. Let's put it like this. If I turn these lights out, what happens?"

"Darkness," Sam replied.

"When I turn the light back on, where does the darkness go?"

"Good question," Sam said. "I guess it's still there."

"Just like evil is the negative to good's positive, so darkness is the negative to light's positive. One cannot exist without the other. It's called The Law of Opposites. The light swallows up the dark negative. It is entirely subject to the light and to the degree to which the light operates. You can believe in the darkness or you can believe it is subject to the power of light. It has no power of its own. The same with evil; you can believe in it or believe it is subject to the one power and used according to the purposes of good."

"It doesn't seem to have any purpose that I can see other than to hurt, to destroy," Sam said.

"Really?" he asked. "The scriptures say all things work together for good to those that love God. Note the caveat: to those that love God. Jesus said if you see with the single eye, your whole body will be full of light. So, the question is, what do you see? If you see evil, then it is as real as real can be. Hard as a rock."

"So, you are saying that God is in everything and no matter what the appearance, we should see God in every situation?"

"Exactly. Let me ask you a question. When you look at all the evil committed in the Bible stories, what was the eventual outcome? What did Joseph say? You meant it for evil, but God meant it for good. That one was more or less obvious, but just because we cannot see God in all situations as distinctly, He is."

"He is," Sam repeated. "I like that. This really transforms one's way of thinking and seeing the world. So, if someone is seeing evil, then really they are just seeing a reflection of themselves, they are reflecting a belief in a false power that has illicitly commandeered them."

"You got it!"

"I think so," Sam replied with a slight smile.

"This is a rite of passage for all who go all the way, Sam," Norman finished. "No one is exempt. To those who navigate through it, all things are possible."

"Wow!" Sam said. He looked over at Mo who had been silently soaking in the discussion.

"And Mo, Pop," Sam said excitedly, "you would not believe . . . well, I guess you would, but she . . . she has seen things that she can't even utter."

"Oh, I would believe," Pop said, turning his attention to Mo. "I would believe."

Mo smiled. "He's right," she said. "When I was technically dead, I did go to a place. It was so beautiful. I think it was like Paul, caught up to the third heaven and heard unspeakable words. Words, he said, that were unlawful to utter. I think what he meant was there were no words that could describe it. Now I know what he meant. I saw the future, too." She beamed. "And the future may not be what you expect, but it is wonderful. As it was shown to me, it was sealed up. I have it in myself, but I don't know how to divulge it if I could. All I can say is everything will be all right."

"That's enough," Pop agreed. "I don't know about you guys, but that's enough excitement for a lifetime, let alone a night. You two sleep in Sam's room tonight. We'll talk more in the morning."

"Amen," they said.

21

WHAT IS HE TO YOU?

JOSE WATCHED SAM AND Mo walk away as if nothing had happened. He turned and slowly made his way down the dark alley in the same direction as Marco. Sirens were blatting loudly from every direction, adding to the confusion. He could see the multicolor strobe lights flickering strange shadows at the end he had just left. He tried to focus. *Just get out of here,* he thought. *Focus. Must get home.* He was drunk with the strangeness of this night. How could these things be? He tried to sort out his feelings in the dark. He started repeating Hail Mary's over and over. "Hail Mary full of grace . . . "

He kept repeating it until he got to the other end of the alley. As the mouth of the alley started to light up by the streetlights, he saw him. Marco! Lying there semiconscious. He was bleeding out. Weak. No longer able to make it another step. Dying.

Marco looked up and saw Jose. Even in his weakness, fear and hate shot out from his face and eyes. He fumbled for his gun, but there was no gun. His face relaxed. He gave up.

"Do it!" he said, resigned to his fate. "Just do it!"

Jose pulled his knife. Marco turned his head away. He heard the click of the knife as it flipped open. Jose walked over to the dumpster Marco was sitting against. He pulled out a piece of rope and piece of wood. He cut the rope to length and tied it around Marco's left arm. Then he tied another knot around the piece of wood and turned the tourniquet tighter and tighter until the flow of blood stopped. Marco just stared at him.

"Why are you doing this?" he asked. "I tried to kill you."

Jose said nothing. He felt Marco's pocket and found a cell phone. 9-1-1. He called in his location in broken English. He waited a few minutes until he could hear the siren of the ambulance.

They stared at one another not saying a word. Marco had never in his life had anyone try to help him, let alone save him. All he remembered was abuse. There had been no Good Samaritans in his life to help along the way.

Jose could feel his hate and fear dissipate. He no longer hated this man. No. In touching him he could feel the pain in this man's life. He could relate. Even have empathy.

As the ambulance got close, he said, "I have to go. God has saved both of us tonight. Better stop and give thanks."

"Wait," Marco said and handed Jose the gold cross.

"Gracias." Jose couldn't believe he had forgotten. He took it and disappeared.

Marco lay there as the paramedics arrived. *God,* he thought. *Where has He been?*

Maria sat at the kitchen table stifling her sobs. Her hands were shaking. The children were asleep. She had been praying all night. "Lord, keep him safe," she prayed over and over.

It was almost three. *Where is he? Alive? Dead?* What would she do? How could he leave her in a strange country with two children alone? Her thoughts roamed to her home in Honduras, such a beautiful place until the drug lords took over and made it hell. Her mother and father were still there. The plan was to make a life in the U.S. Try to get citizenship and be good Americans. Send them money and eventually bring them over.

She looked up at the crucifix in the bedroom. She started to pray. She prayed to Mary, to Jesus, to the Saints, to anyone that would listen. She prayed from her heart an agonizing prayer. "Lord, let him be safe," she prayed. And that was all she could get out. It was out of her hands.

The key lock turned and the creaking door slowly opened. Startled she turned. Standing in the doorway was Jose, covered in blood. She muffled her scream as she ran to him and put her arms around him with deep sobs.

"It's okay," he said. "It's okay. I'm okay."

She pulled back and looked at him over. *How could that be,* she thought. *Is this someone else's blood?*

"You're hurt!"

"No, no, I'm not. Everything is fine. Sit down."

Jose pulled up his chair beside her. He took off his coat and shirt. She could see the wounds. She could see the dried blood around them. But there was no bleeding. The wounds, there were just scars. Healed scars. Maria's mouth opened in amazement and confusion.

"It's okay," Jose said, rubbing her back and soothing her. "It's all over. It's done. I have seen the work of God. And it is wonderful . . . merciful . . . gracious." He proceeded to ignore Sam's instructions and told her what had happened on this night, how he stalked Marco with revenge in his heart, how they fought and killed each other. They were dead men walking. How out of nowhere God sent his servant and healed them both. First Jose, and then Marco through him. The hate, the fear, the evil in his heart could no longer be found. All he had was compassion for his enemy.

"He was lost too," Jose said. "Just like me. Like the rest of us. I was no better. I was just as ready and able to kill as he. Who was I to wreak judgment and revenge? The man . . . I wanted to go after him even after God had so graciously healed me, but the man . . . he said, what is he to you? And suddenly pain and the anger oozed out of my body like a lanced boil and I understood. It was crystal clear. Like God had opened my eyes. Who was I, as he said, to do God's job? What was this man to me? He belongs to God just like us. He will deal with him as He sees fit. All this was for me, for us, to see God as He truly is. Love. And in control. He loves all of us, regardless of what we have done. He brought us here for a reason. Not for us to die or live miserably, but for us to believe and trust in Him. And that is the only thing we need to know."

Maria looked at his face. It was so full of truth she could not help but believe. Where did all this wisdom, this change come from? He was such an angry man. He had believed God let him down. That he was not getting his fair share. Everything was exactly as God planned it. She now knew that also.

She cleaned him up and they went to bed, but there was no sleep. They praised God all night. They got up refreshed the next morning to see what God was going to do next.

Marco lay in his hospital bed full of IV's and monitors. He was making a full recovery. The police questioned him, but he did not see his assailant. It was too dark. He knew they would arrest him for drug possession on release, but he didn't care. It wasn't the first time.

The last two days were tough. Drug withdrawal was far more painful than getting knifed. His head was just now starting to clear. He tried to remember all the events that happened that night. He was out of his mind. Firing bullets like crazy. All he was thinking about was his next fix. That was all he cared about. The other guy was out of his mind, too. Who was that guy? That face. He saw himself in a mirror, full of hate, fear, and anger. Then he came back. That part was a little fuzzy. He was different. *I thought he was going to kill me, but he didn't. He saved me. After trying with all his heart to kill me. Why? Something about God, he said. So God finally showed up on the scene, eh? Where's He been all my life?*

Marco lay there and closed his eyes. There was a time long, long ago, he remembered. A time he believed in God. But his father beat that out of him. There was no God. No God would have allowed that. No God would have allowed all the things he had seen since then. But what was this all about? He pondered this for the remainder of his stay.

When he was released, the police were there with cuffs. They read him his rights. With the third offense, he was convicted and sent to the state prison in upstate New York.

22

BEAUTY AND THE ADULTERER

MARY LYNN KRAKOWSKI SUCKED down one more lungful of smoke on her Marlboro before flicking it against the brick wall of the Pig and Pickle. The lot was starting to get full. She had traded shifts with Marjorie, foregoing the more lucrative evening tips to meet her beau who promised to be at her place tonight with a surprise. Mary Lynn hoped for the question, but she believed in hoping for the best but preparing for disappointment.

The door of the old Dodge Dart creaked as she hopped in, praying it would start. One more time there was a backfire and a muffler-less *varoooom*— announcing ignition. She backed out of the parking lot and headed north to the outskirts of town.

The days were getting shorter. Her headlights caught the reflectors on the two-lane road indicating the narrow road into the trailer park. It was hidden behind the trees. She liked the fact that it was somewhat secluded despite having to slalom the beat-up pickup trucks, tricycles, and toys jutting out from the tiny gravel driveways.

Mary Lynn took a quick shower and started applying her

makeup. It looked a little thick, but the lighting in the trailer wasn't the brightest. The black mascara and the reddest lipstick she could find punctuated her pale face and bleached blond hair. She topped it all off with liberal dashes around her neck and ears with Evening in Paris.

What to wear, she thought, kicking the shoes out of the way and going through her sparse closet. She spied the outfit he had first seen her in that turned his head: a very short red and white skirt with a pink sleeveless top and plunging neckline. She adjusted her bra, admiring her firm breasts. *No need for a pushup with these babies,* she thought. Worth every penny even though the payments were hard to make on a barmaid's wages. Stripping made a lot more money, but those guys were perverted. They will pay off eventually she was sure.

She turned and posed her slim, curvy figure in the mirror. A body to die for, she remembered him saying. It is, she agreed to herself. Sullenness suddenly deluged her as she flashed back to her last beau, her ex-husband. *A lot of good this body did me,* she thought as her anger rekindled. That wife beating, drunken SOB. *He didn't deserve this. This one,* she thought on the other hand, *has promise.*

Sullenness evaporated just as quickly when she spotted a black BMW coming up the road. She smiled and raced to light all the candles. One more dab of perfume and she was ready to meet him at the door.

Steve stood there, roses in one hand and a small box in the other. She had hoped for an even smaller box.

"Hi, sweetie," he said, all smiles as he helped himself through the door. "For you."

"Ohhh, thank you," she said kissing him, the fresh lipstick leaving a mark on his cheek. She wiped if off as she moved over to the kitchen to find a vase.

"You smell good. How are you doing?" he asked.

"Tough crowd today, but I'm here now. How's your day?"

"Oh, not too bad," he said unenthusiastically. "Problem at work. But thinking about you made it all worth it." He leaned over and gave her a long kiss. He stared down at her new double-D breasts busting out over her neckline. He moved closer and started running his hand up her leg.

"Easy, cowboy . . . easy," she said, gently pushing his hand back. "We got all night."

"Well, honey, actually I don't. I told my wife I was working late and would be back before midnight."

Her eyes flashed. *Why does he talk like he worries about what his wife thinks? Isn't he going to leave her?*

Steve, sensing the black mood coming on, quickly moved to ease the tension. "Oh, look what I have for you," he said with an apologetic face, handing her the box all wrapped with a bow.

It worked. Her face muscles relaxed into a smile. She loved surprises.

"Oh, what can it be?" she asked childishly. Her face lit up as she pulled out a long string of pearls. "Oh, thank you," she gushed as she jumped on top of him and started kissing him all over the face.

"Uh, sorry," she said trying to wipe off all the red blotches over his cheeks and face.

"Let's have a drink to celebrate," she said, pulling a couple glasses down from the kitchen cabinet.

"Good idea," he agreed. "Here, I'll make it." He poured her a gin and coke and poured himself a scotch straight up. *Cheap,* he thought, *but it will do.*

They sat on the couch and made small talk for about thirty minutes to finish their drinks, and then she was ready. She motioned him to the tiny master bedroom as she dropped her blouse exposing her curves and the large red rose tattooed on the small of her back. Her skirt fell to the floor. Steve moved up behind her and skillfully unhooked her bra with a snap of his fingers, releasing those breasts from the strangle hold. He slowly caressed them as he slid the bra to the floor. She stood there in the dim light wearing nothing but a string of cultured pearls. Steve stared like a deer in the headlights. She giggled and pushed him to the bed. *These things have power,* she thought.

Afterwards, Mary Lynn lit a cigarette, as they both lay there naked, Mary Lynn covered only to her waist. She offered Steve one to be polite. She knew he quit. Steve declined. He knew that would be a dead giveaway to Sue. She dared him to ever smoke another one.

Mary Lynn turned the night table lamp on so she could see Steve better, and so he could see her as she flaunted her naked beauty. Her infatuation with this slick, classy man was written all over her face and she wanted every advantage. Steve sat up more erect, hypnotized by the view. Noticing something on the nightstand, he pulled his eyes off her for a second to examine a portrait of her and another man. Their arms were around each other.

"Hmmm," he said coyly. "Cheating on me, eh?"

"Oh, Steve," she said, pushing him. "Of course not. You know I love you."

Steve tensed up at those three little words.

"That's my brother," she said.

"Oh. Sorry. I didn't know you had a brother," Steve said.

"Well, there is plenty you don't know about me," she said with a slightly annoyed tone.

Steve, always quick to pick up on body language, interrupted her quickly and said, "I know. I like to savor these things. I don't want to know too much all at once. That way I get to slowly enjoy you just like I savor your beauty, little by little. That makes it last a long time."

He reached over, reassuring her by slowly rubbing her back and kissing her on the cheek and face.

"So," Steve said. "I'm now ready for the next stage of knowing you. Tell me all about your brother. Where is he? What does he do?"

Suddenly she was quiet. Maybe, she thought, she had pushed a little too hard on the subject. There were some things she didn't want him to know.

"Well, he's kind of away right now," she started.

"What does that mean?" Steve asked laughing. "Kind of away where? I want to know all about him."

She hesitated. "He's in prison," she finally blurted.

"Prison?" Steve echoed, sitting straight up now. "Why? What did he do?"

A few more moments passed silently as she tried to figure out what to say. Finally she broke the silence. "Manslaughter," she said, looking over at Steve to see his reaction.

Steve had no reaction. "Really?" he asked rhetorically. "Do you want to tell me about it? It's okay. We all have things in our past."

Mary Lynn looked at Steve's nonjudgmental face. *He can be trusted,* she thought. *Still, better to let it out little by little as Steve said he preferred, just to be sure.*

She loved her brother, but she knew he was actually guilty of first-degree murder. The DA agreed to a plea deal of manslaughter after one of the witnesses got cold feet.

"Well, it's complicated," she started. "Let's just say it was a botched robbery. Guns were involved; bad choices were made. It looks like he will be out on probation in a few months if he keeps up his record of good behavior. He's a good boy . . . I mean man." Her eyes started to well up.

"We all make bad choices at times," Steve said comforting her. "There is good in everyone. I am sure he has learned his lesson." Steve started to think how her brother might work into his plans. He would check out the facts from public records.

"But since you brought it up, I'd like to ask a favor."

"If I can, sweetie," he replied.

"Well, he hasn't done great at the last parole board hearings. One thing that would help is if he had a sponsor when he got out. A job, basically. Can you help? It's looked on real favorable."

"Hmmm, let me see," Steve said thinking. "What kind of skills does he have?"

"Nothin' really." She sighed. "High school dropout. Got in with the wrong crowd ya know."

Steve thought for a second. "Wait. I happen to know we are looking for a custodian. I'm pretty sure it hasn't been filled and I'm pretty sure it doesn't require a high skill level. I'm not in too tight with our HR manager, but he's a bleeding liberal. All for giving second chances. Let me see if I can work on him."

"Oh, thank you, honey," she said, plunking kisses all over his face so he had to push her back.

"You're welcome," he said laughing.

"I'll repay you for this, and you know I can."

"I do, but right now I have to go," he said pulling up his pants and tucking in his shirt.

"Do you have to?" Mary Lynn cried.

"You know I do," he said. "Work tomorrow. It's midnight now."

She put on a sheer nightgown and walked him to the door. "I love you," she said with an expectant kiss.

"I love you too," Steve said, his mind already off somewhere else. "I'll call you."

Steve's bright headlights were very conspicuous at midnight as he meandered through the tiny community. He noticed an old lady peering out her living room window as he drove past. Steve liked discretion, and he knew driving a shiny BMW through this neighborhood wouldn't go unnoticed.

He pulled into his dooryard and carefully closed the car door as quietly as possible. Sue might be asleep and not notice how late he was. After removing his shoes, he made his way to the master bedroom and went to the bathroom, easing the door closed and turning on the light. He checked for any vestiges of lipstick on his face or shirt. He brushed his teeth, put on his pajamas and eased into bed. So far, so good.

Sue's eyes opened as the bed jiggled. She started to turn around but the smell of cheap perfume made her freeze. She wasn't sure before, but now she knew!

23

DARKNESS TO LIGHT

ALMOST A YEAR HAD passed since Sam and Mo's honeymoon in New York. Norman was completely recovered from his stroke. Sue gave birth to a beautiful baby girl. They, or Steve, named her Anastasia Susan Season. Sam and Mo called her Tase. Sue called her Anna.

They often revisited that night in New York. Nothing since could compare. All was normal and very ordinary. The last time Sam had felt and seen the coin was in New York. That didn't stop either of them from daydreaming what God had in store for their future. Yet, they had a lot of questions. Why did it happen then? Would anything like that ever happen to them again, they wondered. It was no small thing. *What was God up to? Was he preparing us for something else? Why us?*

They had shared this with no one except Pop. Sam knew that his Pop was wise in things of the spirit. He remembered Pop saying many things specifically to him in the past, trying to teach him principles, but they were just over his head. Now they made sense. They spent many weekends at Norman's and spent many evenings with their deeper life groups.

Norman had recovered from his stroke. Each year, though, the age in his eyes was more vivid. He spent most of his time on his gentleman's farm. The offer had gone up to four million. Norman had written up another will unbeknownst to Abe Shapiro or Steve. Instead of an even split between Sam and Steve and all going to the survivor if one passed, he split it up between Sam, Mo, Steve, Sue, and Anastasia. There were a few contingencies. If Steve and Sue divorced, their portion would go into a trust for Anastasia. Between Sam and Mo, he made no distinction. She was the daughter he never had. Norman loved Mo. Sam was made the executor. Norman shared this with no one but Sam and Mo.

††

Life was very busy. Sam and Mo had fallen into the American Dream. They had a house, two new cars, and good jobs. They had security, or so they thought. The new house was completely furnished now. They had the tan, leather couch, matching loveseat, easy chair and ottoman, the flat screen TV's, and the cherry dining room suite. John and Molly would look at each other in amazement as the pieces came together like a puzzle in slow motion. They were even talking about marriage, houses, and children.

Sam and Mo were contemplating their first child and already looking toward that larger house in an upper middle class neighborhood. Bigger, better. Yes, life was good. The future looked bright. They were the envy of many. God had blessed them, but it came up short.

Something is still missing, but what is it? They met many in their fellowship groups who had much less but seemed to abound more. As great as things seemed, their hunger persisted.

Could it be we needed more, God? Didn't we have all that God had to give? They thought they did. *Why else would God have used us the way He did?* Sam and Mo went into a lot of silent prayer. Then they would compare notes. They were eerily the same. As great as this life has started out being, there was more out there—much more. God was tasking them with finding that pearl of great price, with finding that lost coin. God had blessed them with knowledge. They knew who they were. Now it was time to move to real faith.

Sam had started to test that faith. Pop had taught him that evil had no power over him other than what power he allowed. That helped. He still wavered from time to time. It was like a freezing and a thawing cycle. Sometimes he would freeze up and be back to his old habits. Then it would thaw. Mo reminded him to stop trying. That was God's job. If he conquered this so-called evil himself, who was he to praise? Himself or God? Sam had no argument.

A new verse kept running through his mind. *Be not filled with wine but be filled with the Holy Spirit*. It kept repeating like his father's scratched vinyl LP's. He couldn't get it out of his head. It was beginning to dawn on him. Something was forming from the deep. This filling of the Holy Spirit had nothing to do with a feeling. Most thought they had to be possessed by a euphoric feeling, an out-of-body experience, speaking in tongues, or some other outward manifestation. But that was false. He remembered New York. He was possessed, yes, but it wasn't something taking control of his being. It wasn't against his will, but totally because of it. He was in perfect union with the Holy Spirit. It was him, but it wasn't. Galatians 2:20 was the only way he could describe it: I live, yet not I, but Christ. It just was. And all he had to do was be. And believe.

The seemingly paradoxical nature of God was constantly blowing up all Sam's preconceived beliefs. Every time he thought he knew God, He would blow it up. Every time he tried to put God in a box, He would bust out. Sam knew that God was preparing him for something. It was time to move from a basic faith to an advanced faith, one that reckons it to be so. One that calls those things that be not as though they are. The one that just knows! Believes! Goes from rote head knowledge to really knowing that God is in control, that He indwells, and that God is the all in all. Sam was just a vessel, the branch to the vine, the container to be filled. One with Christ. One in God. The reason man was made was for God to dwell in them, as them, to enjoy his creation through and as man.

Sam mulled these things constantly in his spirit. The burning coal was applied to his lips. It could not be shared with another. Only God could do that and only to souls hungry enough. One either knew or they didn't. He knew. Mo knew. Pop knew. The vast majority milled about in darkness.

††

It was Sunday. Sam and Mo drove to his parents for a family dinner. Norman, Steve, and Sue were the others on the permanent invite list. Today there were two additional guests, Bill and Liz Morgan. Bill was Joe's college roommate and a hell-raiser by all Joe's accounts. He got his engineering degree and was soaring in his career when it all came tumbling down. Alcoholism was his demise, Joe said. Then he met Liz and something changed him. Joe said he had never seen anything like it in his life. How could a man turn his life around so dramatically? He still worked as an engineer. Liz was an English teacher. Joe had not seen him for years and had never met Liz. He had no idea what he had been up to or what he was doing.

When Sam and Mo walked through the kitchen door, the first thing that greeted them was the thick smell of marinara sauce simmering on the stove and the sound of bubbling spaghetti next to it. A whiff of garlic bread could also be detected. His mother was slaving over all of it while Sue was setting the table.

"I don't want to slobber all over you, but no one, I mean no one, can cook like you can."

"Oh, go away," she said with a laugh and a push. "Go ahead and slobber."

He and Mo gave Sue a hug. Norman was sitting on the couch holding Anastasia. Joe was in another room finishing up a few bills.

"Where's Steve?" Sam asked.

"Working," Sue said.

Sam could feel tension. He had heard rumors that Steve and Sue were having marriage problems. It was over money, and maybe some other things no one wanted to talk about. Sam knew his parents were upset. They loved Sue and they were wild over their first grandchild, Anastasia.

Increasingly, Steve had some excuse why he couldn't be there. Everyone acted like everything was normal. When Steve did finally arrive, the body language between he and Sue gave it away. There was no hiding the strain between the two of them.

A car pulled up behind Sam's Camaro. It was an old Olds 98. Joe came out of his office and looked out.

"That's Bill," he said, going out to meet them.

Bill stepped out of the car with a huge smile. He was middle aged and losing the battle with the belly and mostly gray hair. Joe met him in the driveway with a hug.

"Been a while, eh?" Bill asked.

"You bet, Bill, so good to see you."

Liz was right behind him, a short, petit oriental lady. Joe showed a little surprise on his face. He had not seen Bill in years and didn't know anything about his wife.

"Come in, come in," Joe said, herding them toward the kitchen door. "Dinner is just about ready."

There were introductions, hugs, and handshakes all around. With everything coming off the stove, there was no time to visit before dinner.

Bill and Liz accepted a glass of wine with dinner but only took an occasional sip as they conversed; obviously to be polite, Sam surmised.

They made small talk as they worked through the salad and into the pasta. Joe and Deborah were dying to know where he had been all these years.

"Okay, Bill. Enough small talk," Joe said as they were eating dessert. "Where in the world have you been the last twenty years? It seems like you disappeared off the face of the earth. Ya know, Liz, this guy was quite a party animal in his day."

"I've heard," Liz said with a chuckle. "Not so much these days."

"Why, there was the time . . . " Joe started. "Well . . . let's pick up where we left off. How about that?"

Bill laughed. "It's been a very interesting twenty years, I can tell you that. I met Liz in rehab. She was actually a counselor. I know, I know . . . that's verboten. Nevertheless, that's where we met and that is where my life, my real life started."

"We've seen something similar," Joe said, grinning at Mo.

"Real life?" Sam asked. "What do you mean?"

"Good question, Sam," he replied. "Let's just say that meeting Liz opened up doors I never knew existed. Liz's father was a pastor. He was born and raised in China. Liz's mother was from South Korea. They both came to this country; God brought them together and voila they begat Liz. A miracle in itself but I will save that story. As a result, Liz speaks Korean, Mandarin, and English. Skills that come in very handy in our present occupation."

"And what's that?" asked Joe.

"We have a business. It's in North Korea."

"North Korea? You're kidding? What kind of business?"

"We have a school. Liz teaches English. I teach math."

"That doesn't make sense, Bill," Joe intervened. "How do you make a living doing that, not to mention the possibility of getting arrested for God knows what?"

"They are missionaries, Joe," said the ever-quiet Norman, putting his finger up to his lips and giving Bill a wink.

"I didn't say that," said Bill, smiling and winking back. "That's illegal you know."

"Good God, Bill," Joe blurted. "It sure as hell is. Are you crazy?"

"You bet it's crazy, Joe, and we love every minute of it."

Both Sam and Mo were sitting up straight, hanging on every word of this conversation. Norman observed them with a warm feeling inside.

"Well, I would like to know more about what you are not and what you don't do in North Korea," requested Mo. "Maybe we can move to the living room and talk about it some more."

Liz took over most of the conversation at that point. Bill had hit rock bottom when she met him. He had lost his job and his marriage. Many had written him off, but she saw something in him that no one else seemed to see. A flicker of light that she was sure was inextinguishable. They dated and they married, but they couldn't have children. In her father's church, Bill met all these people he had no idea existed, people who put themselves out there for others, people who were genuinely concerned about him, about people other than themselves. That was all it took to light the torch. It has been burning intensely since then.

They started this school in North Korea; using the Wonchong customs port to cross over from China. Liz had passports from both China and South Korea. Bill slipped in on her coattails. They were met with suspicion every time they crossed. They checked for Bibles coming and going, even checking for missing pages on the way out. What they didn't know was Bill used his engineering and tinkering skills to build a printing press. It was hidden in plain sight at the school. It took him two years to smuggle the parts in. Bill would hum Johnny Cash's "One Piece at a Time" song each time he crossed the border.

Everyone roared.

He told them the press was a physics experiment. It was antique and rudimentary, but it worked. The only real challenge was getting paper, bindings, and not getting caught.

Liz's eyes lit up when she talked about the children in their school.

"These are the most curious children you have ever seen. They are so open and honest. Despite being immersed in the grandest propaganda machine in the world, they are so inquisitive about the rest of the world they are shut off from. Touching on Christianity was always tricky and dangerous. The few other teachers on staff were underground Christians and they knew a slip up could cost them their lives."

Sam and Mo heard nothing for two hours other than the stories of Bill and Liz. Was God tugging at their hearts? Here were two that gave up the middle-class life for something, almost the opposite, that one could see was so fulfilling. Norman watched them and grinned.

Joe and Deborah couldn't believe the transformation.

"My God, Bill," exclaimed Joe. "That's amazing! You are totally unrecognizable. Good for you."

Sue had listened to these two energized people for two hours and didn't know what to make of it. Somehow, she felt life had left her on the side of the road.

"Aren't you scared?" asked Sam.

"In the beginning, Sam, it was a little hairy. But God took care of the fear. Love trumps fear every time. And God is Love."

Sam thought of nothing else for the rest of the evening.

24

DEAD MAN WALKING

BRUCE KRAKOWSKI STOOD OVER the lifeless body. Blood was gushing out of his neck in spurts and running down the drain. Finally it stopped spurting and oozed out. He took the chard of glass he used to cut his throat and broke it up into tiny pieces with the heel of his shoe to eliminate any fingerprints. His inmate guard stood by the doorway nervously looking back and forth, but there was nothing to fear. No one was going to come in.

Bruce turned the shower on and walked casually away like nothing had happened.

"Let's go," he said to his partner. "Last time that SOB'll try that again."

They slipped down the hallway to a room with one guard standing outside.

"Yer late," he groused at the two of them.

"Lose track a'time in here ya know," Bruce said, brushing by him and opening the door.

They took two seats in the last row. There were about twenty men in orange jump suits sitting at attention. The chaplain had already started speaking.

There was nothing new that he hadn't heard before. The chaplain went on about this Jesus and how he could change one's life. How God was love. *Apparently God hasn't visited this joint,* Bruce mused. *Jesus, Shmesus. You have ta be joking,* he thought.

It was difficult, but he managed to keep a straight face and show intense interest as the sermon went on for thirty minutes. He couldn't help but feel relief when the chaplain started to wrap things up.

"Gentlemen, the time is at hand. For those of you who have not received Jesus Christ as your Lord and Savior, there is still time. For some of you this is last call. He is the only one that can turn your life around and save you from your sins. No matter what you have done. All you have to do is invite Him into your heart, confess that you are a sinner, and ask him to cleanse you. All your burdens will be lifted. I am going to recite the sinner's prayer. If God is speaking to your heart right now, I invite you to say it with me. Either out loud or silently. It doesn't make any difference. God hears any way."

The chaplain prayed and then asked if any would like to give their testimony. One young black prisoner came up front in tears.

"I just wanna thank God, thank Jesus, for all He done for me," he said composing himself. "For those who might not know, I'm in here for murder. I done did some mighty bad things. God has shown me dare is nuttin' He can't do. No sin He can't clean." He broke up again. "Praise Jesus," he said as he returned to his seat.

"Praise Jesus," affirmed the chaplain. "Anyone else make a decision today or want to give a testimony?"

Another walked up to the front. "My name is Marco and I'm a recovering addict. I will be out of here soon, and I just want to praise Jesus for all he had done for me. Many of you have heard my story." He proceeded to tell them how a man he tried to kill saved his life and showed the love of God he didn't know existed.

Bullshit, Bruce thought as he made his way to the front. "I just wanna say," he started, "I done some bad things, too. Real bad. Murder. Theft. Vandalism. You name it. But I accepted Jesus as my Lord and Savior when I first came to this prison, and I can't tell ya what it's done in my life. My burdens is lifted.

Even in here, I praise Jesus all day long. It's the only way to go."
He put his thumb up and winked at Jamie.

"Thank you, Bruce," said the chaplain, "for that testimony."
Not that he believed it. "Looks like we are done until next
Sunday. Bruce, how about you close us in prayer."

"Love to, Chaplain," Bruce said and then went on with a
prayer manifesto, asking blessings on everyone in the room, the
prison, his family, and anyone else he could think of.

"In Jesus's name I pray," he ended to the relief of everyone
in the room.

He sure does a pretty prayer, the chaplain thought. *Wonder
how much is real.*

As he and Jamie, his partner, headed back for their cell,
Jamie asked, "Why do we go there every Sunday?"

Bruce looked over at Jamie and shook his head. Jaime
reminded him so much of Lenny in *Of Mice and Men* it was
uncanny, not that he had read it.

"Parole, Jamie. Parole. Good behavior. Remember?
Something you need to think about too. The parole meeting is
coming up this week." But Bruce knew that Jamie would never
see the light of day.

"Ohhh . . . yeahhh . . . right. You sho is smart, Brucie."

"Don't call me Brucie."

Bruce was careful to watch his compadres during lunch. He
sat with Jamie at a corner table in case there was trouble. The
man he killed had friends and even though the warden would be
clueless as to who did it, these guys would know. By now, there
was no one in the rank and file who didn't know.

He could see several taking turns glancing at him from a
table across the room. Not a good sign. If they wanted revenge,
eventually they would get it. If this parole hearing didn't work, he
might be done for. Parole was denied at the last three hearings.
Survivors of the attack kept showing up. Bruce proved he was
rehabilitated, but they wouldn't listen. Denied.

This time might be different. His sister was keeping tabs on
the family members of his victims. Seems some of them may be
out of town for Thursday's hearing. He could only hope.

One huge fellow from the other table got up and sauntered over to Bruce's table. Jamie was as big and as strong. The guy looked Bruce straight in the eyes.

"Dead man walking," he said and slowly got up and walked back to his table.

No shit, Bruce thought. Nothing he could do about it now. It was inevitable. This parole hearing was his only chance. It was two days away.

††

There were two days of no sleep. Every clang of metal, every echoing footstep was tracked. Another weapon had been fashioned for defense this time. Bruce avoided brushing up against anyone or allowing them near. Jamie ran interference. Bruce always got him what he wanted: Popsicles, candy, comic books. Simple things for a simple man—incarcerated for first-degree murder.

The odds makers were giving him almost no chance on making parole. Many took a chance on the odds and laid their money down.

The time came. Bruce tried to remember all the things he was supposed to say. He had rehearsed his lines over and over. Most importantly, he had learned to remain calm, not to fly off in a rage. He got that from some books on yoga and meditation. Just imagine you're not there. Imagine they are talking to someone else.

He was called into the room and sat in a chair in front of the panel. The chairs set aside for witnesses were vacant. He couldn't believe his good luck.

"Mr. Krakowski," started the chairwoman, "this is your fourth appearance before this board. You were convicted of manslaughter. Is that correct?"

"Yes, ma'am," he replied. "But . . ."

"I'll ask the questions, Mr. Krakowski, if you don't mind," she said tersely. "Confine your answers to the questions. I'm sure there were plenty of extenuating circumstances and I'm sure they all came out in the trial. We are not here to rehash old testimony. We are here to see if you have been sufficiently rehabilitated to reenter society as a contributing member."

She stopped and waited to see Bruce's reaction. He remained composed though he really wanted to jump and choke her.

"Yes, ma'am."

"Okay, now that we have the rules established, I want you tell me in your own words why, on this day, after all this time, we should let you out on parole."

"Yes, ma'am," he started. "First of all, I have learned the error of my ways. I done a lot of bad things. I've had lots of time to think about 'em. I know they was wrong. I know I hurt a lot of folks, not just the victims. I am sorry. I wish I could undo it but ya can't undo stuff like that. It's done. I have to live with it the rest of my life. I wish I could trade places, but I can't."

"Okay, Mr. Krakowski," answered another member of the panel. "I get it. You're remorseful. We get it. What are you remorseful for? For the crimes you committed or for getting caught?"

"Sorry, sir," Bruce answered, again maintaining his composure. "I'm remorseful for what I done and what it done to the people I hurt. From the day I walked in here, I received Jesus Christ as my Lord and Savior. I learned that I can't undo that what was done, but there is forgiveness. Maybe not from people, but from God. I turned my life over to Him and it's Him who I serve. If yur think'n I don't deserve to be out of here, I respect that. I don't. But I do think I can go back and do good things. Things I never thought of doing before. I am totally at your mercy and okay with whatever decision you make."

"Any other questions from the board?" asked the chairwoman.

Each either shook their head or voiced no.

"Are there any witnesses here that would like to provide testimony as to whether or not Mr. Krakowski should or should not have a positive outcome from this meeting?"

There was no one present to speak up for or against him.

"Okay, Mr. Krakowski, you may go outside and we will deliberate your future."

"Thank you, ma'am . . . sirs," he said contritely, hanging his head as he left the room.

25

WAIT ON THE LORD

ANOTHER YEAR PASSED AND still no special revelations. It was a very dry period for Sam. He prayed but it was hard. He heard about the wilderness experience and supposed this was it. He wondered why God had used him in such a powerful way and abruptly stopped. The coin, the Lost Coin, did in fact appear lost. He wondered if it was permanently gone. Yet even in his doubt, he knew unequivocally that God had something else for him.

"Patience," Pop would say. "Remember Moses. Remember Abraham. They had years herding sheep, wandering in the deserts before they were ready for what God had prepared. If you want to make an oak, it takes years," he would say. "A ring added each year and then a year to solidify." Sam wondered if they were as bored as he was while waiting.

Pop was the one who made it all make sense. He was another year older, but his face looked like it had aged more than that. *Maybe age becomes exponential at some point,* Sam wondered. But his wisdom also seemed to increase exponentially with age. "God doesn't pop out miracles for any other reason than to expand his kingdom," Pop said. "It's not a side show like you see on TV. Everything He does has purpose. His power and gifts are not there for self-aggrandizement. They are always for someone other than the vehicle through whom he wields his power and grace."

It made sense. He wondered what happened to all those people in New York in the wake of the so-called miracles that happened there. According to Pop they were so-called miracles because he didn't believe in miracles. He believed they were natural, not supernatural.

††

Sam and Mo were hoping for a child, but so far no success. They enjoyed helping out with Anastasia. She was one and a half, walking around, falling, laughing, and crying. Mo thought she was the cutest thing she had ever seen. Her heart longed to have one of her own.

Helping out with Anastasia heightened Mo's motherly instincts—and Sue needed the help. She seemed to be more despondent. Her eyes had aged with the strain. It was clear things were worsening in her marriage. Sue had essentially become a single parent. No one ever knew where Steve was.

At first, Steve's absence didn't bother Sam who never minded avoiding the tension between the two. But now he wished he had more time to spend with Steve. The scars were gone as was the animosity. If anything, he felt empathy for Steve. As involved as he was, or seemed to be, in his church, Steve looked empty, a lost soul searching in the wrong places.

Sam sat at his desk calculating out the head on a new pump he was going to install and the associated piping sizes. After doing the same type of work for three years, he was starting to feel the dull weight of normal living and the routine of it all. The freshness had departed long ago. *There has to be more than this,* he thought as he tried to stay focused on what was in front of him. His mind drifted off as he curiously watched the interaction of his peers and bosses playing out their assigned work roles.

Sam snapped out of his daydream when his boss suddenly opened the door of his office and beckoned Sam to follow him down the hallway. This was typical communication that Sam never understood. The subject was never divulged until the destination, which irritated Sam each and every time it happened. Dan looked at them as they disappeared down the hall, wondering why he wasn't invited.

Pete MacDonald was typical of the company's management. He reminded Sam a little of Steve—ambitious, politically correct, measured temperament, words weighed out, at least in front of those that mattered. He was another that wore these altruistic company principles on his lapel.

Sam followed on Pete's heals. No words were spoken during the trek. They came to the office of Enrique Sanchez, the VP of manufacturing, and stopped. *What is this?* Sam wondered. *This could be very good or very bad.* Pete knocked.

"Come in," could be heard from the inside.

"Hi, Enrique," Pete said with a broad smile, reaching forward and shaking his hand. "This is the one."

Enrique got up out of his chair and shook Pete's hand.

This is the one? thought Sam. *What does that mean?*

"So, Mac, this is the one, eh," Enrique said with a slight smile, shaking Sam's hand.

"He's the one you asked for," replied Pete.

"Sit down, Sam," appealed Enrique. "Just want to have a chat. Has Mac said anything to you?"

"Uh, no, sir," Sam stammered.

"That's okay," Enrique said. "I have heard some good things about you and your work. One is your honest, and two is when you put it in, it works. Those are two great attributes that fit with our company culture."

"Thank you, sir."

"But I'll get right to the point. We are going to build a new plant and we are putting together a team of engineers who we think can really do this on time and on budget and bring it on line successfully. You would be working directly for the project manager from one of our other divisions from whom you can learn a lot. It would entail a promotion, more money, and bonus. Interested so far?"

Sam was excited. "Yes, sir," he blurted. This is what he was waiting for, a major project. *A whole plant! Wow,* he thought. *What great experience for an engineer only three years out of school.*

"Great. I'm glad to hear that. But there is more. This project is obviously not here. It's overseas. You would have to relocate for at least a year, maybe a year and a half."

"Hmmm," Sam murmured caught cold, "let me think. I would have to discuss this with my wife and, of course, know where the job is." In his excitement, he hadn't thought of the obvious.

"Of course. This is certainly a family matter. We are going to build it in Iraq," Enrique said.

"Iraq?" Sam asked rhetorically. "Hmmmm. Well that will be a lot to mull over."

"Of course," Enrique agreed. "Take it home. Discuss it with your wife. Mac will go over the financial details. It's pretty lucrative for someone as junior as yourself. Iraq is a pretty good place right now. Obama has just pulled the troops out, but it looks like it is a sustainable peace."

"Thank you, sir," Sam said, shaking Enrique's hand to leave. "I'll discuss it with my family and get back to you."

"Excellent, Sam, and I am glad you are part of our family."

As they walked out, Mac said, "Congratulations. That is quite an opportunity that just fell in your lap."

Sam walked back to his office stunned. *What will Mo say?* he wondered. He felt a lump in his pocket and pulled it out. The Lost Coin. This time it had the throne on one side and a woman sweeping the floor searching for something on the other.

Sam rushed home to tell Mo about the great offer. She saw the excitement in his eyes. He explained how it was such a great opportunity for his career and how, after only three years, he was feeling stale.

"That does sound exciting," she said. "Where is it?"

"Iraq," he said. "Mosul to be exact." He watched her eyes for a reaction. There was none.

"Ok," she said without hesitation, "let's go."

"Wait," he said, excited and surprised at the same time. "Are you sure? How can you be so nonchalant about it? I'm not sure if I've made up my mind."

"I don't know," she said, shrugging her shoulders. "I just know."

"Shouldn't we pray about it?" he asked.

"We just did," she replied. And that was all there was to that.

Mo was always so sure but Sam not so much. He questioned, hesitated, and doubted, but she . . . well it was like someone was always whispering to her just behind the ear giving constant assurance. She always heard it first, then he usually through her.

"Okay, off we go into the wild, blue desert adventure," he joked, giving her a kiss on the cheek. "You have such a way of simplifying everything, making it easy and never over thinking it. Just knowing, eh?"

She laughed. "Right. You're learning. I doubt the reason for this opportunity is to enhance your career. Better keep your eyes open."

Mo took a leave of absence and researched nursing opportunities with the Red Cross in Iraq. They were delighted to have her.

Sam mulled Mo's words over for the days following their decision. There was something mystical in the way she said things so simply with such sureness. What should he be looking for? Should he even look for it? Wouldn't it just come and stare him in the face? Did God have some other purpose?

26

THE LAW AND THE LAWLESS

STEVE PACED AROUND HIS office. He looked at the pile
of mail on his desk. Bills. He had changed his mailing address
to a P.O. box to hide all the past due notices from Sue. Things
were getting dire. The thought of his BMW being repossessed was
unthinkable. He had to come up with a plan. He had a few to start.

The Masterson case finally met its resolution. Good for
Masterson but bad for Steve. Dick Masterson got restitution
of two years back pay plus interest, legal fees, and lost future
income. All told, it cost MacNeil and MacNeil close to one
million dollars. They were not happy. Pay increases and bonuses
were frozen over the last two years for Steve who was paranoid
they would try to oust him.

"Bastards," he said out loud to himself. "We'll see about
that."

Steve had one plan in the works. He had teamed up with
Abe Shapiro on a horse-betting scheme. Abe said it was a sure
thing. He had insider information. An old bookie friend of his
from Brooklyn, referred to only as Freddie, was betting money
for the mob. The mob had paid off several jockeys, so out of a
field of eight horses, three were dead, meaning they would pull

back leaving only five horses in actual competition to finish. The odds were astronomical for anyone in the know. Once or twice a month, they would rig the race and this bookie would take the mob's money up to this track and make the bets he was given. The last set of bets yielded two hundred grand on a twenty-five grand investment.

Abe shared this betting scheme with Steve. The deal was for Steve to take his and Abe's money and place the same bets as the bookie Freddie. Abe would do it himself, but he was afraid guys from the old neighborhood might recognize him if they were to show up. Freddie would give Abe the bets. Steve, Abe, and Freddie would then pool their money. Steve would go up and place the bets and come back with the cash.

Steve was broke. He sat at his desk and started pouring over the books. He quickly spotted an account he could loot, or borrow from, as he preferred to call it. This was a sure thing. As CFO he had the authority to write checks without a counter signature. He would cash a check for $50,000 in the morning in enough time to make it to the track with the cash. Then he would have it back in the account by Monday morning. Things were looking up.

Steve pulled into the Pig and Pickle. Abe, as usual, was there early scarfing down drinks. Steve wouldn't take long to catch up. Mary Lynn was serving a corner table, looked up, and smiled as he entered. Steve smiled back. He was in a good mood.

Abe was bellied up to the bar with a rum and Coke, chatting with the bartender. Steve placed his hand on his shoulder. Abe smiled.

"All set?" he asked.

"You bet," Steve replied confidently.

Abe handed him an envelope to put in his jacket pocket. "Ten grand in here," he whispered looking all around the bar. "Five from Freddie and five from me. Freddie said we should start out small, not try to kill the goose laying the golden eggs. Try to be as inconspicuous as possible. There will still be a huge payoff. Remember who we are dealing with. Both the law and the lawless."

Steve thought about that for a second. He needed big money and he needed it now.

†††

Mary Lynn walked by and whispered in his ear, "Gotta minute?" and walked over to a vacant corner of the bar.

Steve sauntered over with his drink. "Sure, babe. What's up?"

"Just wondered if you are coming over tonight. Have some things to talk about."

"Sure thing, sweetie, I'll be there."

"Wonderful," she said as she planted a huge smooch on his lips.

"That sure tasted like another one." He laughed. "See you tonight."

"Tonight."

Steve went back over to Abe at the bar. "Let's get a table," Steve said. "Bit more comfortable and private."

They grabbed a corner table and started talking.

"I guess you know about your grandfather, eh?" Abe asked.

"Know what?" asked Steve. "I haven't heard anything. What are you talking about?"

"His will. I thought you knew. He's going to change it."

He had Steve's attention. "Change it? Change it to what? It's already not fair, giving half to that worthless Sam. Has he come to his senses and decided to leave it all to me?"

"I doubt it, buddy," replied Abe, "but to be truthful, I don't know."

"How would you not know?" Steve asked. "I had him put you as the executor."

"That was then. This is now. I guess I've been fired. He just said he was revising the will and doing it with another attorney. I don't even know who. Probably some small-time lawyer."

"God. Do you know what his estate is worth?"

"I can guess, given where his land is and the fact that a bunch of different developers are bidding on it," Abe said

"God dammit!" Steve cursed. "I don't know what the old man did but I'm pretty sure Sam sold him some snake oil and poisoned him. Where's the old will?"

"I still have it," Abe said.

"Where's the new will?"

"I don't know. He probably has it in his house somewhere. It will supersede any previous versions."

"What if it gets lost?" Steve asked.

"Well, in that case, the existing will would prevail in a court of law," Abe replied.

"That's all I need to know," Steve said heatedly.

"Just as long as I don't know anything about it, Steve, and I mean it."

"Not a problem."

It was late as usual when Steve weaved his way through the trailer park. That black BMW always drew attention, even in the dark as the streetlights reflected off the shiny metal. That one light from the trailer across the road always seemed to mark his comings and goings. Occasionally he would see her face in the window. Just an old biddy, he thought, a harmless busybody. He pulled into the drive locking up his brakes. The car growled to a halt as it skidded over the loose gravel, stopping inches from Mary Lynn's Dodge. He carefully got out, steadying himself with the door. A man shouting at his wife could be heard a few doors down. *Maybe that drowned out the skid,* he hoped. He looked over across the street. Sure enough, there she was leering. He tottered to the front door.

Mary Lynn swung the door wide open wearing nothing more than a see-through negligee and a smile. She handed him a drink and a kiss. He didn't react with his usual "Oh, baby, baby" singsong. She could see he was preoccupied with something and he was . . . well . . . smashed. Abe's update had taken its toll on him. He was tired and had too much to drink.

Mary Lynn quickly picked up on his downcast mood. She wondered what had happened from their brief conversation to now.

"What's the matter, honey?" she asked.

"Nuthin I can't handle," he slurred. "Don't worry your pretty little head over my problems. Everything's under control. Things are looking up."

"Maybe I can cheer you up," she said, pulling him up off the couch. She had slipped off her negligee and stood in front of him stark naked.

"Maybe you can," he said as his eyes dilated.

Easy as pulling a bull by his nose ring, she chuckled to herself as she herded him toward the bedroom.

Steve teetered on one leg as he tried to pull the other one out of his pants. Gravity prevailed and he fell backward on the bed. He reached over to grope Mary Lynn as he tried to kick the pants off but didn't make it.

"Zzzzzzzz . . . zzzzzzzz . . . zzzzzzz." Passed out.

She looked over at him in disgust. *Brother, I can't believe this,* she thought. She turned her face to the wall and tried to go to sleep, but it wouldn't come. Was she wasting her time with this guy? He was supposed to be her ticket out of this mundane dead-end life she so hated. Waiting tables for groping men, lousy tips, lousy pay. He said they had a future, but she hadn't seen anything change. He was still married and clammed up every time she approached the subject. Maybe she was being taken for a ride, she thought.

She lay there staring at the paneled bedroom wall thinking. The more she thought the more agitated she became. She pulled the covers up over her naked body to get some warmth. It sure wasn't coming from him. The only time that occurred was when he wanted something.

An hour later she was still staring at the wall. Fatigue finally set in and began to save her from a night of insomnia. She was just about to doze off.

Bang . . . bang . . . bang in rapid succession. Someone was rudely rapping at her door.

She looked at the clock. It was two in the morning. *Who the hell could that be this late,* she wondered. She reached into her nightstand and pulled out the .38 she kept loaded there.

Bang . . . bang . . . bang came the incessant knocks. She put on her robe, slipping the pistol into the pocket with her hand around the trigger. No safety. Double action. *Point and shoot,* she reminded herself.

She slowly approached the door from the side. She looked out the side window to see if she could recognize the intruder.

She saw a young man standing on the stoop. She relaxed her grip on the gun and opened the door.

"Hi, Sis," he said and walked in.

27

PARADISE AND JUDGMENT

SAM AND MO WERE hunkered down in the dank basement of a mud and stone house in the middle of Qaraqosh. The shelling was getting louder. Most of the resistance had fled, but there were a few who would stay and fight to the death. There were a dozen other people huddling in the middle of the room lit by only one propane lantern. One mortar shell exploded on the next block. There were quiet screams.

Sam looked at Mo. "Sorry," he said.

"About what?" she asked as if surprised.

"For bringing you here. ISIS. Who would have known? We never even heard of these people before we left, and now look. An army of thirty thousand? How in the world could our government not know? This was supposed to be a liberated country. Good job, eh? Now an unknown terrorist offshoot occupies entire regions of the country and we can't get out."

"Sam," she said, holding his hand tenderly, "you have nothing to apologize for. It was as much my choice as yours. You didn't exactly twist my arm. We are here for a reason. Maybe we don't know exactly why, but that's God's job. Not ours. He has us exactly where he wants us."

"Yeah, between the proverbial rock and a hard place." He tried to laugh but the best he could do was a smile. She amazed him. How could anyone stay so composed? Just looking at her relieved the anxiety in his body. Yet he could still feel the fear. Not so much for himself, but for her. He remembered Bill's words, "Love conquers fear."

Here was a country steeped in religion, yet they seemed to be looking through the wrong end of the telescope. They were busy little ants not even trying to earn God's love but just trying to avoid His wrath without realizing He is love. He can't be anything but. Everything He does has to stem from love. That is who He is. Maybe that was what God had in mind for the two of them. To be missionaries like Bill and Liz.

If this was what God had in mind, Sam certainly had a way of coming at one sideways. He remembered Mo telling him that whenever you think you know what to expect, think you know what God wants, look out. It never comes the same way a second time. Now they were totally at God's mercy and totally unable to extricate themselves from this situation. Maybe that was right where God wanted them to be, but it didn't feel good.

The job site was shut down. All Sam's U.S. colleagues had high tailed it back to the states. Mo could see the extreme need for health professionals in this crisis and knew she needed to stay. Sam knew she did, also. Despite rumors of beheadings and crucifixions of Christians, he volunteered to remain behind to clean up the job site, get everyone paid, and secure it as well as it could be given the precarious environment.

With Mosul falling to ISIS, they fled to Qaraqosh, a Christian enclave, but that bought little time. Now ISIS surrounded them. No way to get out.

The room was filled with some of Sam's Iraqi coworkers and wives, Aadila, a nurse's aide to Mo, and Raheem. Raheem was a Christian convert. He was in hiding before ISIS became a threat. His brother had been searching for him to kill him. Converting from Islam was anathema to the family, a disgrace that must be eradicated. His courage was already evident in his commitment to Christ despite the dangers from his family. He was probably more prepared for a stand against ISIS than any of them, Sam thought, including himself.

Aadila was on the cusp of believing. She loved Mo. Mo had shared the good news with her, the liberating news of Jesus Christ, how grace already saved her and washed her sin away. All these rituals wouldn't save her. It could not be earned, only received. Aadila had spent several nights secretly away from her family to have dinner with Sam and Mo who used every minute to teach her the truth.

"It seems too easy," Aadila would say. "No, you have to pray five times a day, fast, and give to the poor. This doesn't sound like it's enough."

"It is enough, Aadila, and it is that easy," Mo would assure her. "That's why it so difficult for the self-righteous to ever come to Christ. Works will never get anyone to heaven. They would have to confess that all their righteousness is as filthy rags, not good enough to earn God's love, and that is a tall glass of water for them to drink."

The rest were Shiite Muslims, but they were no safer than the Iraqi Christians who fled to the mountains. ISIS sent out letters warning everyone in their path to convert, pay a tax, or die.

And that was what ISIS was doing, beheading everyone and anyone that did not convert immediately to the Sunni faith. The tax, for those that could afford it, had limited results. Many were decapitated anyway. These were not people of their word. If any who professed to convert didn't sound sincere, off would come their heads also. The bodies were left in the streets for the vultures, dogs, and ravens.

Sam had tried to lead them out of the city earlier, but it was too late. They were cut off. ISIS had the village surrounded. The rumors of what happened in the other villages had their desired effect. They were terrorized. They bowed toward Mecca and flooded the room with their rote prayers. Sam and Mo could not understand what they were saying. They just quietly prayed in their hearts, waiting to see what God was going to do next.

The bombs were getting closer. The last one blew part of the roof off. The women screamed. The men prayed louder.

Aadila started to cry.

"It's all right," Mo said. "God will take care of us."

"How?" She sobbed. "I don't know what to do. This Jesus," she blubbered, "He sounds so loving. I just don't know. I don't want to die without knowing."

Raheem stepped up and said with authority, "Aadila, you can know. I know. Just confess with your mouth the Lord Jesus and believe in your heart that God raised Him from the dead and you will be saved."

The bombs stopped. The room went silent. All eyes were on Aadila.

"I do believe," she confessed with tears. "And I do believe He is the Son of God and that God raised Him from the dead that we might live."

As she said these words, the fear fell from her face and it radiated peace like a beacon that everyone in the room could see. They all stared silently and marveled. Could this be true, some of them wondered?

Hussein, a contract worker for Sam's company, yelled, "No! Don't do that. Stay with our faith. Today you will be in paradise. Don't do this."

"I will be in paradise, Hussein. I know that now. And you can, too."

Hussein was shocked by her confidence. He turned his head away.

Leyla, Hussein's wife, was rereading the ISIS letter. *Convert, pay, or die.* She looked at her husband, then Mo and Aadila. She crumpled it up and let it fall to the floor and started pacing in circles.

There was a loud blast that shook the tiny basement and filled it with smoke. The wooden bulkhead door came crashing down the narrow wooden steps. Behind it came three masked ISIS fighters. As the smoke cleared, they saw them standing in front of the exit with pistols, automatic weapons, and swords. The women screamed again. Sam and Mo stood in the corner with Aadila, staring at these oddly dressed soldiers. The only thing visible was their dark eyes, full of hate.

A soldier started yelling and giving orders in Arabic. They were lined up against the wall. Their heads hung low, accepting their obvious fate. The leader walked up to the first one, Raheem.

"Shiite, Sunni, Christian?" he asked.

"Christian," Raheem replied, staring into his hidden face.

The leader motioned for the other two. They pulled Raheem to the center of the room.

"On your knees," one commanded.

Raheem made no attempt to obey. They kicked his legs out from under him and forced him to kneel. One drew a sword while the other held his head down.

"Convert, pay tax, or die," the leader said.

"I am a Christian," he said. "I will not renounce my Lord and Savior Jesus Christ. And you too can come to know God . . ."

Before he could finish the sword came down across his neck with such force his head plopped to the dirt floor with a thud. His body collapsed. Blood spurted over the three of them. They did not move. They looked around at the rest.

Terror had no sound. They were paralyzed.

The leader walked slowly along the wall, stopping in front of each one and staring into their eyes. He was pleased with what he saw.

When he came to Sam and Mo, he said, "I know who you are. I'll deal with you later."

"All Shiite over here," he said, pointing to one corner. "All Christians over here," pointing to the opposite one.

Sam, Mo, Aadila, and, to everyone's surprise, Leyla, moved to the Christian corner.

Hussein tried to grab her and pull her back. As he stepped out from against the wall, one of the ISIS killers pulled out his pistol and shot him in the head.

"So," the leader said, laughing at Sam, "you know Arabic."

"No," said Sam not realizing until then he understood every word and it wasn't English.

"Sure," he said. "I see you little missionaries been busy. That's fine. Hell has plenty of room for you and all your little infidels."

He jerked Aadila out to the middle of the room by the hair. She made a muffled sound.

"Let me show you what we do with harlots, infidels like this." He laughed again and tossed her to the other two.

"No," Mo said in a loud voice. "I don't think so."

The leader laughed even louder. "Ha, you don't think so?" He started to reach for her but something stopped him. He couldn't move his arm. It was like there was a force field between them.

"No, I don't think so," she said confidently. "Don't you see?"

"See? See what?" He snarled, reaching for her again. Again something stopped his arm.

His two soldiers had Aadila in a corner trying to rip her clothes off. She was kicking and fighting back. One held her down while the other tried to smack the fight out of her.

"See that," Mo replied, pointing at the two. "Look around you." The two soldiers looked stricken and gasped for breath. They grabbed their throats and dropped to the ground like rag dolls.

The leader stared, stunned. He walked over and kneeled down by one of them. He felt for a pulse. There was none. Perplexed, he walked back over to Mo and just stood there looking at her, trying to figure out what just happened. His eyes were not so confident.

Suddenly his demeanor changed. If terror could be seen only in one's eyes, it was right there in his. He was looking through Mo. He pulled out his handgun and then dropped it, paralyzed. He put his arms up in defense as if being attacked, but it was too late. His eyes lost all expression. He dropped to his knees and a few seconds later fell over. Dead.

"It's time to go," Sam said, gathering everyone and starting up the stairs.

"To where?" one asked.

"God will lead. Don't worry," he said. "Just move."

They hurried up the broken wooden steps and piled out on the street. It was dark. ISIS fighters could be seen herding more victims. Gunshots rang out randomly. Women were screaming.

A military transport appeared around the corner out of nowhere and stopped in front of them. They turned and were set to run, assuming they were ISIS reinforcements when they heard the driver yell frantically in Arabic, "Get in! Christian!"

The back of the truck was full, but they packed in tighter to make room for the new refugees. Sam helped each of them get up in the back and waved the driver forward as he ran and jumped in.

The smell of fear and body odor was inescapable as the torn, canvas-covered cabin tossed back and forth and rumbled down the side streets. It made no more stops as it found a main road out of town and, picking up speed, drove through the night, jarring the necks and backs of the passengers with frequent jolts as the wheels fell into the ruts.

††

No words were spoken on the midnight voyage. There was no need. Everyone knew the importance of putting as much distance between them and Qaraqosh. As the night aged, they could feel and hear the engine labor as the incline increased. Several grabbed their children and moved away from the rear of the truck fearing they would be tossed out as it jostled and bounced.

"This is good," Sam whispered to Mo. "We must be heading up into the Kurdish mountains. We should find help there." Mo made her best effort to smile.

The sun could be seen through the holes in the canvas peeking over the slopes. A few could actually nap in the noise, dust, and jerking motions of the truck. Sam was wide eyed trying to see what was in front of them. Finally, around mid-morning the truck came to an abrupt stop. They could hear a multitude of people cheering.

They crawled wearily out of the truck one at a time. Sam felt like he was a hundred years old. But their aching bones and muscles were warmed when they saw the smiles of their fellow refugees approaching them with food and water dropped by the U.S. Air Force.

The refugees were all given water and food and a place to sleep. Sam and Mo wanted to talk, but exhaustion overwhelmed them as they passed out in a makeshift tent. Sam's dreams went back to the night before. What he didn't see then, he saw in his dream: Raheem's spirit going up into the joyous bosom of the Lord. His work was done. Raheem and the Lord's angels watched over the one truck caravan as it careened through the night and up the mountain on almost impassable roads.

It was evening when Sam opened his eyes. The camp was starting to quiet down. Children were being roped in for the night. He looked over at Mo lying on the cold ground and adjusted the blanket over her. He couldn't wait to talk to her, to hear what she saw in that basement that so terrorized the terrorists leading to their ultimate death. It was unbelievable.

Sam decided to explore and round up some water and rations for when she awoke. He ran into a peshmerga officer and tried to get some intel as to how long they might have to stay. The young Kurdish warrior had little news other than to say the U.S. had no plans for evacuations as far as he knew, but he heard the U.N. was working on a way to get people out and to safety. They would have to be patient.

When he got back to their tent, Mo was sitting up. Her face showed exhaustion and contentment at the same time.

"Guess you got the adventure you asked for," she said and laughed.

"I guess so. I didn't know it included a sword fight, though." He laughed himself. "That was so amazing. I told you God had you reserved for some great things. To be honest, I didn't see anything other than the terror in their eyes and them keeling over. I can surmise what happened but you need to tell me."

A serious look came over her face. "First I saw Reheem pass over. An angel, or a man like the Son of Man, came and received him in his arms. That dark basement turned into the most beautiful light you can imagine. There was an explosion of joy and beautiful music as Raheem entered into His bosom and became one with Him. Then the light left. I mean it literally left the room. In its place was the blackest black imaginable. Everyone was visible, but no light existed in that room except for you, Aadila, and Leyla. Suddenly it was filled with angels. They were there for one purpose. It was not to save. Their garments were so white it hurt the eyes to look upon them. They were girded with flaming swords. Their eyes were on fire like burning coals. They stood between Aadila and the two barbarians. I could see them reveal themselves to the attackers. Their eyes opened wide as the angel of the Lord ran his flaming sword through their hearts. Another stood between the leader and me. The angel revealed himself to him like the others. The leader could see that there was no paradise waiting for him. Nothing was waiting for him after this death but the second death. That is what killed him. The revelation of the truth swallowing up the lie."

Sam felt the old familiar object in his pocket. He pulled out the coin and handed it to Mo.

"Is that them?" He asked, pointing to one side of the coin. On one side sat God on his throne, on the other side stood angels of death with flaming swords and burning eyes.

"That's them," she said.

Sam relayed what he knew about the current situation. There were a few other Americans in the camp and no one was optimistic about getting out. In the meantime, ISIS knew where they were and had not forgotten about the infidels on the top of the mountain.

"I don't know when we will get off this mountain." He shrugged.

"No rush," she said almost cheerfully. "I think we have plenty to keep us busy right here."

He smiled. Even if his failed, he thought, she had enough faith for both of them.

It was dark now. They lay down as sleep started to overcome them again. The muffled sound of a solitary missile could be heard hitting a target in the lowlands below. They fell asleep.

28

ROLLING HIGH

IT WAS A SUNNY Saturday. Steve had to drive a few hours to the target racetrack across the line in New York State. It was a popular track with enough high rollers to make for above average payoffs.

Steve was a gambler, but he had never bet on horses. Abe gave Steve a crash course. With his financial background, it didn't take long for Steve to figure the odds. Three of the eight horses were dead, leaving five to run the real race. With the number of contenders reduced from eight to five, the number of combinations to come in first, second, and third went from three hundred thirty-six to sixty, an astronomical advantage. A two-dollar trifecta bet boxing in five horses would cost one hundred twenty dollars and be guaranteed to win. The only question would be the amount of the payoff.

The net pool and the amount bet minus the track's take would be equally divided between the winners. Given the dead horses were the favorites, there would be few winners to divide the spoils. Those that knew the horses would place their bets on the tried and true. Abe gave Steve five thousand for himself and another five thousand for Freddie. He told him to bet an equal amount for himself. Freddie would be betting more than that for the mob

"Don't be greedy. We just want to skim the winnings," Abe reminded Steve. "There are eyes all around. The mob will be there. There could be feds. And there are thieves. Be innocuous. Blend in with crowd. Show no excitement."

Steve was excited. He pulled out the envelope with sixty grand in it, his fifty plus their ten. *Abe is overreacting,* he thought. *How many times can you pull this stunt off? Better go for broke now.*

Steve pulled into a full parking lot. *Good sign,* he thought. *Lots of bets.* He had about an hour to spare before the post time for their race. He wanted to get there early to walk around and get the feel of the place. He spent most of his time watching people make their bets, their reactions, and betting protocol. He knew Freddie was there, but he didn't know what he looked like. That was by design. How better to pretend you didn't know someone than if you really didn't.

Steve memorized the horses on his list, not that there was any point other than to kill time. They all had funny names. *Who dreamed these up?* he wondered. One on his dead list was called Getupngo. *Seriously?* He laughed to himself. *Not today.*

Steve sauntered up to the lady on the other side of the glass with his list of trifecta boxes. He noticed she never looked up at the patrons as they placed their bets. When he pulled out the sixty thousand to bet on these boxes of five horses, she looked up and stared right into his face. Steve got a little fidgety. *Am I doing something wrong?*

She printed out his bets and handed them over without saying a word. "Thank you," Steve said, giving her a sideways glance as he left. She was still staring but said nothing.

Now he was nervous. Maybe he should call Abe. He pulled out his cell phone. It was dead. He had forgotten to charge it. *Okay,* he thought. *I was going to call him with the payout, but now I'll just give him the good news in person.* He made his way to the stands. His race was about to start. He looked back one more time at the lady who took the bet. She was gone.

The horses bellied up to the gate, which flung open and they were off. *This is kind of exciting,* Steve thought to himself.

Wonder why I never got into this before.

The crowd was going wild. They were all yelling out those crazy horse names like it would make any more difference than body English would turn a bad putt. Steve was amused. The field stretched out. The veterans watched through binoculars. Steve couldn't wait for them to come back around. The announcer's voice boomed over the crowd's cheers. *So far so good.* He watched them as they rounded the back corner. *Nothing to worry about. In the bag.*

Around the backstretch, the announcer yelled off the first three horses in quick succession. Steve looked at his sheet. *Good,* he thought. *This will be over quick.* As they came back around his ears perked up when he heard the announcer yell the name Getupngo running number five. Steve tensed up. Getupngo was a dead horse. It shouldn't even be in the first five. He sloughed it off, thinking the jockeys had to make it look legitimate. *He'll pull back at the last minute.*

"Getupngo, look at that horse go," the announcer yelled excitedly. Sure enough, Getupngo was passing the other horses on the home stretch. "Rein him in," Steve yelled silently to himself. "Rein him in!"

But Getupngo didn't pull back. He crossed the finish line third.

Steve stood stunned with his mouth open, staring at the dirt track. His legs were about to give out. He hung on to the railing for a minute to gather his strength and his thoughts. He had no idea what to do next but to get out of there. Fast! He turned. There were a couple of men in suits looking at him from the upper stands. He could see them turn and head to the stairs. Steve moved quickly.

As he hurried down the stairs to the parking lot, he could he hear the announcement for the trifecta payout on the last race. A two-dollar bet paid seventy-six dollars. Steve couldn't believe it. All the money he had lost, all the money the mob had lost, just got divvied up between a few lucky winners.

Steve made it to his car, started it up, and spun his tires on the gravel as the door slammed shut. He hit the highway and held it at a steady speed while he tried to think through what to do next. He pulled the car charger cord from his console and plugged his phone in. Three missed calls! From Abe!

God, these calls were three hours ago. What did Abe want? He listened to the voice mails. Each one was the same. Call him back, each one having a more frantic tone than the other. Steve knew that Abe wouldn't leave any voicemails for evidence, nor would he say much on the phone.

Steve dialed him back. "Why didn't you call me back," Abe yelled.

"The phone was dead," Steve replied. "What the hell just happened?"

"Meet me at the Pig and Pickle," Abe said and hung up.

Steve had three more hours of driving to think about his dilemma. He wondered again if he was setup. *For what he purpose?* He tortured himself moment by moment. He could hide the stolen money from the company for a good long time, he figured. That wasn't an immediate problem. But this was also mob stuff and now he was involved. He theorized about what Abe wanted to tell him before he got to the track. *Did the horses change? Did one of the jockeys back out? Was the mob wise to their scheme?* He played them over and over like a worn-out recording for four hours.

He pulled into the Pig and Pickle next to Abe's Mercedes. He was tired. He was mad. He was confused. His brain was totally wiped out from trying incessantly to analyze all that had happened. In the end, he gave up. There was no logic to it.

Abe was sitting at the bar. Mary Lynn gave him a smile. He paid her no notice as he zeroed in on Abe. He pulled him around by the arm and stared at him menacingly.

"Easy, Steve," he said. "Let's get a table."

Steve motioned to Mary Lynn to get him his usual. She knew what that meant and turned her frowning head away to get his drinks.

It was clear Abe had already had a few too many.

"What in the hell just happened?" Steve demanded. "You don't know how much money I just poured down the drain, and I'm not uncertain that either the law or the mob is on my tail!"

"Easy, easy, Steve. I tried to call and stop you. You didn't answer. There was nothing I could do."

"Why stop me? Stop me from what?"

"Freddie called in the morning. The mob has plenty of cops on the take. They got word that the feds had figured this all out. They got wise."

"How?" Steve asked.

"That hole is all fished out," Abe said. "They ran the statistics. There were too many races that losing horses should have placed but didn't, and too much money bet and won on the remainder. It's not rocket science. The feds interviewed all those jockeys this morning. They got scared. They weren't going to jail over a thousand bucks. The mob pulled back just in time. I was trying to get the word to you."

"Shit!" Steve cursed.

"Well, all you lost was five grand," Abe said. "Not the end of the world."

"I wish," Steve lamented. "I bet fifty grand."

Abe looked over at him in unbelief. "You didn't? Tell me you didn't."

"I did. Why? What's the big deal?" he asked.

"The big deal is if the mob finds out you boxed the same horses, which they very well may with that kind of bet, they will assume they were jinxed by Freddie and any co-conspirators. Like I told you before you left, the mob doesn't believe in killing the goose that lays the golden egg. They like to keep it alive. They hold their greed in check for the long haul."

Mary Lynn set two doubles of straight bourbon down in front of Steve. He downed them instantly.

"Two more, hon," he said glumly. Frowning she went back to the bar with his order. *Another one of those nights,* she thought. *Don't bother coming over.*

††

It was Sunday morning. Steve awoke confused. All he could see was a blur. His head was about to explode. He could feel the rough fabric with his hands as he tried to focus. He made out the tiny kitchen and a shapely figure standing over the stove. It was Mary Lynn. He threw the cover off. He was still in his clothes. He sat up, rubbing his face.

"Mornin, sunshine," she said sarcastically. "How ya feelin?"

Steve shook his head and said nothing. He tried but couldn't remember what happened the night before. He remembered talking to Abe, but not much after that. But the subject of their conversation came back immediately. *Shit,* he thought. *Could things get much worse?*

He held on to the arm of the couch as he raised himself and walked tenderly to the kitchen cabinet where she stored the Advil. He poured a glass of tap water and popped three in his mouth. He sat down at the kitchen table. Mary Lynn placed some black coffee in front of him. "Great, sweetie," he said returning the sarcasm, "just great."

"What the hell was your problem last night?" she asked sitting in front of him.

"Nothing. Don't worry about it," he replied.

"Well, it sure looked like it was something to worry about the way you was pounding down those bourbons."

"Just a few problems with work. Nothing I can't handle. Just blowing off a little steam."

"I guess so," she said.

A door opened from the spare bedroom at the end of the trailer. A tattooed young man with long hair came lazily out in his skivvies, yawning and scratching his butt.

"Morning, bub, rough night, eh?"

He laughed.

"Who the hell is this?"

"Meet my brother, Bruce," she said, getting up from the table. "He's going to take you back to the bar to get your car."

29

THE TREE OF LIFE

SUE SNAPPED THE LAST strap in place, locking Anastasia in her car seat. *Like roping a steer*, she thought and laughed a little to herself. But she was in no laughing mood. Steve was AWOL for another weekend. *No call, no text, no nothing.* His discreet behavior had disappeared long ago.

She drove to the church for the eleven o'clock service. *This parking lot seems to have fewer and fewer cars in it each week*, she thought. She dropped Anastasia off at the nursery where there was only one other child. She just beat the procession as she entered the sanctuary. Down the center aisle came the choir followed by the priest led by the cross bearer. They were swinging the incenses on both sides of the aisle. She always held her breath when they passed by her. She couldn't stand the smell. It reminded her too much of her college days. The sickening mixture of incense and pot would incessantly seep out from under the dorm doors into the hallway.

The service started with announcements. Songs from the marquis sung in order. The rote chanting of scripted prayers. Her lips were moving, but her heart was not. She felt like she was caught in a snare. No way out. The marriage was over, she was sure. She had an appointment with Father David after the service. She was not so optimistic about sharing her problems with him, but she had no other place to go. Her family was split up and on the other side of the country. She seldom talked to either one of her parents. She couldn't go to Steve's family. They would just protect him. *Maybe Pop,* she thought.

The sermon was half over when she realized she hadn't heard a word. Then again, when she did listen there wasn't really anything to hear. Another sermon on doing unto others as you would have done unto you, sort of. Be good. Do the right thing. Those were his boilerplate sermons.

It seemed his sermons were more don't do unto others what you wouldn't want done to you than the other way around. *Sounds like seeing it through the wrong end of the telescope,* she thought. Sue had been paying attention to those dinner discussions between Sam, Mo, and Norman. She didn't quite understand all of it, but it sure sounded like there was more to this faith than quid pro quo.

Father David ended his sermon with an odd story. "Once upon a time, there were two men who died. When they awoke, they were in front of St. Peter's gates, the entrance to heaven. But they were not free. They were bound with cords, opposite to one another, face to face. In between them laid two apples from the Tree of Life. Each could reach the apples with their hands, but their wrists were restrained in a way that prevented them from bringing it to their own mouths. The cords did not restrict them, however, from reaching the apple to the mouth of the other man they were facing. St. Peter came in and spoke to the two men.

"He said, 'You cannot enter the Kingdom of Heaven unless you eat of the Tree of Life. I must now leave. If you are still here when I come back, it will be because you have not eaten of the Tree of Life, and you will be cast into hell. If you are not here when I come back, it will be because you have partaken of the Tree of Life and have been welcomed into heaven as one of God's faithful servants.' St. Peter left the room.

"The two men stared at one another and panicked. What would they do? They could not feed themselves. Each could see suspicion in the other's eyes as well as a reflection of their own distrust.

"When St. Peter came back, the two men were gone. They had eaten of the Tree of Life and entered the kingdom of heaven."

"How did they do it?" Father David asked rhetorically. "They could not help themselves."

He waited a minute. Silence.

"The answer is though they could not feed themselves, each could feed the other. In that moment, they had to put their faith in one another and put the holy fruit up to the other's mouth so the other could eat and enter heaven with no promise the other would reciprocate. They learned the lesson of Jesus: Do unto others as you would have done unto yourselves." He smiled.

The congregation ah ha'd ever so slightly at this wisdom. Sue was not so sure.

Father David started the Holy Communion, blessing the wine and bread. Sue stood in line. Her mind was far from the sacraments being offered. As she partook of the wine, she looked up in Father David's eyes hoping to see some glimpse of an answer. She saw none.

After the last sip was taken and all were in their seats, Father David ceremoniously consumed the leftover wine so no drop would be wasted. The exodus then started in reverse order to the processional. Sue remained in her seat.

Finally she got up and found Father David standing near the exit.

"Father," she said calling to him. "Do you have time?"

"Oh," he said, snapping out of his trance. "Sorry. I almost forgot. Please. Come to my office."

Forgot? Sue doubted.

They entered his plush, leather upholstered office. The bookcase behind his desk was filled with many volumes of books. They sat erectly on the shelves like little soldiers. None were out of place.

"Please, Sue, sit," he said pleasantly, pointing to the overstuffed chair in front of his desk. "I am so glad you came to me. I haven't seen Steven in a few weeks. Is he traveling? There are some discrepancies in the books I need him to take a look at."

"No," Sue said, "he's not traveling. That is what I needed to talk to you about. He is missing a lot."

A tear started down one cheek. Father David didn't seem to notice.

"Okay," he said, "tell me what's going on."

"You have not heard of any problems with Steve at all?" she asked.

Father David stopped to think for a second. "Hmmm . . . well, no. Not really."

Sue wondered how something so blatant and widespread could not have made it to his ears. Even those that were so proud of their ability not to gossip couldn't help themselves.

"Our marriage seems to be over," she said, starting to cry. "Infidelity, alcoholism, you name it. It's destroying our life. He has a mistress. He is gone many nights and this weekend he never came home."

"Oh," he said. "I'm so sorry to hear that. I can see why you are so upset. Can we get him in for counseling?"

"You can try," she replied, "but I think it's beyond that. He won't talk about it. His mind is constantly on other things. He ignores his family. He's not at home when he's at home. What does the church say about divorce?"

"Well, of course, we try to avoid that," he said. "But it is understood there can be irreconcilable differences at times, and the bishop has the power to forgive that. Hopefully it won't come to that."

Sue looked at him. His eyes were glazed over, and it didn't sound like he had much advice to give.

"Let's hope, Father," she said. "But what about his salvation? I know his sin can be forgiven, but he doesn't seem to be too repentant. What about heaven and hell like you were talking about this morning in your sermon?"

"I wouldn't worry about that," Father David said. "There is no real assurance that either exists. They are metaphors of how we live this life. We don't really know what happens after that."

"I see," she said, sensing the futility of the meeting and looking toward the door. "Before I leave, I wanted to discuss this morning's sermon. I had a little twist to it that might change your point of view. I was thinking that there might be a better way to portray how to truly follow Christ by slightly changing the story line."

His eyes lit up. "Well, I'm glad someone is listening. Please, how would you change it?"

"Let's say that one of the men in the story had his wrists bound behind his back. He could neither feed himself nor feed the other man. The other man would be, like you say, able to feed the other but not himself. How do you think Christ would have worked that one out? Do you think there would have been one person, two persons, or none when St. Peter returned?"

Father David looked at her quizzically. *Was this a trick question?* he thought.

After a couple thoughtful moments he said, "I don't know, Sue. I suppose he would have returned and found both of them. They couldn't help each other. How do you think he would have worked it out?"

"I think . . . no . . . I know," she said, "that when St. Peter returned, he would have found one man. That man is Christ. He is the only one that would go to die for another. The only way anyone will get to heaven, which, by the way, is very real, is for someone else to go to hell in our place. No one on earth has the power to get to heaven on their own by good works. We are totally helpless. The only way we can get to heaven is to have Christ feed us from the Tree of Life, which he did at the cost of his own life."

She glanced at the stunned Father as she got up to leave. She extended her hand. "Thank you for your time," she said.

"You're welcome," he replied, rising to shake her hand.

Sue walked to the nursery to get Anastasia. She wondered where in the world that confident oration came from. A weight had been lifted.

Father David thought about her words for a few moments as the sound of footsteps faded down the hall. Then he opened a drawer and pulled out another bottle of wine.

30

THE LOST COINS OF IRAQ

It was a year since Sam and Mo left for Iraq and six months since Norman had heard from them. He prayed daily for the itinerant missionaries, but he knew in his heart they were okay. Finally a letter arrived. It looked like it had literally been around the world, tattered and crumpled. Norman poured himself a hot cup of coffee and took it out on the porch to savor both. It was dated a month earlier.

> *Dear Pop,*
>
> *I pray you are in good health. Let me say right off, we are doing fine. Please let everyone know. Things are very dangerous, but as you have quoted, "A thousand may fall at your side, ten thousand at your right hand, but it will not come near you." And that is literally true here. Death and dying are the norm. Yet God is so amazing. He has protected us in ways that are nothing short of miraculous. I know you don't like to use that term. It's natural to you, not supernatural. I am coming to believe that myself. Mo, of course the one with the most amazing gift of faith, never doubted. It's*

hard to believe His Love and Grace can dwell in such a hellacious place. But it does. We see it every day. He dwells everywhere. There is no escape.

I know nothing I say will surprise you. We have seen angels of judgment, angels of mercy, and guardian angels. They are everywhere. Mo sees them. I don't see them, but I know they are all around us.

When ISIS started taking over regions, we shut the job down in Mosul. I was ready to leave but Mo felt compelled that we stay and tend to the injured. It wasn't long before these killers got closer and closer. Shells were falling on the city. Everyone was awed by their power. Where did they get it everyone wondered? They were obviously very sophisticated and well funded. They say they do this as Jihad, for Allah, but they kill and rape without compunction. They are totally opposites of what they say they stand for.

We fled Mosul the night it was being taken. We went to Qaraqosh, a Christian stronghold. But in a few days it was under siege. ISIS fighters actually had guns on us, but Mo rendered them impotent with the Lord's Army. I'll tell you more about that when we are face to face. It was such an overwhelming experience. Suffice it to say the Spirit was so mighty in her.

We had no way to flee, but the Lord sent a transport literally to our door and we made it to the Kurdish mountains to a refugee camp. We stayed there for several days. There were many sick and injured. Mo worked night and day.

We prayed every night seeking God's will. It didn't take long for the Lost Coin to appear. It had Jesus on one side. It's interesting that the face is starting to resemble mine. On the other side was the same likeness carrying a lone injured lamb on his shoulders through thorns and thistles. The flock could be seen in the distance. The message was clear. God has people here. We had to stay.

I must admit. These people here are so hardened. The darkness is great. Pray for them. They know God only *as a vengeful god. One only to be feared and obeyed. There is no love in their god, only retribution for failing him or paradise for those willing to obey and give up their lives. Except they are obeying the commands of men, not God. Grace is an unknown concept. Love never enters the equation. We have offered the good news to many. Many have been almost persuaded. They remind me of King Agrippa. But the fear of being killed, as you can imagine, usually wins out. They are slaves to their culture and upbringing. Not too unlike the cloned beliefs in our own culture. But for them, it is life and death. They, like lemmings running to the ocean to die for no explainable reason, do so without question. They lunge into the black abyss obediently. There is no thought or questioning of the truth. To convert to Christianity is anathema, punishable by death. That is paramount on their minds. It's not just fear of ISIS. Family members kill each other for honor. To be a Christian here is serious. There are no lukewarm Christians. Standing for the truth can and will get you killed. In the U.S. one can get away with it. Not here. It's all or none. Yet I know that all that will come will come. Pray that God will give them the courage to find and hold on to the truth.*

I said I would wait and tell you about our experience in Qaraqosh, but I need to tell you about some that have come to know the Lord. One such person was our friend, Raheem. We saw him lose his head for Christ, and we saw him, or Mo did, ascend into Christ's bosom. It was so odd to feel God's love in that room when such a seemingly evil thing happened. But it was for God's glory. At the same time, there was nothing but hate exuding from the eyes of those fighters. They were blind and didn't see it. They were totally given over to the lie and lost their lives believing it. I fear that is where they will spend eternity.

Then there was Aadil and Leyla. They are still with us. They stood firm in the basement that dark hour, not wavering. Leyla was a blessing I didn't see. At the last moment, when it was now or never, she stepped out in faith like I have never seen. She could have remained silent, but she stepped out in Christ confronting the ISIS fighters ready to die for a faith she had only just heard of. No doubt she had been listening to our teaching, but God's inner working of the Holy Spirit, the work we don't see with our eyes, gave her the victory.

I also know now why we haven't been blessed with a child. It is because we have been blessed with hundreds. The eager eyes of all these children shows they are so hungry to learn, so hungry to please. They are fascinated with Mo. They follow her all day. She has to wade through them wherever she goes. She teaches them what she can, but we are all under watchful eyes. There are some Christians here, but those that are not are very suspicious.

The gleanings may be few, but God will not leave them behind. That is the job He has given us. I don't know when we will be back stateside. We certainly know how Bill and Liz Morgan feel, compelled to do the Lord's work without fear of appearances around them.

The company gave me a leave of absence without pay, although I don't know if there will be a job when we get back, if we get back. That's up to the Lord. I did get a pretty good bonus for staying and closing up the job site. That allowed us to keep payments on the mortgage for a while, but that's gone now. We used what little we had left for medicine and food for those in need. We are totally broke, and what a blessing that has turned out to be. Of course I know you know what I am talking about. God provides everything we need on an almost hourly basis. We have no lack. We have food, clothing, and shelter. It just appears when needed. It is glorious.

I wish you could be here. I know your spirit yearns for this work. But God has other things for you to do. I need to interrupt all this to talk to you about some housekeeping issues. I have attached a Power of Attorney. We will need to sell the house. I don't know when we will be back, and I think it is best to get rid of any assets. Do what you think best for all the contents. We won't need them. Perhaps you can line up a realtor to sell it.

This is a short letter. We will write when we have more. Right now we are moving from place to place. This ISIS threat is much bigger than anyone imagined but pretty small to those who know Christ. God will keep us to do His work. Our faith is the faith of the Son of God in us. He does the works. When I forget, I have Mo to remind me. Pray for us. We love you.

In Christ,

Sam and Mo.

Norman read the letter several times. His heart grew warmer as his coffee grew cold. The sun was setting. The reds and pinks became more and more prominent as it hung lower in the sky. He felt the age in his bones as he rose to go back into the house. His setting sun was not too far in the future he knew. He was ready. To see how the Lord had possessed Sam and Mo so totally was his reward. Even he had never imagined.

Norman looked around the old house. The furnishings had become quite sparse. It was one thing or another. One young couple needed a coffee table. Another needed a divan. This one needed some lamps. The cost was never counted, except by Steve who would shake his head each time he came by and saw something missing. "How many chairs do I need," he would say. *It won't be long,* he thought and laughed to himself, *when I won't need any chairs.*

The house was getting to be too much to keep up. The last offer he had was four and a half million dollars. That was a number too much for Norman to wrap his mind around, but he knew it could do a lot of good things. He had been offered a contract to sell in principle, allowing him to maintain residency for whatever time he specified. He hadn't signed it yet, but he was seriously considering it. He had enough cash for the time being to keep payments on Sam's house. He knew they would be back. He also knew that no one in his family needed that much money, so he changed the will once more giving the bulk of it to missions. The rest of the estate would be divided up equally as originally stated in his will.

Norman stared into the mirror as he brushed his teeth. He looked at the old man staring back at him. He laughed.

31

FREDDIE'S DEAD

DEBBIE SEASON SAT AT the kitchen table reading a letter. It was from Sam. He was letting her know they were all right and would be home soon. It was short on specifics. He mentioned this stuff about the Lord's will, saving these people, but she couldn't understand why he was putting himself in harm's way. He wasn't a soldier. He wasn't a missionary. The news said ISIS was about ready to take over Bagdad. *Is he crazy? Putting his life out there for a bunch of ungrateful butchers. What about the mission field here at home?*

Sam had always been unpredictable. She couldn't say he was anti-establishment, but he sure didn't go with the crowd. Always daydreaming. Always thinking. About what, she didn't know. Head in the clouds for sure. She wasn't sure how he got through school. The teachers said he was smart but not engaged. They couldn't figure it out. She wasn't even sure he had the focus to safely drive. Now this. She shook her head. Should she be proud or just cry? Steven was always so different, so predictable, and so steady. He was at least up until the last few months. Now she worried about him.

She passed the letter over to Joe as she slowly got up and

went over to the stove to check on Sunday dinner. Joe read it quickly and just raised his eyebrows in wonder. No comment.

Debbie heard a car stop in the driveway. Sue, and hopefully Steve, would be there with Anastasia. She didn't recognize the old Chevy Sue got out of alone. Sue went to the backseat and removed Anastasia from the jungle of straps and started walking to the kitchen door all smiles.

"Hi," she yelled from the car.

"Hi," said Debbie a bit surprised. Sue had been more depressed lately, but not this time. "Where is your car? In the shop?"

"No," she said. "Repossessed." She laughed.

"Repossessed?" Debbie echoed.

"Yes, guess our financial issues, which Steve is keeping to himself, are a little more serious than I thought."

"What about Steve's car?" she asked. "He was so proud of it."

"He's still proud of it." Sue laughed, again. "He had to pick one to go and it wasn't his."

"That doesn't make sense," Joe interjected. "By the way, where is he this time?"

"I think you probably know, Joe," Sue said candidly. Joe didn't reply.

"I thought you were going to have a talk with him," Debbie said leering at Joe.

"I did," he replied. "He listened. That was about all. He made no comment or excuse. He just walked away. I don't know what to do at this point."

"Sue, I am so sorry," Debbie said. "I never imagined Steve would ever act like this. We raised him to be a good boy, a good man. You seem to be handling it much better than I would."

"Well, to tell you the truth, having you as my family really helps. Thank you for your support. He is your son. This has given me a lot of time to think. To think about what life is really all about. It's not about how much stuff we can get, pretty designer dresses and fancy cars. I kind of like driving that old car. It's refreshing. It makes me feel like an honest woman for the first time in a long while."

"What makes you feel honest?" asked Norman, entering through the kitchen door. No one heard him drive up.

"Well, it's this whole financial thing. To me it's a blessing in disguise. We were yoked to this lifestyle we couldn't support. Steve, on the other hand, is fighting tooth and nail to hold on. He won't share our situation. I don't know how much money we have, and I can't help him. I've stopped worrying about it. It's a huge burden lifted off, I can tell you that."

"Good for you," said Norman.

"So you talked to Father David?" asked Joe.

"Oh, yes, for what good that did," she replied wryly.

"Oh?" responded Joe. "He didn't help?"

"Let's just say he isn't quite with it, spiritually or mentally."

Joe let it go there. Father David, he knew, was not exactly a shepherd of the flock.

"What's for dinner?" Norman asked, changing the subject.

"Your favorite, Dad. Pot roast," replied Debbie.

Norman ambled over to the easy chair reserved just for him. Anastasia waddled over with her little smile.

"That's my girl," he said, leaning over to pick her up. It was an effort.

The dinner conversation had a bit more damper on it than usual. Steve's parents were becoming increasingly concerned about their son's mental state.

Sue, however, seemed unconcerned and chatted away. "Anyway, I've found a teaching job locally and a great childcare facility for Anastasia. I'll be starting in a month."

"That's great," cheered Norman. "You need to put those brains to work. I've seen how you work with Tase, and you are good, really good."

"Thanks," she replied smiling. "I'm really looking forward to it."

Norman looked at Sue. She had always been a beautiful woman, but even more so now. In the midst of all her issues, she radiated something new, something different.

While Debbie was preparing dessert and coffee and Joe had an errand in the garage, Sue and Norman had a little private time to talk. She relayed her experience with Father David.

"All my life, I believed in the church," Sue said quietly. "I thought they knew it all and we could trust them. But . . . but this priest, well . . . he isn't even sure of salvation and if he isn't, what about all those people under his guidance? Is this all fiction? Made-up? Isn't that what atheists say, an opium for the masses? I just couldn't believe it."

Norman listened intently. He could see her eyes opening, truth being revealed. When she relayed the story of the two men at St. Peter's gate, he smiled broadly. He knew then she was close.

Joe came back in from the garage. They quietly enjoyed their carrot cake and coffee. The sun was starting to set.

"I need to get back before dark," Norman said slowly rising from his comfortable chair. "I don't see as well as I used to."

"Thanks for coming," said Debbie, helping him up and giving him a big hug. "Pray for us," she whispered in his ear, "and Sue."

"I will," he said.

"I need to get Anastasia home, also," Sue said, kissing each one. "Thanks for everything. Hate to go. That house is dark and lonely these days."

Sue fastened Anastasia in and off she went down the road. She revisited the moments of the afternoon, how relaxed it was being with a family that loved each other. Then her mood darkened as she realized she was going to a place where that did not exist.

As she pulled down look-alike row, she spotted her house at the end of the cul-de-sac. A black car was sitting in the drive. It was Steve's BMW. *Home at last?* she wondered. *This should be interesting.*

She had Anna on her hip as she breezed through the door. "Hi," she said without making eye contact, "long time no see." She set Anna in her playpen and went to the kitchen to boil some water for tea. Steve paced around like a caged animal.

"What's up," she asked uninterestedly.

"Can't stay," he said nervously. "I have some things to do tonight. I'm just waiting on a phone call."

"What's wrong with your cell phone?" she asked. "I never knew you to wait for a land line."

"Just better this way," he mumbled. "Waiting for Abe to call me."

"Abe?" she asked. "What is he up to? I never cared for that man. There is just something about him . . ."

"Duly noted," he said, curtly cutting her off as the phone rang. "Abe?"

Steve listened intently for a couple of minutes. His expression registered increasing concern.

"What? Are you kidding?" he almost yelled. "Freddie is dead?!"

"Who's Freddie?" asked Sue innocently.

Steve stared at her for a second and headed for the door.

"Wait," she said, "we need to talk."

"Don't have time," he replied as he ran out the door.

"What about your daughter?" she yelled as the car door slammed. His tires squealed as he backed out of the drive.

32

IT'S ME OR HIM

STEVE SEASON WAS GETTING squeezed from all sides. He was shuffling accounts around at work to hide the fifty thousand, but he was running out of ways to cover up. All those transactions were bound to make the partners suspicious. *Or maybe guilt is making me paranoid,* he thought. And then the church. He had not returned the calls to Father David. He was inquiring about some odd transactions there. *Don't worry about that old fool,* he thought. *He'll never figure it out. That's the last of my problems.*

He popped one bourbon after another to quiet the noise in his head. He sat alone in the corner of the Pig and Pickle waiting for Abe. *Where the hell is he,* he asked himself repeatedly. *Why is he keeping me waiting?*

Finally he could see Abe come in the front door with his hat pulled down over his face. Abe looked the place over from one end to the other before sitting down across from Steve.

"Well?" Steve asked impatiently. "What's going on? You said Freddie's dead. What happened? What does that have to do with me? Or you?"

"It has a lot to with us," he said quietly. "More you than me."

"Why?"

"Why? Because you got greedy and put that very conspicuous bet on a fixed horse race!"

"So, that was months ago," Steve said. "Besides, it wasn't me . . . us that ruined their game. We came in late. The jig was already up."

"Maybe so, Steve. But they don't know that. With that bomb you bet, you're the poster child that screwed it all up. They don't know you from Adam, but they know you were the one who placed the bet and, in their minds, ruined a very good thing."

"Like you said," Steve said trying to whip some optimism, "they don't know who I am."

"These guys have better contacts than the FBI, Steve," Abe replied. "They have patience, they have time, they have resources, and, most importantly, they have no inhibitions about how they get their information. Maybe you don't know what they are capable of, but I do. I hope you are not so naive as to believe that Freddie went silently to his grave."

Steve stared at Abe in disbelief. This trouble was not one he had added to the list. He tilted his head back and gulped a full glass of bourbon.

"What . . . what am I . . . are we . . . going to do?" he asked.

"Well, we are going to lay low for sure," Abe said. "Freddie knows me, but he never met you. I didn't give him your real name. I have no idea what he said before they sized him for concrete shoes, but you can bet he told them everything he knew. With my name on the list, I'm getting out of town for a while. I have some of my own contacts."

"Well, you wouldn't rat me out would you, Abe?" Steve asked, staring him in the eyes.

"Of course not," Abe said breaking eye contact. "Why would you ask?"

"I know, Abe. Just jerking you around a bit. Always need some humor in any situation, eh?" he said, putting his arm around his shoulder.

"Anyway," Abe said getting up to leave, "I have some things to do before I leave town."

"Hey before you go, anything new about Pop's will?"

"Nothing that I know of."

"You mentioned we might be able to interpret some of the legalese to change the allocation? Like I said before, that little shit doesn't deserve any of it. He's been a thorn in my side since he was born," Steve said not disguising his disgust.

"It's a stretch, but there is some case law. But I can't help you now. I have more important things to do now . . . like self-preservation."

"When do you plan to leave?" Steve asked.

"In two days. I have to get some tickets," Abe said.

"Well, maybe I'll see you again before then," Steve said shaking his hand.

"Maybe," Abe said as he turned and left his eyes furtively scanning the room one more time.

Maybe, thought Steve. *Count on it.*

Steve ordered a cup of coffee to get his bearing before heading over to Mary Lynn's. This was going to take some thought. He needed to clear his head. Abe was the only one who could finger him. *But what can I do about it,* he wondered. Then it came to him.

Steve pulled into the trailer park. The same light across the street came on as usual, and a hoary head poked her face to the window. *Gaawd,* thought Steve. *Give me a break. Nosy bitch.*

Mary Lynn was off that night. She had been expecting him and, these days, expecting him to be late. Dinner was cold. He didn't care as he wolfed it down. She could see something was weighing him down.

"What's the problem, honey?" she asked. "You look awfully down in the dumps."

"Oh, nothing," he said glumly. "Nothing I can't handle. Say, where is Bruce tonight?"

"He'll be back late. Out with the guys. I hope he doesn't do something to violate his parole. You gett'n him that job was what got him out. We sure is thankful. I hope he's doin okay."

"Yeah," Steve said, "no problem. He's showing up every day. There isn't much more to being a janitor than that."

Steve grabbed her around the waist. "You say we're alone, eh?"

Her face lit up. She gently grabbed his index finger and led him into the bedroom.

Steve was about to doze off when he heard Bruce's old Dodge pickup slam it breaks in the gravel. *Hope that idiot didn't hit my car,* he thought. No clunk. That was good. A creaky door slammed shut.

Bruce teetered noisily up the wooden steps and fumbled with the lock. He couldn't find the hole. Steve jumped up and met him at the door to save the entire neighborhood from waking up. A light from across the street lit up. He wasn't surprised.

"Steady, buddy," Steve said, grabbing Bruce before he hit the floor. "Little too much to drink."

"Wush you talk'n bout?" slurred Bruce. "Just coupl'a beers with the guys."

"Right, right," Steve agreed, "just a couple of beers. What say you go sleep those two beers off? You can't miss work without violating your parole." Steve grabbed him around the waist.

"Let go'a me you faggot. I ain't gonna violate no parole," he mumbled, shaking himself loose from Steve's hand and then grabbing on to a chair. "I can put myself to bed."

"Okay," Steve said, watching him weave back and forth toward the bedroom door. *Can't believe he made it,* Steve thought as he disappeared behind the door.

Steve showered while Mary Lynn made coffee. "Make it strong," he said. Then he went into Bruce's room and shook him out of bed.

"Let's go, man," Steve said, "can't be late again. My ass is on the line for your job you know."

"Yeah, yeah, yeah," Bruce growled sitting up.

"You ride with me this morning," Steve said. "I need to make sure you get to work on time and there are some things we need to talk about."

"Talk about what?" asked Mary Lynn standing in the doorway.

"Just guy stuff," Steve said. "Let's see if we can deflate his face with some coffee."

Bruce washed his face and came out to the kitchen table to the waiting coffee.

"Gaawd," he said burning his lips, "what is this shit made out of?"

"Just fine Columbian coffee, my boy," Steve said, stuffing some toast in Bruce's mouth. "Eat up. We need to go."

"What's the hurry?" He took a few more sips of the coffee as it cooled then a couple long gulps.

"Let's go."

"Mighty fancy car," Bruce said getting in the passenger side. "I feel quite extinguished."

"Glad you brought that up," Steve said pointing to Bruce's rusted out Dodge. "Looks like you might want to upgrade yourself."

"That'd be mighty nice," Bruce said. "Matter of fact, me and the guys got a few ideas."

"Forget about the guys," Steve said. "Those dummies will just get you caught and back to the big house you'll go."

"You gotta better idea?" Bruce asked skeptically.

"I do," Steve said, turning his head and staring him in the eyes. "Twenty five big ones, not this dime store stuff."

Bruce's puffy eyes got large. "You got my attent'n. Whatta I gotta do?"

Steve pulled a picture of Abe Shapiro out of his suit pocket and handed it to Bruce.

"But it needs to be done within the next two days. After that, he's gone," Steve instructed.

Bruce studied the picture over. He stared straight ahead silently for a couple of minutes.

"Okay."

33

LOVE IS GOD

SATURDAY MORNING STEVE PICKED up his newspaper from the driveway and whisked into his study and started reading. It wasn't on the front page or the second. It was a few short paragraphs on the third page: *Local Attorney Murdered in Home*. It appeared to be a robbery, the article said. The body was stripped of watch, jewelry, and cash. The house had been ransacked. Mr. Shapiro lived alone so there was no one to identify what might have been missing, but it was clear there was little of value left. It appeared Mr. Shapiro was packing for a long trip.

Steve turned the TV on to the local news. Yes, they also had it covered. It basically said the same story as the paper, but then they slipped in some little known information about Abe's history in Brooklyn and mentioned alleged associations with the mob. *That's interesting,* thought Steve. *How did they know so much about his personal life? Hmmm, that would be great if they think it's a mob hit. Won't be looking for anyone else. What luck.*

Steve had spent the last two nights at home. His alibi. To Sue's surprise, he showed up both days right after work, sober.

He even played with Anastasia, bouncing her on his knee. For two evenings, strained as it was, Steve sat with his family for dinner and helped cleanup afterward. *Why couldn't it always be like this,* Sue wished.

Steve came out of his study with the paper. He had a satisfied look on his face as he tossed the paper on the coffee table and was looking toward the door. Sue could see he was getting ready to go somewhere.

"Steve, we need to talk," she said.

"Can't right now, Sue," he replied. "Things to do."

"Look," she said, "it's time to make time. This cannot continue. Living like this. This . . . this lie."

Steve stopped in his tracks, turned, and looked at her.

"What do you want to do?" he asked knowing the answer.

"I . . . I don't know. Either we get some counseling or it's over. I have been trying to avoid using the word divorce, but it doesn't look like you are giving any options," she said as a tiny tear started its trek down her cheek. "I can forgive everything you've done if you let me."

"Let you?" He laughed. "Okay, I'll let you. Look, it's up to you. Draw the papers up if you want. I won't contest it. You can have everything. Course it all comes with payments."

Sue started to cry. Steve showed no emotion. He was already thinking how well this was working out. He still had his eyes on the bulk of his grandfather's estate. If he was still married when he inherited millions, he would have to split it with Sue. Not so if they were separated. More luck.

Steve walked out the door without looking back. He drove off. Sue knew it would be days before she saw him again, if ever. She didn't care. It was over. She was now sure.

Sue sat in front of Anastasia feeding her some creamed peas. She spit every spoonful out of her mouth while making the most awful face. Sue just kept putting them back in her mouth as she stared into space wondering what was going to happen to the two of them.

She barely heard the doorbell. It was Norman.

"What a surprise, Pop," she said, almost cutting off his air with her hug. "How did you know I needed someone?"

"Good question." Norman laughed. "Been wondering about

that myself for years. Actually, I stopped wondering a long time ago. No such thing as coincidences. It's called knowing. That's all."

"Well, I'm glad someone does," she said starting to tear up. "These aren't exactly good days. Sit down. I'll get you some coffee. Black, right?"

"Right," he replied, slowly sinking himself down into the wooden chair. He wiped Anastasia's face with a napkin from the table. "Looks like Tase isn't exactly helping either."

"Oh . . . right," she said, setting a hot cup of coffee in front of him. "She's the last of my problems, that's for sure. Probably the only thing keeping me sane. Isn't that crazy?"

"I'm so glad you're here, Pop," Sue started. "You just missed Steve. He walked out. Didn't care about me or Tase. Said if I wanted a divorce, just go draw up the papers. What's going on? How did my life get to be such a mess? Does God hate me? Is he punishing me? Help me!"

Sue broke down in deep sobs. Norman reached over and grabbed her hand.

"Sue, honey, God is not punishing you. He loves you. Look, I know these past several months you have been really seeking some truth, questioning everything. Your lifestyle. Material wealth. Spiritual reality. All the events happening in your life, as dire as they may seem, as painful as they may feel, are all for one purpose."

"What purpose is that?" she asked starting to calm down.

"Let me ask you a question first. What is God?" he asked.

"What is God?" she repeated. She thought for a moment. "Well, He's love, the way, the truth, the life . . . I guess. But you know, other than what I have been taught, I really don't know what that means."

"Honest answer," Norman said. "Those answers are all correct, but you are right. But let's start with the first and most important one—Love. God *is* Love." He looked at Sue's eyes to see if there was any reaction.

"Okay," she said, "God is Love. Now what?"

"Well," he continued, "love is not something God has. It is something God is. That is why I emphasis the word *is*. Let me turn it around."

"If God is love," he said slowly, watching her face, "then love is God."

He could see her eyes open wider in recognition.

"You see love is a person—God—not a thing or an attribute. It is who He is."

"I see," she said, "sort of."

"Well, it will become more clear to you. But what is important to understand is that God cannot do anything that is not an outflowing of who He is. Love."

"So you are saying that all these bad things aren't bad if God is in them? They aren't meant to hurt, to punish?"

"Right. God is in everything. He uses what we call evil for good. Where would you be right now in your relationship with God if he let you keep the course you were on?"

"I think I see what you are saying. But this course doesn't look like it is going to have a Godly outcome. Maybe I don't have the faith, but I sure can't see with my eyes or my heart Steve turning and repenting. I don't know what I married. He is so different than the man I thought I married. What about divorce? I know the Father never really answered my question. Is God for that?"

"God is for you, Sue. And for Steve also. Whether Steve repents or not, that is up to him, and if he does it will be because God brought him to his knees. No, He is not for divorce. But He is for Sue. Whatever that takes. He has a plan specifically for you. That may include Steve and it may not. Don't be taken by some church dogma. God works in so many ways."

"Thank you, Pop," she said, leaning over and hugging him. "You have such a way of making even us simple ones understand. You don't know how that lifts a weight."

He smiled.

The doorbell rang again.

"Wow," she said, "lots of company today."

Standing there was a young man in a suit holding out an ID.

"Hello, ma'am," he said politely. "I am Detective Joseph McCarthy. Is this the residence of Steven Season?"

"Yes, it is," she replied blankly.

"Is Mr. Season home?" he asked.

"No, no, he left about an hour ago."

"Do you know where we might find him?" he asked.

"Actually, no. He doesn't exactly keep me informed."

"I see," he said. "May I come in? I am investigating a case. Maybe you can answer some questions."

Sue thought for a moment. She looked over at Norman. He nodded.

"Sure, please come in. This is my grandfather-in-law, Norman Season, Steve's grandfather."

"Please to meet you, sir," he said dipping his head. "Sorry to intrude."

"That's okay," Norman said.

The detective walked slowly into the living room, his subtle skills scanning the walls, the floor, and the open door to the study with the TV on and the paper on the coffee table.

"Nice place you have here," he said.

"We're having coffee," Sue said pointing to the kitchen table. "Can I get you some?"

"Thank you, no, ma'am," he said. "I really don't have much time."

"What questions can we answer?" she asked.

"Do you know a Mr. Abraham Shapiro?"

"I met him once," Sue said. "I think he is an attorney. I believe he worked for Steve's firm."

"I know him," Norman said. "He did one of my wills. He was recommended to me by Steve."

"Well," the detective started as he watched their faces, "Mr. Shapiro is dead. Last night. It appears to be a homicide."

"My goodness," said Sue. She thought for a moment. "You aren't thinking Steve had something to do with this are you?"

"We just want to talk to his clients, ma'am," he said reassuringly. "I understand that your husband has spent quite a bit of time with him at a local bar outside of their professional relationship. We just want to talk to him to see if he might know anything that would provide some leads. That's all."

"That's a relief," she said.

"If I may ask," McCarthy asked, "can you tell me where Mr. Season was last night between nine and midnight?"

Sue immediately understood there may be more to this than just collecting leads. "He was home all last night," she said.

"He came home the last two night right after work, had dinner, watched TV, and went to bed. That's all."

"Hmmm, you say the last two nights. Is that unusual? Doesn't he spend every night at home?"

"Well . . . no, not exactly. Things around here haven't been all that normal for the last several months."

"How often does he stay out?" McCarthy asked.

"Sorry," she replied. "A lot, but I don't keep a journal."

"That's okay," he said. "Here is my card. I will try to locate him at work or wherever he might be. If you would, give that to him when you do see him. Please tell him I need to talk to him about his friend."

"He doesn't know, I guess," Sue said. "He wasn't that upset when he left."

"Doesn't know?" asked the detective, pointing to the newspaper on the coffee table open to page three. "It's right there."

Sue picked up the paper and read the short story. She looked up at the detective and then over at Norman, her mouth slightly open.

34

MAE WEST

IT WAS SUNDAY MORNING. The congregation was swaying with the beat.

I got a robe, you got a robe
All o' God's chillun got a robe
When I get to heab'n I'm goin' to put on my robe
I'm goin' to shout all ovah God's Heab'n
Heab'n, Heab'n
Ev'rybody talkin' 'bout heab'n ain't goin' dere
Heab'n, Heab'n
I'm goin' to shout all ovah God's Heab'n

The walls of that old, white clapboard church reverberated in perfect rhythm. Mae West was singing out of tune at the top of her lungs in the front row, but no one could hear or would care. There was silence when the preacher came out, open Bible in hand.

"Please turn to Romans chapter 5 verse 19," he said. Pages rustled for a moment, and then he began. His impassioned sermon lasted an hour, interspersed with "Praise Jesus" and "Hallelujah." The pitch picked up in the final minutes, until the crescendo of a final plea to the lost to receive Jeeeesus. His energy spent, he held out his arms as the invitation was given.

After some final announcements, he headed to the exit as they lined up to shake his hand.

"That was a mighty fine sermon, Pastor," Mae said when her turn came.

"Thank you, Mae. That's what you always say. Do you have a ride home?"

"I'm walking today," she said.

"Hmmm," the pastor said looking at the threatening sky. "Maybe I better give you a lift."

She thought for a second. "Guess it would be a good idee to give these old legs a rest."

She sat down on the park bench overlooking the cemetery as the line melted away. Finally the last car pulled out.

"Ready?" He smiled.

"Sho is," she said, slowly pushing herself up while he held her hand. He opened the passenger door of his Chevy sedan and put her in.

"Well, Mae," he said holding back a laugh, "where'd you get such a fine name as Mae West?"

"Well," she started, "oh, Pastor, youse just pull'n my leg. I'd blush if'n I could."

"Well, it is a pretty name," he said. "Even if it was stole from some ole white woman."

"Oh, stop it, Pastor." She laughed.

He pulled into the trailer park. "You know, this is quite a walk for anyone, Mae. Plus walking alongside the road. How about I get you a ride each Sunday?"

"That's mighty nice of you, Pastor, but it's good exercise. I don't get out much. Maybe when the weather's not so good."

"That works," he agreed, helping her out of the car.

Mae was looking across the street as she sat at her kitchen table while having coffee. There was what appeared to be an unmarked police car in Mary Lynn Krakowski's driveway. A man in a dark suit was standing on the stoop talking to Mary Lynn who was standing inside the doorway.

Mae began mumbling to herself. "Them people makes me nervous. Comings and goings all night long it seems."

Mary Lynn paused for a moment as she saw her nosy neighbor glaring from across the street.

Detective McCarthy asked Mary Lynn what she was looking at.

"Neighbor?" he asked.

"Well, she lives right there," Mary Lynn replied pointing. "She's a busy-body. Spies on everybody and writes things down."

"I see," the detective said. "Anyway, back to the question. You know a Steven Season?"

"Why do you want to know?" she asked.

"Do you mind if I come in and we can talk?" he countered. There was some movement in the back of the trailer.

"We can talk right here," she said. "Yes, I know Steven. He comes over sometimes. What about it?"

"Easy, Miss Krakowski," he said. "We are investigating a homicide. I'm still looking for Mr. Season. He was a friend of the victim's. He may have some information that might help us get a lead. At the moment we have none. We want to interview the victim's friends and acquaintances."

"Well, if he shows up, I'll tell him," she said starting to close the door.

Detective McCarthy held his hand against the closing door.

"What now?" she asked.

"Just a couple more quick questions, if you don't mind. Let's see, is your brother living here? I have this address from his parole officer."

"Yes," she said dryly.

"Is he around?"

"I don't keep track of him," she said.

"I see. Was he home last night?"

"Didn't you hear me? I said I don't keep track of his comings and goings?" She started to close the door again.

McCarthy bravely stuck his hand in the closing door with his card. "Ma'am. Please give that to him if you see him. Thank you."

She took the card and shut the door.

The detective stood at the door for a moment before returning to his car. He could hear some muffled talk inside the trailer. Then he looked over at Mae's trailer. *Why not,* he thought.

Leaving his car in Mary Lynn's dooryard, he walked over and knocked on Mae's door. She peeked through the small glass window in the door and then opened.

"Hello, ma'am," he said showing her his ID. "My name is Detective Joseph McCarthy. What is your name?"

"Mae West," she said.

"Well, that's a pretty name. Do you have a few moments?"

"Sure do," she said always excited for company. "Come on in. Sit down. Can I get you some tea? Just mak'n a fresh pot."

This is much better, he thought.

"Thank you, no, ma'am. I'm investigating a homicide. Nothing that happened around here I assure you. I was trying to find a Mr. Steven Season. I understand he frequents your neighbor's house across the street."

"Well, I don't know no Mr. Season, unless he's the gentleman caller that shows up there almost every night. Got a real fancy car—a black shinny one."

"I see," he said pulling out a photograph. "Is this him?"

"Yessuh, it is," she said glancing at it.

"When was the last time you saw him across the street? Friday night maybe?"

"No, sir," she said, pulling out a diary. "I write down all the comings and goings over there. They always seem suspicious. He was there last night, but not Friday. Left this morning . . . let's see, at eight twenty-three. Now her brother's been there almost every night. He usually come in late. I'm a light sleeper. I write all that down, too. I think her brother is on parole, but you'd never know it. Comes in drunk. Saw him Friday night putting a gun in his pants as he was leaving."

"Well, that is very serious for a parolee. That would send someone back to prison for a very long time. Are you sure?"

"I sho is," she said. "With all the racket he was making. I's sure."

"Okay, Mae. This has been very good information. You keep on writing down all those comings-and-goings."

"Are you gonna do anything about dat boy over there?"

"We will, ma'am," he said. "We just have to move slowly to make sure we have all the evidence we need before we make any moves. We'll keep an eye on him for now. I certainly appreciate your help."

Detective McCarthy walked back over to his car. He could hear some louder voices coming from Mary Lynn's trailer but still not loud enough to make out what they were saying. He stood there for a few moments and then decided he had better leave rather than let them think they were suspects. *A lot going on here,* he thought staring at the trailer as he drove off. He found a little cul-de-sac near the entrance and backed in and waited to see what would come out of that trailer.

"Where the hell were you Friday night?" she demanded, thumping him on the head. "And where in the holy hell did you get that gun?"

"What gun?" he asked fending her off.

"Don't give me that shit, what gun?" she said pulling out the dresser drawer in his room and holding a police issue .38 in his face. "This gun!"

He hung his head. "Don't worry," he said.

"Don't worry?" she screamed. "Don't worry? You want to go back to jail? After all I did to help get you out? After what Steve did? If you go back you know you won't be coming out next time."

"I mean, don't worry. It's just there. In case we need it. I don't plan on using it for anything."

"Really?" she said glaringly. "Well, just where was it Friday night? Cuz I'm pretty sure I saw you trying to hide it when you went out the door."

"Just protection," he said. "Some of these guys can't be trusted."

"I don't know what guys you're talking about, but the guy that was just here was a detective. And he's investigating a homicide. I guess you know what that is?"

"Don't worry," he protested. "Has nothin to do with me."

"I hope so," she said. "He didn't say who the victim was, but I know it was that Abe Shapiro. He and Steve hung around the Pig and Pickle all the time. You better be sure you wasn't involved in this thing."

"Didn't you read the paper?" he asked. "They say it was a mob hit. I ain't no mob."

"Right," she said. "You sure ain't. They wouldn't get caught."

"I have to go," he said, abruptly heading for the door.

"Look," she said, "I don't know what yer up to, and I don't wanna know. But I'm telling you, if you get into trouble one more time that's three strikes, and I won't be looking for you in my rear view mirror."

"Whatever," he said slamming the door.

35

CONSIDER YOURSELF SERVED

MONDAY MORNING, STEVE WENT in to work, late as usual, with sunglasses on as usual.

"Morning, Elsa," Steve said, grabbing his mail and whisking by.

"Morning, Mr. Season," she replied sunnily. "Alan was looking for you. Said to tell you."

"Okay," he said not missing a stride.

"I think it was important," she said. Steve did not hear.

Steve turned on his computer and then went to the kitchenette and poured himself some hot black coffee. "Man, I need this," he said to himself. He took his mug and walked slowly to his office and closed the door. He dreaded opening his outlook. That was always a disaster on Monday mornings. To his surprise, not many e-mails. He tilted his head back and almost drifted off to sleep.

His head was splitting. He grabbed some Advils out of his drawer and popped them in his mouth followed by a slug of hot coffee. He started dwelling again on all the raw deals he had been dealt.

I played by the rules, he complained. *But the rules didn't work. I tried the God thing. I stayed with God for so many years from altar boy to confirmation to leader in the church. But God let me down. Where the hell has he been after all I've done for him? All I wanted was the American dream. Work hard. Be successful. Nothing was working. And Sue of all people. After all I've done for her. Now she shuns me over what? A little tryst? Big deal. That's what men do. Bitch! And my grandfather. What a back stabber he turned out to be. Splitting his, no my, inheritance with that shiftless Sam who never lifted a finger to help him. How many times did I cut his grass, paint his barn, and make repairs. I was always there. Something's not right. Not fair. Then that damn Shapiro. He would've finished me off, given my name to those thugs after he set me up. It was me or him. He was a dead man walking any which way. This way, only one of us had to go, not both. Mary Lynn, for what she is, I have to give her credit. At least she's stuck by me through it all.*

The ring from his phone startled him. Snapping to, he hit the speaker button. "What, Elsa?"

"Mr. Season, there is a Detective McCarthy here to see you. He doesn't have an appointment."

Can't avoid this, he thought. *Might as well get it over. Compose yourself, Steve.*

"I'll be out in a minute," he said finally.

Let me see, he thought. *Let's get ready for any questions. He'll ask how well did you know him? How long have you known him? When was the last time you saw him? What was your relationship with him? Yeah, that should be about it.*

McCarthy sat in the waiting room for thirty minutes. He wondered if this wait was for real or if Steve was trying to wear him down. *Could he have a meeting this early on a Monday morning? Doubt it,* he thought. *Most of these guys are just recovering from the weekend. Anyway, I'm patient. Or I better find another job. Better make the most of it.* He picked up *Entrepreneur* magazine. The lead article was "Have You Saved Enough for Retirement?" *No.*

"Detective McCarthy?" Steve asked knowingly as he reached out his hand to the solitary resident of the waiting room.

"Yes," McCarthy said standing up and shaking his hand. "Thank you for seeing me on such short notice."

"Not a problem, Detective," he said showing him to his office and closing the door. "I did get your message. Sorry I didn't get around to it. I was going to call you this morning. Things were just so hectic this weekend. The news of Abe really shook me up."

"I understand," the detective said. He started to pull out his ID.

"Don't need that," Steve said smiling. "I'm sure you're the real thing. I have a talent for judging people by sight."

"Great," McCarthy said. *Me too,* he thought. *That's my job.* "I won't take up much of your time. Just need to get some information. Hopefully you can help us get a lead, because we don't have much at the moment."

"Sure. I'll help all I can."

He followed Steve into his office.

"Please sit down," Steve said, pointing to the couch.

"Thanks," McCarthy said, recognizing the low position of the plush leather seat. "I spend enough time sitting as you might imagine. I'll just stand."

"I understand," Steve agreed. "Tell me about it. What can I do for you?"

McCarthy walked inconspicuously around the office. He observed the cherry desk, the leather chairs, the huge globe in the corner, and the trophy case. "Wow," he said, "looks like you were quite the football hero," pointing to the trophies and awards on the wall. "MVP of the state championship? Wow!"

Steve smiled broadly as he was drawn away for a moment to times past. "Well, those were the days. Days long gone now. I guess you would call these the remnants. This is the day after," he said. His smile disappeared.

"Mr. Abraham Shapiro," McCarthy started as he got down to business. "A friend of yours?"

"Yes," Steve said. "More of a business acquaintance."

"I see. A business acquaintance. Can you tell me about this business relationship?" he asked.

"Sure. I met Abe a few years ago. A mutual friend introduced us. We were looking for an attorney to put on retainer. I interviewed him. He had all the qualifications we were looking for, so I recommended him to the firm and he became our attorney."

"Did you know him socially?" Joe asked.

"Not really," Steve said. "We met a few times away from the office to discuss some business. Things get busy around here, you know. Sometimes we would meet for drinks to catch up."

"At the Pig and Pickle?" he asked.

"Occasionally," Steve said.

"Is that the only place you met?" McCarthy asked.

"I'm missing something, Detective. I thought you wanted to know about him. Sounds like you are more interested in me."

"Sorry," he said, "I didn't mean to give you the impression we were investigating you. These are standard questions. We want to know as much as possible about the victim's acquaintances and friends. We dig into details that might provide answers or leads the layman off the street wouldn't think might be connected to the case. Places you met him. People you met or you might have seen him talking to. This sort of thing. We are looking for any shred of information to move the investigation along."

"Oh, I see," Steve said somewhat disarmed. "We did do some other personal business. I recommended him to my grandfather to do his will. We met at Pop's, I mean, my grandfather's house. Other than that, a few meetings here or there and the occasional drinks at the Pig and Pickle, I can't think of any other rendezvous. He wasn't exactly a close friend. As I said, more of an acquaintance."

"When was the last time you saw him?"

Steve deliberately thought for a minute. "Hmmm, Wednesday," he answered.

"Where was that?" McCarthy asked making notes.

"The Pig and Pickle," he said knowing the detective already had the answer.

"The purpose of your meeting?"

"Well, actually, it wasn't a meeting setup. We both liked that particular bar, so sometimes we were there at the same time. He just happened to show up at the same time."

"I see," said McCarthy, keeping eye contact with Steve as he jotted down his notes. "Did he act differently when you saw him? I mean in your opinion?"

"Well, now that you mention it, he was a bit on edge. He sat down at my table. I bought him a drink. But he kept looking around the room like he was expecting something. And the fedora he always wore . . . he never took it off. Actually, he even pulled it down more than usual over his eyes. Interesting that you would ask that question."

"Thanks," McCarthy said. "This is good information. What about his conversation? Did he say anything to make you suspicious or that he had a problem?"

"It was pretty much small talk, actually. He was kind of preoccupied for sure. He mentioned something about his contacts back in Brooklyn. Kind of asked me to lie if I needed to. Like if someone were to come in asking about him, just to play dumb."

"Contacts in Brooklyn, you say," McCarthy continued. "What did he say about them?"

"Not much, really," Steve answered. "It was pretty clear he didn't want to meet any of them. Said he was going to leave town in the next couple days. Didn't say why. Just said if I needed him, to call him on his cell. That's about it. He got up and left. That was the last I saw of him."

"Did he talk to anyone else in the bar that night?"

"No, not really. He came in, had a couple drinks, and left."

"Thanks, Mr. Season. This has been very helpful. I won't take any more of your time," he said.

"No problem, Detective. Anything I can do to help, you let me know. Abe was a fine man."

McCarthy shook Steve's hand and went back to the waiting area to jot down a few private notes.

Steve closed the door behind the detective. "Nailed that," he said to himself.

McCarthy was busy finishing his thoughts on paper. *The interview was a little too clean,* he thought. *Based on interviews with the bartender and some of the waitresses at the Pig and Pickle, their rendezvous were more frequent and intimate than he professed. What's he hiding?*

McCarthy lifted his head just as Bruce Krakowski walked past Steve's secretary's desk. Eyes of mutual recognition. Bruce glanced toward Steve's office and hurried off.

Steve went back to work. He had figured out a way to siphon off more of the firm's money by setting up a faux company called Shapiro Legal Services. The company would assume this was Abe Shapiro, and the money invoiced was for services and a retainer for its namesake. Except it was Steve's company. They were his invoices and the payments were made to Steve. He just finished an invoice for twenty-five thousand to pay off Bruce and put it in his outbox to accounts payable.

Damn, he thought. *Why did I offer him twenty-five grand? He would have done it for ten. Probably five. Too late now. I may need him later on.*

His phone rang again. "What now, Elsa?" he asked.

"You have another visitor, Mr. Season," she said. "No appointment. Do you want to see him?"

What the hell, Steve thought. "Send him in."

Elsa brought the young man in.

"Mr. Season?" he asked.

"Yes," Steve replied. "What can I do for you?"

The young man shoved an envelope into Steve's hand. "Consider yourself served," he said quickly and just as quickly made an about face and was gone.

Stunned, Steve sat, pulled out his silver letter opener and slit the flap. He pulled the pages out and laid them on the desk. He stared at them for several minutes. A court injunction. He had two days to get his things from his house and keep one hundred feet distance between him and the house and Sue. "That bitch," he swore. *Who does she think she is? She'll pay for this. She can start by making those mortgage payments. Lots of luck.*

36

HEAVEN KNOCKING

NORMAN SEASON WENT AHEAD and signed in principle to sell his property and received a substantial sum of earnest money. The contract allowed him to remain in residence for six months while the developer obtained all the permits and approvals necessary to build. Five million dollars even for twelve acres, for a man who lived a simple life, was more money than he could comprehend and much more, in his opinion, than anyone needed.

He sat at the kitchen table going over the new will he had his attorney draw up. Sam and Mo had already told Norman they didn't need the money. It would be far better used giving it to missions, churches, and charity. Wherever Norman's heart led him, Sam had written. Sam had learned the secret. He would always have whatever he needed. Steve had a high-paying job. He didn't need it. His son, Joe, and Deborah, would soon retire with a comfortable pension and investments. They didn't need it. *No,* Norman thought, *the Lord has other things in mind.*

He read it over one more time. He would leave one million in trust for Anastasia and one million in trust for the child, or children, of Sam and Mo. The rest would go in a trust for Sam, as the fiduciary, to disburse, as he felt led. Norman paid off Sam's house so that he and Mo would always have a place to come back to. He also paid off Sue's house. This, in his mind, was his last, best, and final. He folded his hands and prayed over the paper.

"Lord," he said, "bless this last will and testament. May it be to your glory . . . No." He paused. "Thank you, Lord, that it is to your glory even now before it has even been realized in the world. Amen."

Norman's prayers were always short, words never wasted. His life was a prayer, totally absorbed and possessed by Christ.

He knew that he was really Christ in his Norman form on earth. He knew that when he was walking, Christ was walking. When he was talking, Christ was talking. When he was praying, Christ was praying. The Bible was so clear in so many verses. He loved First Corinthians 6:17: But he who is joined to the Lord becomes one spirit with him. One spirit. One being. A union between the two. One person, yet each one individual in their duality.

This was the secret that so few knew. God's intention all along was to live and enjoy his creation through man, as man. Norman had led many people to this water, but very few took a draught of the life that was there for the taking. It was so clear, he thought, percolating throughout the entire Bible: Old Testament and New Testament. Then God finally just spelled it out. The mystery that men had wanted to know all through the ages. Galatians 2: 20: I am crucified with Christ, nevertheless I live; yet not I, but Christ liveth in me, and the life which I now live in the flesh I live by the faith of the Son of God, who loved me, and gave himself for me. It is not I who lives, it says. *Christ lives in me! Pretty simple,* he thought.

He poured himself another cup of hot black coffee and stepped out on the porch to sip it and reread the latest letter from Sam and Mo. The coffee and the letter warmed his heart. Sam and Mo learned the secret, and so quickly. "It took me years," said Norman to himself. *I knew the day they pulled him out of that wheat field in the crumpled-up aluminum can that God had set him aside for great things.* His letters confirmed what he knew.

Sam and Mo were ready to come home. ISIS had been attacking Bagdad for months and had come perilously close to taking over the airport. That was not the reason for their return. They didn't have anything left to pack, which made it easy. They would see Norman in a week or two.

Norman relaxed in his chair sipping on his coffee as it cooled. The sun was starting to dip over the hills. He loved to watch that yellow ball become vibrant orange as it extinguished over the horizon. *That is how my life will end,* he thought to himself. *Perhaps invisible to the world around, but all life in Christ ends in a blaze of glory.*

The coffee grew cold as he reminisced. How things had changed. Now the encroaching strip malls and housing developments surrounded him. The gentleman's farm would soon be another memory. The John Deere tractor was setting in the barn rusting. It had mowed grass, plowed snow, and tilled Ann's one-quarter-acre garden, the lower forty as Norman loved to call it, faithfully for many years. He remembered with amusement when he first bought it. He heard it fire up and there came little Joe crashing through the barn door in first gear, his face saying it all. Fear and excitement all amassed in one little expression as he swept the broken wood off his lap. Norman ran him down and jumped up in the seat, engaging the clutch. The tractor slowed to a stop. Little Joe stared straight ahead waiting for the worst. Norman said nothing. He tried to look sternly at Joe who looked back and grinned. Norman broke out in laughter.

Yes, he loved the view, his gentleman's farm, the barn, the tractor. But the lower forty had not seen much activity since Ann had passed away. She loved that garden. Norman had to laugh. True, she did love to plant. But, oh, how she hated to weed. Norman could see his job in the making every spring. He could see her out there on her knees and cotton gloves planting those seeds and seedlings in a world of her own. Visualizing her out there in the garden evoked a huge smile. He no longer remembered those hot summers working by the sweat of the brow as she walked out to check her "crop," as she called it. How he missed Ann and her garden. "It won't be long, Ann," he whispered.

The coffee was stone cold. It was dark and Norman had lost track of the time. As he started to raise himself, he could feel a weakness come over him as a sharp pain stabbed him in the chest and traveled down his left arm like electricity. He could feel himself hit the deck. Just before he lost consciousness, he pushed the life alert button on his wrist.

A dim light started getting brighter. Everything was a haze. He was disoriented. It was clear there were figures in the room. The haze slowly cleared. He thought he was seeing an angel looking down over him.

"So this is it," Norman said out loud. "Heaven. An angel."

"Not quite, Pop," said a sweet voice hovering over him. "But I'm told I have that effect on people."

Norman could feel a warm kiss on his cheek. It was Mo. His eyes cleared and he could see Sam and Sue standing beside the bed.

"Well, it's as good as," he said slightly embarrassed, "seeing all of you."

They all laughed the same reserved laugh.

Norman tried to sit up, but Mo quickly held his shoulders. It didn't take much pressure. He gave up quickly as he felt a resurgence of pain.

"Easy, Pop, you're not ready to go anywhere just yet."

"What happened?" he asked. "When did you get back? I thought it was going to be a week?"

"It's been a week, Pop," Sam said. "That's how long you've been here. You had a heart attack."

"They don't have me on life support, do they?" he asked. "You know my living will . . ."

"No, Pop, just IV's and standard things. You held your own. But it was touch and go."

"We've been praying the entire time, Pop," said Mo with her effervescent smile. "I knew it wasn't your time."

"I'll go get Joe and Deb, Pop," Sue said, leaning over and kissing him on the cheek. "They're down getting a cup of coffee. They are worried sick."

"Where's Steve?" Pop asked as Sue left the room.

"They say he stopped by quickly," Sam said. "Talked to the doctor. But we didn't see him."

Just then the doctor came in. "Hello, Mr. Season," he said as he pulled out his stethoscope. "You certainly gave us a scare."

"So, I heard," Norman said. "What's the prognosis?"

"Well, that's a good question," he said. "I'll be honest with you. You defied the odds making it through this. That was a massive heart attack. The Life Alert saved you. When the ambulance arrived, it took a little time to find you out on the porch, which delayed treatment. It was black all through the house. Right now you need surgery, but you're too weak to sustain it. We are going to monitor and do what we have been doing and see if you can get enough strength back so we can perform a bypass. To be truthful, I'm not sure how successful we will be."

"It's okay, Doctor," Pop said. "Everything will be fine. It's not in your hands. Or mine."

The doctor gave him a funny look. "Errr, right," he agreed. "Anyway, we will have to ask the visitors to leave for a while. You need to get rest, and we need to do some more tests."

As his family left, the nurse came in with a shot. "This will help with the pain, Mr. Season, and help you relax."

It did just that. He drifted off to sleep. He felt the presence of Ann closer than ever.

37

CAIN AND ABLE

STEVE SEASON WAS IN his office. He pulled out a copy of the old will that Shapiro had given him and read it one more time. "What was Pop thinking," he said, steaming. "There is no way this is going to happen. I'll be damned if I let him get a penny of this."

Steve knew his grandfather had signed a contract. He wasn't sure of the sale price, but he knew it was in the millions. Now he was in the hospital, in and out of consciousness, they said. The end was near. *Another stroke of luck,* he thought, *the planets in alignment again.*

Steve sensed the firm and the church were about to catch up with him. They were asking more questions. More auditors. He had to get that money back. He owed money to his divorce lawyer. Sue wasn't the pushover he thought. She had her own lawyer and her own demands. He had no idea where she got the money. He thought the bank would have foreclosed by now. She must be getting help from somewhere, he surmised. He was sure she had no help from her family. But then again, he never really paid much attention to her life story.

"Whatever," he said to himself, dismissing the whole thing.

My problems will be over soon. The only thing standing in my way is Sam. And I have a cure for that. He looked out the window and saw Bruce Krakowski making the trashcan route.

"Get your trash, Mr. Season?" he asked, cracking his office door.

"Yes," he said staring at Bruce. "Come in. Close the door."

Bruce walked over to the trashcan, emptied it, and replaced it with a fresh bag.

"We need to talk, Bruce," Steve said quietly. "Got another job for you."

Bruce hesitated. "I dunno," he said. "Maybe that there detective ain't stalk'n you, but he sure is stalking me. I don't think I can do anything right now. I'm going by the book. Reporting in everyday with the parole officer, showing up for work, not making no raucous. And I certainly ain't do'in it for what you shelled out the last time."

Greedy bastard, he thought to himself. "We can work out the price. No problem. You name it," he said, calling his bluff.

Steve could see the wheels turning in Bruce's eyes. He waited for an answer. Steve's phone rang. He diverted it to voicemail as he stared at Bruce.

Bruce spent at least three minutes pondering how he would answer. *This rich bastard can afford a whole lot more'n he paid the last time,* he thought. *Big ole shiny BMW, Brooks Brothers suits, fancy dinners and presents for Mary Lynn.*

He looked over at Steve. "One hundred thousand dollars," he said.

Steve stared back and said without hesitation, "Okay." He knew this could be worth millions. *What's a hundred grand?*

Surprised, Bruce immediately started planning in his mind, not how to do the job, but how to evade Detective McCarthy.

"Half now, half after the job is done," Bruce said to Steve.

Steve hesitated. He didn't know this redneck would actually try to negotiate. "That might be a problem, Bruce," he said. "The money is on the other side of completing the job, if you know what I mean."

"No, actually I don't."

"Okay," Steve said exasperated. "I'll spell it out. The hit is on my brother."

"You serious?" Bruce blurted.

"Shhh," Steve cautioned. "Yes, I'm serious. Not as though it's going to be some big loss to humanity. He and I are in my grandfather's will, and my grandfather is on his deathbed. Right now the old man's estate is split between the two of us. If my grandfather dies while Sam is still alive, half the money will go to Sam's estate. If Sam is dead before the will is executed, it all goes to me. Time is of the essence here. Right now, Pop is in a coma and can't change the will if he wanted to."

Bruce stared in unbelief. Had he just found someone more evil than himself? *What a son of a bitch.*

"Two hundred thousand," Bruce demanded. "Take it or leave it. To be paid after the job as you want."

Steve hesitated, but not for long. "Okay. But this has to be done tonight. Sam is back from his mission, or whatever the hell they call it, in Iraq. Pop isn't going to last. It has to be tonight."

"Tonight it is," Bruce said as he and Steve looked out in the lobby to see if anyone had noticed this rather long rendezvous. Bruce grabbed the trash and hurried out and down to the next office.

††

"Where the hell you think you're going this time of night?" Mary Lynn demanded as Bruce headed for the door.

"None of yer business, Sis," he yelled back nervously. "Jus stay out of it."

"Stay outta what?" she asked as a knowing feeling swamped her. She ran to the bedroom and pulled out the drawer. "Where's that gun?" she demanded.

"Don't worry about it," he said halfway out the door.

She ran out on the stoop and grabbed his arm. He jerked it away.

"Gimme that gun," she yelled.

"Shut up!" he said, looking all around. A light came on in the trailer across the road. "Dammit, Sis. Why don't you run down the street and yell it out to everyone."

"Sorry," she said sheepishly. "Look, Bruce. I don't know what yer up to, but it's no good. Yer gonna find your ass back in the slammer for once'n for all if you keep this up."

"Our problems is about to be over," he said, giving her a whiskey-laden kiss on the cheek. "Trust me."

She let him go. He hopped in his new truck and squealed on down the road. He plugged Sam's address in his GPS. It was midnight. He would arrive about one. The plan was similar to Shapiro, a robbery gone wrong. This house had been empty for months. They would assume someone decided to burglarize an empty house and unfortunately there were people in there sleeping. When asked about Mo, Steve just told him to do whatever he had to do. No more money for killing two, though.

††

Mae was wide awake in her trailer and heard Bruce and Mary Lynn's loud voices through her open bedroom window. When she heard the word gun, she knew it was time to call Detective McCarthy. He had told her he suspected there was a gun in the house, but he didn't have enough evidence to get a search warrant. Now he would.

It was midnight, and Mae called the detective's cell phone. McCarthy shook off the grogginess. "Hello?"

"Detective McCarthy?"

"Mae?" responded McCarthy, recognizing her voice.

"Yessuh," she said. "You said ta call ya if sumpin really strange happen."

"Yes," he encouraged. "What is it Mae?"

"Dat hooligan just screamed outa here . . . an he's gotta gun!"

"A gun?" McCarthy asked. "How do you know?"

"I heard him argu'n with his sister. She were 'a yellin at him to give her the gun. I could see him stuff it in his pants and leave and get in his truck."

"Any idea where he's going, Mae?" he asked.

"Nosuh," she said.

"That's okay," McCarthy said. "We can find him. Thank you so much, Mae. I'll be back in touch."

"Yer welcome," she said, hanging up the phone. She wondered what would happen next.

††

McCarthy threw the covers off the bed and hastily put on his shirt and pants and called dispatch as he got in his car. Bruce's truck had a GPS tracking device installed by the dealer who was concerned about the lack of credit. After identifying himself he said, "We have a GPS tracking device on a pickup truck, tag number AVE608. I need to know its location, direction, and speed, and I need some backup."

He sat in his car with the engine warming. A few minutes later she came back on the radio with the coordinates. McCarthy radioed in his intention and set a heading to intercept him. Fifteen minutes later he was on Bruce's tail; his backup stayed a mile behind so as to not tip him off. He followed him as he exited the interstate and headed toward town. He navigated through some neighborhoods; circled one block twice and then pulled over between two streetlights and stopped.

The truck looked out of place for this neighborhood, McCarthy thought. Probably doesn't want to raise any suspicion.

Bruce sat parked for a few minutes. McCarthy could see him tip a bottle. Then he could see him holding up what looked like a gun up to the dim light and cocking it. "Gotcha," McCarthy said as he called in his backup.

Bruce was stepping out of his truck and slipped between two houses in the dark. McCarthy followed and could hear the sirens getting close. Bruce paid no attention. He crept through the backyards, coming up on Sam's house, which was dark. As Bruce started to pick the lock, he realized those sirens and flashing blue lights were stopping on this street where his truck was parked. A backyard light next door came on, stopping Bruce in his tracks.

"Freeze," McCarthy yelled, pointing his flashlight in his face. "Police."

More house lights started to flick on up and down the block.

Startled, Bruce reached for the gun in the back of his pants. Two officers appeared from each side of the house with guns raised.

"Police, drop the gun," one officer announced. Bruce froze in his tracks when he realized they were fully intentioned on pulling the triggers. McCarthy walked up behind him and removed the gun from his hand. Bruce was mute as he was cuffed. He had a dazed look on his face as they read him his rights. The only thing on his mind was the third strike and what that meant for his future.

The officers took him around to the front of the house. McCarthy rang the doorbell. No answer. He knocked loudly on the door several times. No answer.

"No one home," he said to the officers.

Bruce looked up. *God! All this for nothing,* he thought.

"Take him in. I'll follow you."

When they got to the station, they took him into the interrogation room and placed a hot cup of coffee on the bare table in front of him and left him alone to mull his situation over for about an hour, which he did. Bruce's feet twitched constantly as he slugged down the coffee.

Finally McCarthy came in with one of the officers and sat right in front of him. "More coffee, Mr. Krakowski?"

"Sure," he replied nervously. McCarthy beckoned to the officer who stepped outside.

"Do you understand what the charge is?"

"Not really sure," Bruce replied. "Not good, I reckon."

"You reckon right. Possession of a firearm is unlawful for a felon and most certainly unlawful for a parolee." McCarthy looked down at a file and paused. "Looks like, Mr. Krakowski, this is your last strike. Do you understand that?"

"Yeah," Bruce said, hanging his head trying to conceal his anger. "Got it."

"The only chance you have is to be straight with us. What were you doing in that neighborhood? What were you planning to do? What was the gun for? You might as well tell us. It's down at ballistics now. That will tell us the story."

Bruce froze. He knew they would quickly tie it to the Shapiro murder.

This is it, he thought. *All my life I've had the short end. Not fair. But he's got me. Do I give a damn about Season? What the hell is he going to do to me? Nuthin compared to where I'm headed. Hell!*

His eyes fell down to the cup of coffee. He lifted it and drained it in one gulp. He had his story concocted and was ready.

"What do ya want to know?"

38

No Honor Among Thieves

"HELLO," STEVE ANSWERED the phone.

"Hey, buddy," said the voice on the other end. "You're my one phone call."

"What? Bruce? What the hell's going on? What do you mean one phone call?"

"Didn't go as planned, buddy," he said. "They caught up with me on your brother's street. Before I could do the deed. I need you to help me get a lawyer."

Silence. Steve immediately sensed something was not right. He knew that if he was in jail, the call was being recorded. *How stupid does he think I am,* he thought.

"Deed? What deed? Why were you on my brother's street? Look, man, I've done all I can for you. I got you a job. Got you a chance to clean up your act. If you threw it all away that's your problem. I can't help you anymore. You've blown your one phone call. You should have called your sister."

"Why you sonofab . . ." Click!

"Well, that didn't go well." McCarthy grimaced. "You don't pay attention, do you? I told you not to confront him. Let the conversation unravel however it goes. We have time. We could have had you out on bail and put a wire on you. Now you are no use to us. No bail."

"Shit, you lied to me you sonofabitch," Bruce said. He continued cursing as they led him back to the cell.

McCarthy walked away shaking his head. He wasn't sure whether to believe Bruce's story. *Why was he on Steven Season's brother's street?* He checked into Sam Season and learned that he had been overseas. *Maybe he was just planning on robbing a vacant house. Maybe Steven gave him a tip there was something there worth stealing.* It didn't make sense.

††

The next morning Sam went downstairs to make some coffee. It was unusual for him or Mo to sleep that late, but they stayed very late at the hospital. It was still touch and go for Pop. He knew his time was about over. In his lucid moments, they could see the glow on Pop's face. Sam wanted to be there when he passed over. He expected it to be a glorious moment.

Mo surprised him with a kiss on the cheek. She never seemed to make a noise when she walked.

"Man," he said, startled, "now I know you have some Indian in you."

"Wonder what all that commotion was last night as we were coming in? Blue lights, sirens, the works. At least it didn't last long," he said.

"I don't know," Mo said. "It was sure close to the house. Looks like the police took care of it very quickly."

"They did," he agreed. They both sat down at the kitchen table to talk. "It's nice to have a few minutes to relax, isn't it?"

"That is for sure," she agreed. "I noticed there was something on your mind last night. Anything you want to share?"

"Well, I've been thinking about Steve a lot. Actually for a long time, before we went overseas. I've come to realize that he's just another lost soul. Anything he did to me he couldn't help. I'd forgive him, but there is nothing to forgive."

"So, you finally let it go. I knew you would. A relief, isn't it?"

"It is," he said. "I harbored a grudge for a long time. It was like a cancer gnawing away. He doesn't realize that he's enslaved and has no choice but to act out the nature that possesses him.

He's just blind to the fact that he, like all of us, is a vessel that contains a deity or, in his case, a false deity, and we act out the roles given us by that deity. It was never personal. It wasn't about me. It was about him and him being drawn into himself. He just became more and more self-centered and doesn't even realize it. Delusional. It just saddens me now. I've prayed about if for months. I know, like you, we can't save anyone. That's God's job. But ours is to act and pray as he leads us. Do you remember the last time you saw him? You could see in his eyes that he was close to the point of no return. He was getting darker and darker. But, yet, I believe there is still hope."

"I do too," she agreed. "I've had it on my heart to pray for Steven, also. I also feel somehow there is hope."

They bowed their heads and prayed for Steven.

The doorbell rang just as they finished. Sam opened the door.

"Good morning," said McCarthy, holding out his ID for Sam to see. "I'm Detective Joseph McCarthy. We had an incident here last night. Mind if I come in."

"No," Sam said, "certainly not. This is my wife, Mo. We've been out of town for several months."

"Please to meet you, ma'am," McCarthy said, nodding. "That's my understanding. I was surprised when you answered the door. I tried knocking around one last night, but there was no answer."

"You just missed us. We were at the hospital with my grandfather. He had a heart attack. We passed the police cars on our way home. So, you probably just missed us. What's going on?"

"That was very lucky for you. I hate to alarm you, but it appears a man was getting ready to burglarize your house."

"Seriously?" asked Mo.

"I'm afraid so. What I am trying to find out is why he picked your particular house. Have you ever heard of a Bruce Krakowski?"

"No," both said at the same time.

"I see. Well, he's an acquaintance of your brother, Steven Season."

A concerned look came over both their faces.

"We have him in custody, so you don't have to worry about him," McCarthy said. "We're just trying to fill in the gaps. His story is your brother tipped him off that the house was empty and ripe for the picking."

"That's hard for me to believe," Sam said. "Steve knew we had been back a few days ago, or at least I thought he knew. I haven't seen him. And the house has nothing of any value. You can see that for yourself. It's been slowly emptying itself out."

"I can see that," McCarthy said. "The other disconcerting part was he had a gun. That didn't really make sense if he was burglarizing a vacant house. Particularly for a parolee."

"I'm sorry, Detective," Sam said. "I wish I could help you with that, but we've been gone so long and I haven't exactly been on speaking terms with Steve. I have no idea who he's seeing or what he's been up to. I know he's in the middle of a divorce. But I don't see how that has anything to do with us. I hope to see him soon, though."

"Well, thank you for your time. We'll keep investigating this. We'll talk to your brother. We actually had to interview him while investigating the murder of one of his acquaintances. Abe Shapiro. Do you know him?"

"I do," said Sam. "What happened? He was once the lawyer for my grandfather, recommended by Steve. He drew up his first will, but he's changed it using another lawyer."

"He was allegedly murdered during a burglary. At least that is what it appeared. He did have some unsavory connections. Anyway, the leads went cold. We were keeping an eye on this Bruce Krakowski and one other person of interest. But we don't have any real evidence at this point."

"Wow," Sam said. "Looks like a lot of things happening while we were away."

"Job security for sure. Here's my card. If you think of anything, please give me a call. Or if you see anything suspicious around your house."

"We will," Sam said, holding the door. "And let us know if you get any more information."

"Wow, do you believe that?" Sam asked Mo.

"Not really. Do you think that Steve had something to do with this?"

"Let's just say we hope not. I really need to see Steve and find out what's going on. He really does need our prayers. Why don't we get fixed up and have breakfast on the way to the hospital?"

††

Sam's mother and Sue were sitting beside Norman, who was awake but very groggy.

"Has Steve been by yet?" Sam asked.

"I haven't seen him," his mother replied. "But I keep hearing that he is keeping up on your grandfather's condition. Norman says he hasn't seen him, but he may have been by when he was asleep."

"I sure do want to talk to him," Sam said.

"I'm so glad to hear that, dear," Deborah said. "I hope the two of you can get back together."

"I don't know if we were ever together, Mom, but he really needs help. We've been praying for him. When we left it seemed like his life was getting darker and darker, and from all you have been saying, it sounds like he is so deep inside himself, he must be unrecognizable."

Then Sam told them all that happened the previous night and about the visit from the detective. They listened intently. Norman's eyes perked up as he told the story. When Sam was done, everyone was silent. His mother's eyes stayed focused on the floor.

"I know what you are saying," she said. "His whole being has changed. His eyes are drawn. Always preoccupied with something. That's just the few times I've seen him in the last several months."

"When I married him," Sue started, "he was so full of ambition and hope. He wanted everything. But it seemed like he couldn't wait. He believed in hard work, but I guess it didn't work fast enough to get him all he wanted. He was driven for more and more things. It was like he was a slave to his own desires, and it has distorted his outlook on life and even his face. He is so full of anger at me and at everyone. By the way, what was that man's name they say tried to break into your house?"

"Bruce Krakowski," Sam replied.

"Well, all I can tell you is his mistress's name is Mary Lynn Krakowski. There has to be a connection."

Sam and Mo looked at each other.

"Do you think he might be home, Mom?" asked Sam. "I really need to talk to him."

"I doubt it. He always works late and then no one knows where he goes after that," his mother replied. Sue nodded.

"Well, maybe I can catch him tonight."

39

TRUE LOVE

STEVEN SEASON GOT OFF the phone with one of the nurses on Norman's floor. Norman wouldn't last much more than twenty-four hours. That's not what the doctor said, she told Steve. That's what she said. Steve knew the nurses were always right.

Time was running out. He read Shapiro's will one more time. Rage seethed. He had to take care of Sam tonight or his chance to inherit all of Norman's estate would be lost forever. *And that sniveling little shit would be rich. For what? For doing nothing.* No, it had to be tonight.

Steve stayed late that night, waiting until everyone was gone except the janitor. That was going to be his alibi. He would come back and sleep in the office. Never went home, he would say. Worked through the night. He knew he was in the crosshairs because of that weasel Bruce. "What happened to honor amongst thieves," he mumbled to himself. "After all I did for him, for him to rat me out. He made this far more difficult than it should be. I'll be a suspect no matter what happens. The alibi needs to be rock solid."

All the lights were out except for his office. He pulled out a .38 from his drawer. The serial number was filed off. He cleaned it one more time and carefully placed it in his briefcase. Leaving his lights on, he snuck past the janitor and headed for the basement parking lot, being careful not to be seen and avoiding any cameras.

Across the street from his office sat Detective McCarthy in his cruiser. There was too much smoke surrounding Steve Season, both in the Shapiro murder and this incident. Also parked down the street was a black Lincoln with New York plates. The man inside was reviewing a file while he waited. There was a picture of Abe Shapiro and another of Steven Season. He also had a description of the 740i black BMW and license plate number. He pulled out a .45 with a silencer and laser scope and checked the magazine for the third time. He never missed.

The garage door opened. A black BMW slowly pulled out onto the street and started heading uptown. Joseph McCarthy pulled out behind him. The black Lincoln's lights came on as it pulled away from the curb behind McCarthy's car. The detective noticed the lights almost immediately pull up on his tail. *What's this,* he wondered.

The caravan headed uptown toward the hospital. Steve knew Sam would be at the hospital. He would wait there in the garage for Sam. He would use gloves and drop the untraceable gun next to the body and saunter off like nothing happened. He looked down at his hands. There was a slight shake. "Better get steady," Steve said to himself.

Steve pulled up on the parking deck. Most of the cars were gone. It was just past ten at night, and normal visiting hours were over. He was able to find Sam's red Camaro parked in a corner by itself. He pulled in beside one car several spaces over and parked. He didn't notice two other cars pulling up on the same level and parking away from him. He was preoccupied with the task at hand. They all waited.

They didn't wait long.

Steve couldn't believe that Sam magically appeared so quickly. His hands started to shake more. He wished he could hit him from a distance, but he knew this would have to be up close, eye to eye. As Sam got closer to his car, Steve jumped out of his car and ran over to him pointing his gun at Sam's chest.

"Sam," Steve called to him.

Sam turned. "Steve," he said, "I was just coming to see you. We need to talk."

"Talk," Steve said. "Are you serious?" They were ten feet apart. *Doesn't he see this gun?* Steve thought.

"Yes," Sam said. "There is a lot we need to discuss. I love you, Steve. That's what I wanted to tell you. I forgive you for everything I ever thought you had done to me, and I want you to forgive me for whatever I've done to you."

"Forgive me? For what? Forgive you? For what? For being a thorn in my side since the day you were born. I doubt there is enough forgiveness to go around for that." Steve couldn't believe he was standing there conversing and arguing with a man, his brother, who apparently wanted him dead.

"Steve, it's okay," he said, pointing at the gun. "I don't understand what you are getting ready to do or why, but it's okay. I love you. God loves you. My prayers, even my last prayer, goes out for you, brother. It's okay."

Sam pulled a coin out of his pocket. On one side it had a man, a mortal man, entering a door. On the other side it had a man, an immortal man, coming out of a door.

"What's that?" Steve asked, not believing this conversation had lasted this long.

"It's the truth, Steve," he said as he handed the old coin to him.

Steve had a puzzled look as he flipped it over in his fingers.

Suddenly a red dot appeared on Steve's chest.

"Steve!" Sam yelled as he jumped in front of him.

Steve froze. There was one shot, hardly audible. Sam fell to the ground. Dead.

Then there was one un-muffled bang. The hit man fell to the ground. Dead.

Detective McCarthy appeared with gun drawn at Steve. "Drop it," he said.

Steve immediately dropped the gun and kicked it away.

"Hands in the air, on your knees," commanded the detective.

Steve hit his knees. But he didn't raise his hands. He bent over Sam. His body was lifeless.

A tear fell from Steve's eye and plopped on Sam's cheek.

40

REDEMPTION

NORMAN SEASON DIED AT three minutes past eleven. The time of death for Samuel Season was determined to be the same. Norman had handed Mo his coin just before he passed. On one side was an old man being lowered into a grave. On the other side was a young man rising from the dead. A flash of light lit up the room as he ascended. Mo was the only one who saw it. At the same time she saw a huge flash of light out the window. It was the parking garage. She was the only one that saw that, too. Sadness overwhelmed her just as the life inside her womb jumped.

It was a twin funeral. There were four headstones lined up. First Ann Season, then Norman Season, then Samuel Season, and one unmarked. Joseph Season sat in the front row with Deborah, Mo, and Sue and Anastasia. In a single moment he had lost his father and two sons. His face said it all. He watched mournfully as the two caskets were let down simultaneously into the ground. He looked down and then he looked up. He didn't understand.

Mo had no tears. She wondered why she wasn't there for the man who brought her back to life. God works in a myriad of ways, she knew. It's never the same way twice. She didn't know what went on in that parking garage.

Steven was arrested. Attempted murder, they said. Yet he wasn't the one that killed Sam. It was some mob guy, and then he was shot dead by Detective McCarthy. It was all very confusing, but one thing she was sure about, whatever happened in that garage had a purpose. God's word never returns empty, but always accomplishes what it was meant to do. Sam was God's word. Maybe it was a short life, but it was fulfilled. She felt her belly. She hadn't told the family yet that there might be another Samuel Season or Samantha Season on the way. It would be better to share the good news after the sharp edge of this grief had a chance to subside.

Steven Season confessed to everything including the conspiracy to kill Abe Shapiro and embezzlement. They dropped the charge of attempted murder of his brother. He waived the right to a trial and relied on the mercy of the court. Thirty years to life with the possibility of parole was a better sentence than he expected or thought he deserved.

Bruce Krakowski pled not guilty. The trial took a day. His gun matched the weapon that killed Abe Shapiro. The jury came back in one hour with guilty verdicts all around, including first-degree murder. He got life without the possibility of parole.

One year later, Mo was changing diapers and fixing bottles for four-month-old Sam. She and Sue were the best of friends. Anastasia wondered why little Sam wouldn't play. Joe and Deborah visited both of their grandchildren often. To them, the children were the faces of their sons, the only thing they had left. And they visited Steven quite often, also. Deborah would always remark on the change in Steven.

"You would think he would be angry and bitter," she told Mo. "But it seems to be the opposite. He's joined some church group and he talks about it all the time. He talks about what he is going to do when he gets out. He never mentions money. It's like whatever possessed him before has been exorcised, if I can use that term, and he's possessed by its opposite." Joe nodded in agreement.

Mo knew what that was. "Well, all things work together for good to those that love God," Mo said. "That always holds true. Most people might disagree, but this is probably the best thing that could happen to Steven."

"All things work together for good?" Joe asked, the pain coming back over his face. "How can you say that? Didn't Sam love God? Look what happened to him. And I don't see how this is so great for Steve either."

"Easy, dear," Deborah said, patting him on the arm. "It is hard, but somehow you have to turn it over to God. His ways are not our ways."

"Everybody's keeps quoting Bible verses," Joe said. "What does all that mean? All I see is one dead son and another who might as well be."

Mo decided to change the subject. "You know, I have been having this urge to visit Steven myself. That would be ok with you, wouldn't it?"

Joe suddenly calmed down. "Of course, dear. Sorry. I didn't mean to go off. I just don't understand. You know my father would speak this stuff to me, but I guess I just never got it. Sam seemed to. I'll just have to accept it. Sorry. I'm rambling. I do believe. But it's harder for me I guess."

Saturday morning Mo drove upstate to the prison on visiting day. Joe and Deborah were very happy to babysit and let Mo take her time with Steven. Mo was nervous sitting there alone at the table. She jumped when she heard a buzzer. The steel door creaked open. A guard led Steven in the room with shackles and sat him down in front of Mo, his head hung down. Steven fidgeted with his hands, which made him sound like the ghost of Mr. Marley.

Mo reached over and steadied his hand. "It's okay," she said.

Steven finally made eye contact. He could see the forgiveness in her eyes.

"That's what he said," Steve said softly, a tiny tear emerging from the corner of one eye. "That's what he said."

They remained silent for a few minutes. Steven was expecting Mo to ask why, but she just sat there looking at him. She didn't say anything.

"You know," Steve said, breaking the silence, "I never really got to know Sam. I don't know why. The day he was born . . . it just seemed all the attention went to him and all of a sudden I was in second place. How I hated that. Up until then, it was all about me. I never gave him a chance. I was determined to hate him for messing up my life. Even though he never did a thing to me. It was my mission in life to make his life miserable. And I did a pretty good job of it until he met you. Then everything changed. He seemed to be invulnerable then. He ignored my taunting. I don't know that I actually never loved him. There was always something there. But I did a good job with that, too. Burying it deep, out of sight. It was contrary to what I wanted to believe."

Steve's voice started to break up. He sat there quietly for a few moments to regain his composure. Mo continued to hold his hand while the guard watched.

"But," he continued, "in the last few minutes of Sam's life, I got to know him. I mean really know him. I had never looked into his eyes, into his soul, to see who he was. All I ever saw before was this thorn in my backside. But his eyes . . . I don't know how to explain it."

"I know," Mo said. "You can't put that into words. You just know."

"Yes," he said. "Exactly." Their eyes were now fixed on each other. "I had never seen anything like it before. It wasn't the Sam I thought I knew. It was something . . . something mystical. I realize now I was shackled, in bondage to something much stronger than these cuffs," Steve said, raising his wrists. "Sam freed me. He died for me. It's totally unbelievable. You know, the Bible says that barely will one man die for a righteous man let alone for a sinner. But Sam died that I might live. He was my Christ here on earth. And even though this place looks like death to everyone else, it's life to me. That is what Sam gave me. I have a new mission in life."

Steve broke down in tears.

"Thank you, Steve," she said, tears finally coming to her face after a year. "That is what I came to hear. I don't need to say it, but maybe you need to hear it. I forgive you. Sam forgives you. God forgives you."

She got up to leave and bent over and kissed his cheek.

"Thank you," he said. The guard moved over to escort him back to his cell.

Mo walked out the locked doors to her car. She reached into her pocket for the car keys and felt the familiar shape of the lost coin.

She pulled it out and looked at both sides. A smile spread across her lips as she started up the car and drove off.

ACKNOWLEDGMENTS

In my 27th year, I came to know Christ as my Lord and Savior. I thank those who God used to lead me into His truth. But after a few short years of eagerly devouring the Word, I hit a ceiling and was left with an unquenchable thirst. Working for Jesus and trying to be a "good person" was a wearisome task laden with constant failure. Wasn't our burden supposed to light and our yoke easy? It was time to let go of the old and search for the new.

So, to the dismay of many, I "fell away" only to be caught by God and led to another group who at the time called themselves Union Lifers. This merry band seemed to be led by an old missionary named Norman Grubb, the author of many books on what he called "Total Truth." There was something different about him and these people. You could see it in their eyes and demeanor, their confidence and non-judgmental attitudes. You could only call it Love. The Total Truth they had learned was that we were never intended to live the so-called Christian life. Only Christ can do that. And He did, through them, but more importantly "as them." We are Christ in our human forms, simply containers for Christ to dwell in as us. That was God's plan all along. It is just that easy. This book is an "out of your belly will flow rivers of living water" story that had no choice but to be written. It's a different way of unveiling these truths through a fictional story with characters just like you and me, filled with drama and suspense.

yetnotibutchrist.com